DRAGON'S MASK

ADAM KWIAT

THM

Ten Hut Media
tenhutmedia.com

This is a work of fiction. Names, characters, businesses, places, events and incidents are either the products of the author's imagination or used in a fictitious manner. Any resemblance to actual persons, living or dead, or actual events is purely coincidental.

ISBN: 978-1-964007-34-2

AUTHOR'S NOTE

A number of characters with Chinese names appear in this novel. In most instances, their full names are presented according to Chinese naming conventions: family name first, followed by their given name. Only in scenes where an English speaker is referring to a Chinese character is the name order reversed to English naming conventions.

The People's Republic of China and Taiwan use different systems for the Romanization of the Standard Chinese language. China uses the Pinyin system, while Taiwan utilizes the Wade-Giles. This novel primarily reflects Pinyin, as most characters and locales are from or in mainland China, but for Taiwanese characters or locations, the Wade-Giles system is used.

PROLOGUE

2025. Somalia, East Africa.

The long-troubled nation once again finds itself in the throes of civil war. The Islamic Courts Union (ICU), a Taliban-style political and military organization, seriously threatens the rule of the Western-backed but weak central government. The ICU was once a major force in the country, and its ideology and affiliation with terrorist groups made it a target of the global War on Terror in the early 2000s. Dissolved in 2007, it has now been re-established and consolidated under new leadership. After rapid advances, the ICU now controls huge swaths of territory east and south of the capital Mogadishu.

The United States and its allies, seeing parallels to Afghanistan in the lead-up to 9/11 and sitting on vital international shipping lanes, have decided to intervene. They now provide military aid and support to the Somali government in its fight against the ICU, primarily in the form of air power and special operations personnel. The mission is known as Operation Eastern Promises.

PROLOGUE

October 8, 2025. 02:17 hours local time.
Kurtunwaaray District, Somalia. ICU Controlled Territory.

We must be close.

Master Sergeant Mike Harrison of the United States Air Force Special Operations Command, or AFSOC, thought as he and the three men with him moved silently in the moonless night through the sandy, scrub-brush-laden landscape of rural Somalia. It was the sudden presence of the smell that triggered the thought. The unmistakable odor of butchered meat and offal.

He was with his longtime teammate from AFSOC, Master Sergeant Randy Thomas, and two scouts from Somali special forces, known as the Danab Brigade. The two Somalis, Yusuuf and Ismail, led the way, both carrying battered AK-47s and donning only their battle fatigues and secondhand night vision the US Department of Defense had donated. It was a stark contrast with the two Americans, who were armed with heavily modified M4A1 assault rifles, armor plating beneath their desert camouflage—both chest and back—and backpacks filled with the latest in military gadgetry.

Despite being poorly kitted, Yusuuf and Ismail were necessary scouts.

The two Somalis, who appeared to be in their late thirties—not an easy age for anyone in the Somali military to reach—both spoke passable English and knew the terrain. They also knew where they were going and what they were looking for.

The four men were looking for an abattoir used to slaughter camels. During their mission briefing at the Somali Army forward operating base, or FOB, Harrison and Thomas were told that Somali military intelligence had recently learned from a local informant that ICU units were using the slaughterhouse as a makeshift ammunition and material depot. Supposedly, the ICU even had a couple of T-62 tanks, most likely captured from Ethiopian forces during their invasion in 2006 to combat the ICU's previous incarnation. Those too were housed under the abattoir's roof, away from the prying eyes of American aircraft. The slaughterhouse was in a good location for business—almost equidistant from the capital Mogadishu to the north and the large city of Baraawe to the south—meaning it served the teeming meat markets of both cities. But it was not far from the current front lines to the north, which made it logistically useful to ICU forces. Somali military positions and towns near the areas of engagement had been experiencing heavy amounts of shelling in recent bouts of fighting. The ICU appeared to be moving material to its frontline fighters quickly.

After Somali military intelligence passed this information along to their American counterparts, US Air Force drones performed reconnaissance over the area. Photographs and video from the recon revealed what appeared to be ICU activity in and around the abattoir. Camels were led in and did not come back out, but covered trucks came and went, usually with black-clad figures armed with assault rifles hanging onto the back or standing on the vehicle running boards. Technicals, the pickup trucks or jeeps fashioned into fighting vehicles by mounting a heavy machine gun in the back that had become virtually synonymous with Somalia, were also present at various intervals. The intel from the informant looked solid. The camel slaughterhouse was now dealing in multiple kinds of death.

The two AFSOC men and their Danab Brigade companions were coming to the facility to do what AFSOC did best: targeting. They were tasked with moving behind enemy lines, locating the target building, and scanning it with precision laser equipment they carried in their backpacks.

The laser would provide exact coordinates to a US Air Force F-15E Strike Eagle circling somewhere above them in the night sky, thus enabling it to hit the slaughterhouse with a payload of Guided Bomb Units (GBU) and take it off the face of the earth.

The abattoir sat on the edge of a medium-sized village called Baran. The proximity of the village was part of why the higher-ups at US Special Operations wanted AFSOC targeting men on this mission. Precision guidance would reduce the risk of civilian casualties and damage to civilian infrastructure. An ancient Somali Air Force AS532 Cougar Helicopter, apparently a gift from the Netherlands from some time ago, had dropped the four men into the scrubland roughly three kilometers from the village under the cover of darkness. The surrounding area was sparsely populated and nearly pitch dark. Still, the team trekked through the sandy terrain a couple of hundred yards from the only road—or what passed for a road—that ran to Baran. They did not want to run the risk of a chance encounter with the enemy. This was ICU territory after all.

Harrison and his squad came to a small berm rising from the desert. The stench in the air led Harrison and the other three to draw their weapons. He gave a low whistle to capture the attention of Yusuuf and Ismail. When they turned towards him, he motioned for them to fan out. The four men crept up the berm and, as they came to the crest, Harrison and Thomas instinctively went into a prone position, prompting the two Somalis to do the same.

Looking over the berm, Ismail muttered, to no one in particular, "Baran."

The slaughterhouse was before them, about five hundred meters away. Harrison took a pair of binoculars from his kit, positioned them at the end of his night vision gear, and proceeded to scan the vicinity.

It was a nondescript cinder-block building with a flat roof and three vehicle bays, which were facing southward, toward Harrison and his team. The bays were large enough for trucks carrying camels on their way to be butchered, or perhaps T-62 tanks. The flat roof was surrounded on all sides by a waist-high cement wall. Harrison could make out a lone ICU fighter positioned up there. Hardly any light came from the town at this hour and, from what he could discern, the fighter had no night-vision gear. Harrison continued to study the building and the grounds around it. A handful of much smaller buildings were nearby. He could not tell if they were homes or somehow linked to the slaughterhouse. There were no other ICU men posted outside that he could see, but their presence was indicated by two technicals parked along the side of the building.

It was a quiet night.

Harrison brought down the binoculars and turned to Thomas. "Sniper on the roof. Two technicals this side of the building. Not seeing any other movement, but this is it."

He handed the binoculars to his partner, who took a brief look for himself.

Thomas returned them to Harrison and said, "OK, let's go."

Thomas turned to his left to the two Somalis, both of whom had been silently staring out towards the target. He said, "You two, take up positions. One to our left, the other on the right. Give us some over watch while we do our work."

Yusuuf and Ismail nodded their understanding and lifted themselves up from the ground. Ismail crouch-walked around the two Americans to take up a position, while Yusuuf shifted farther down to the do the same. Harrison had set down his backpack and removed their AN/PEC-1C Ground Laser Target Designator. This lightweight camera-like apparatus would hit the target building with a laser that the F15E, call sign Sandman, would be able to read and use as a guide to perform its strike.

Harrison had the Designator nearly set up when both he and Thomas paused at the same time.

A sound was emanating from the darkness behind them. A cackling of some kind.

"What the hell is that?" Harrison said in a low tone.

Yusuuf responded from his position off to the left, "Hyenas."

The two Americans stole a glance at one another.

Yusuuf spoke again, "They smell blood. From..." He gestured toward the slaughterhouse, not knowing the word for the building.

Harrison turned his head to look behind their position and peered out. He could make out three or four sets of glowing green eyes floating in the darkness. The cackling grew louder.

He turned back to his task.

Time to rock and roll

"Alright Randy, let's light this thing up for Sandman and get the hell out of here."

"Roger that."

Thomas fired up the Designator. Through their night vision, they could see a thick green laser beam hit the side of the slaughterhouse, and a large green circle appeared on the building.

After waiting a few moments, Harrison spoke into his comms, "Sandman, this is Alpha-1, copy."

A voice came back in his ear, "Alpha-1, this is Sandman, I copy you, over."

"Sandman, target building is lit up for you. It's your show now."

"Alpha-1, roger that, ordinance inbound, over."

The four men waited, not saying a word. The laughter of their canine companions continued to break the silence of the night. A minute later, however, that was drowned out by the *whoosh* of a jet engine far overhead, and seconds later, the AFSOC men and their Somali scouts watched as the abattoir burst into flames and lit up the area with a huge plume of fire. Immediately, secondary explosions followed as the ammunition and mortar shells the ICU kept in the building went off. Where a slaughter-house once stood there was now a boiling mixture of flames, dust, and smoke.

Harrison spoke into his comms, "Sandman, that was a direct hit. Target building is dust, over."

"Roger that Alpha-1, get home safely."

Harrison and Thomas quickly disassembled the Designator and packed it back into Harrison's backpack. Yusuuf and Ismail had already joined them, ready to make their way back. Shouting could now be heard from over the berm. Harrison stood and turned to head out, the darkness in front of them now illuminated by the fire rising behind them.

The green eyes were gone.

1

October 8, 2025. 08:16 hours local time.
Air Force Office of Special Investigations Headquarters, Quantico, Virginia.

Special Agent Henry Purcel flexed his right hand open and closed, trying to shake off the jolt of pain that had just shot from his elbow down his right arm.

Goddamn.

As he let the pain ebb away, he used his other hand to pick up a steaming mug of coffee from his desk, his second cup already this morning, and took a long sip. The aroma helped him forget his troubled appendage for a second. Next to the mug was his large lined yellow legal pad, filled with the chicken-scratch handwriting characteristic of a southpaw. He looked back at his morning's work: typing up the handwritten notes he had compiled for his current case, which involved an Air Force officer, who really should have known better, downloading personal material onto a government computer system.

Purcel turned to look out his office window overlooking the building's front parking lot at the gray October morning. He sighed and shook his head, remembering he also had to look into allegations of exam cheating among several cadets at the Air Force Academy.

So, this is it for me now?

For Purcel, it hadn't always been this desk-jockeying, burdened by a caseload of mundane investigations. He had been an agent with the Air Force Office of Special Investigations, or AFOSI, for over two decades. Originally, he had hopes of following in the footsteps of his father and uncle and serving his country as a pilot. But during initial training all those years ago, he found he didn't quite have the stomach for the G-forces. He also discovered a dormant fear of heights. Despite his family's storied Air Force history, the "right stuff" gene must have skipped Henry, and he came to the realization that he was just more suited to *terra firma*. His 6'3" frame wasn't meant to be crammed into a cockpit, anyway.

It didn't take long, however, for him to establish himself as one of the top agents at AFOSI. Accolades and praise from further up the chain piled up quickly. Spurred partly by his inability to achieve anything in the air, Purcel was dogged in his pursuit of the truth and facts on the ground. *Brilliant investigative mind* was one line that he still remembered fondly from an early performance review. After impressing his superiors early on with his work ethic and eye for details, he would end up working some of AFOSI's toughest cases, often finding himself in the field collaborating with the FBI or ATF. On more than one occasion, it had become necessary to make use of his weapons training.

In recent years, his standing at AFOSI earned him some overseas postings, where he was tasked with helping to train agents from friendly intelligence services in investigative methods. Back in May, he was put on assignment in the dry desert heat of Jordan. It was there that things took a turn for him.

The Royal Jordanian Air Force was creating an investigative branch of its own, one modeled on AFOSI. Purcel had been sent there as part of a three-week stint to help get it off the ground, lending his expertise to the unit's first class of agents. One morning, the day before he was set to head back home, he was seated with four Jordanians at a long table, holding an impromptu question-and-answer session in the mess hall at King Abdullah Air Base. Partway through the sit-down, a young Jordanian Air Force cadet, who would later be discovered to have been radicalized online by extremists in the region, marched into the room and opened fire with his service sidearm. Luckily, Purcel had been seated facing the entryway (an old habit of his: he always needed to see who was coming and going in whatever venue he found himself) and immediately saw the action unfolding. While flipping the table to provide some form of cover, however, Purcel's right arm caught two bullets that ricocheted off the floor. Security forces quickly took down the shooter, but not before one of Purcel's companions lay dead and another critically wounded.

The fleeting moment of discomfort in his arm caused him to reflexively look from the window and up at the fabric pinboard that took up much of the wall space above his desk. To one side of the board, next to sheets of paper containing phone numbers or notes on cases, Purcel had pinned a photo of himself standing next to a serious-looking Arab man. Behind them rose the rock-cut façade of Jordan's famous archeological wonder Petra. Purcel's companion in the photo was Hani Khatib, an officer in Jordan's intelligence agency, the General Intelligence Directorate. Khatib had been assigned as both a translator and "cultural liaison" for Purcel during his stint in-country. Despite his dour appearance in the photo, Khatib had a warm and welcoming demeanor, and the two men had formed a friendship during Purcel's short stay.

The trip to Petra had been just days before the shooting incident. Khatib had been with Purcel in the mess hall that day. In the photo, Khatib stood with an air of authority that almost made up for the several inches in height that Purcel had on him. He was now unlikely to ever walk or stand again. While the result of the shooting for Purcel was severe nerve damage to his arm and, for now, an end to his time in the field, Khatib had been struck in the spine by one of the shooter's bullets and had his entire life impaired forever. Purcel tried to remember this whenever he began to feel sorry for himself over his current work arrangement.

He also tried to remember the operative part of his situation, the "for now." Despite the pain he still felt in the arm, he could use it normally, and he had recently gotten through all the mental health checks that the agency required following a traumatic encounter. Purcel looked back out the window, trying to shake the memory of that day at King Abdullah.

Purcel knew that any number of his colleagues at Quantico, had they been in his position, would have more than welcomed a stint of easy desk work and the comfort of the office. But Henry Purcel wasn't built like that. He wanted to be back on real cases, and to him, real meant out of the office, traveling to different areas, conducting interviews, investigating matters that had real security implications. This other stuff, like investigating cheating on tests or someone plugging a USB into the wrong computer, was the province for other special agents. He was now approaching his third month back on duty, and he was ready to be working on something real.

He continued to look out the window at nothing in particular. After another moment, he sighed heavily and turned back to his work.

2

October 8, 2025. 21:17 hours local time.
Creech Air Force Base, Indian Springs, Nevada.

A pleasant evening breeze broke through the Nevada desert air. Lieutenant Devin Moore closed his eyes and tilted his head upwards, sighing as he did so, enjoying the feel of the wind on his face. He held that position for a brief moment before bringing his head back down and taking one last drag of his cigarette while looking out at the huge flood-lit runway stretching before him.

He was standing outside his "office," as he called it, a small, unassuming building about the size of a shipping container, comprised of one room and a bathroom, tucked away in the corner of Creech Air Force Base. While there appeared to be little to the "office" from the outside, it was actually what was known in military parlance as a Sensitive Compartmented Information Facility, or SCIF, housing a bank of computers and servers that helped run some of the US Air Force's most advanced technology. It was from here, seated in a leather office chair in front of a large high-definition monitor in the climate-controlled space, that Moore and one other Air Force specialist operated reconnaissance drones around the world from various US military bases and staging areas. Three years prior, when

Moore was assigned to this particular unit, the 44th Reconnaissance Squadron, he had started his new job by performing surveillance and gathering intelligence supporting the Afghan National Army—before the US military completely pulled out of that country in 2022—and then for special operations in Syria and West Africa. The current tasking, though, was Operation Eastern Promises. Somalia.

Moore was standing in a small pool of a yellow halogen light, given off by the floodlight perched just above the entryway into the building. He glanced up to see a single moth dancing around the bulb. He flicked his cigarette into the darkness and turned to punch his entry code into the pad to the right of the door.

He stepped into the small workspace. His approach caused the other specialist on duty that night, Lieutenant Andrew Gajewski, to turn around in his seated position in front of his monitor and speak to Moore.

"Good timing. Call just came through for you."

Moore walked over to his workstation to the left of Gajewski's, took a seat, and clicked on his monitor. He said to his partner, "What do we got?"

"The Colonel wants the BDA done on that bombing run from the other day. The slaughterhouse."

A "BDA" was Bomb Damage Assessment, sometimes Battle Damage Assessment, which was as it sounded: evaluating the level of damage on a target and the surrounding area after a bombing run. Moore had been tasked with flying his drone over the target site of a strike mission that had taken place a little over twenty-four hours before. The target had been hit just after midnight local time, and while the new drone that Moore operated, a Lockheed Martin Ocelot, had night-vision technology, it was preferable that the BDAs be done in the light of day. When daylight broke the morning of the bombing, however, a large dust storm had kicked up in the area, rendering attempts at aerial imagery impossible. Moore's commander had told him to see if the following morning would have better weather. While a delay of that length wasn't ideal, it was unlikely that the enemy could do any real clearing of the site in that time frame, especially since any operations on the ground would be hindered by the dust storm as well. Given the orders he had just received, it was apparent that a new day had brought clear skies around Baran, Somalia.

Moore responded to Gajewski as he fitted a large headset over his ears. "Roger that. Let's get this bird in the air."

———————

A half hour later, Lieutenant Moore's screen was filled with a clear view of what used to be Baran's camel slaughterhouse and erstwhile ICU munitions depot. The Ocelot drone that he manipulated with a joystick from his desk hovered about five thousand feet above the site. While he piloted the craft, he was also taking pictures using a trigger on the joystick that activated the drone's onboard high-definition camera. The pictures would not only be saved on the drone's internal memory but also downloaded automatically onto Moore's PC. By holding down the trigger, video clips could be captured as well. Moore had operated a number of different drone classes during his time in the 44th, but the Ocelot was, by far, the best. It was no surprise. The Ocelot was the newest addition to the Air Force's drone fleet, and it came equipped with some of the most cutting-edge technology the defense industry had developed. Lockheed Martin had sold only a small number to friendly foreign militaries, but those lacked certain features carried by the US Air Force's Ocelots. In order to operate the machine and be briefed on some of its capabilities, Moore had to have his already high-level security clearance moved up an echelon. The Ocelots contained technologies that very few knew about. It remained strictly need-to-know.

The introduction of the Ocelots was so recent that Operation Eastern Promises was the first deployment of one overseas during a US military operation. Moore understood that his Ocelot was the only one currently in Somalia. There was another at Camp Lemonnier, a US-Africa Command base in Djibouti, but it had yet to arrive at the Somali military FOB from where Moore flew his missions.

Moore captured several images of the target site. The strike had done its job; very little of the slaughterhouse was left. The knock-on explosions from ICU munitions had furthered its demise. He could make out twisted and burnt metal and smoldering tires and treads, the remains of whatever combat vehicles the ICU had stowed away. After more than a half hour of studying the area and typing notes onto a screen adjacent to his drone monitor at the same time, Moore was satisfied with the intel he had gathered. He swung the Ocelot slightly southwest, passing the outskirts of Baran to see if there was anything of interest beyond the town.

At first glance, there was virtually nothing attention grabbing. The scrubland and desert landscape ubiquitous to rural Somalia soon filled Moore's monitor, with no sign of human activity. After a minute, Moore was ready to call it quits and bring the drone back to base. He had what he needed. There was nothing to see outside of Baran. ICU units in the area had run off somewhere with their tails between their legs, but it wasn't for him to go searching for them at this time.

Just as he was about to move the joystick to prompt the drone to fly west back to base, his monitor began to beep, a sound like a common alarm clock, and on his screen, on the desert floor, thick gold lines began to appear, spreading like veins. Three, then four, then five...

The lines were part of a computer-generated overlay coming from the drone. They were similar to what one would see on a mapping app to show traffic density on the roads when searching a route. This was the drone activating a capability that Moore knew of but had yet to see come to life.

The beeping stopped, as did the appearance of the new gold lines. Moore leaned into for a closer look at his screen and counted the number of different lines, some of which were connected. Eleven in total. Moore leaned back in his chair and paused for a moment.

"Holy shit," he said out loud.

He rolled his chair to the far-left end of his workstation, where a landline telephone sat. He picked up the receiver and punched in a number.

He tilted his head to rest the receiver between his ear and shoulder, freeing up his hands, which fidgeted with a pen. One of his legs bounced with nervous energy while the phone rang.

"This is Colonel Chavez," a voice said from the other end when the call was picked up.

"Yes, good evening, sir. This is Lieutenant Moore down in the UAV SCIF. I think I have something here you should see."

3

October 16, 2025. 20:24 hours local time.
Outskirts of the village of Dhayo, 75 kilometers west of Baraawe, Somalia.
Islamic Courts Union territory.

Mahmoud and Jama, two young ICU fighters, stood outside a large, mud-walled compound that belonged to the head of a prominent local clan. The two men, AK-47 assault rifles slung barrel-down across their chests, their heads wrapped in checkered keffiyehs, stared out into the still, pitch-dark night of the Somali hinterlands. Very little went on in this part of the country after sunset, particularly outside the village center. In between the evening calls to prayer from the town's lone mosque, there was not much to create noise. At times, one might hear the discomfiting laugh of hyenas on the hunt or the rustling of other nocturnal wildlife. But apart from the low metronomic hum of the clan leader's generator somewhere in the compound behind them, tonight, it was quiet. No roaming packs of hyenas. At least, not yet.

They both served as personal bodyguards to Mohammed Said Hassan. Hassan held many titles in the ICU: Minister of the Interior, Minister of War, Chief Propagandist. They did not know in what capacity he was serving for the meeting happening in the compound behind them. This new edition of the ICU was a secretive organization, even amongst its own.

Sheikh Hassan, as his fighters all knew him, was a notoriously arrogant man, sure of himself and the support that the ICU had in Somalia, particularly in this part of the country. After all, during its first manifestation in the early 2000s, the ICU was widely popular. He always traveled with light security, usually just Mahmoud and Jama and an older lieutenant, who was inside attending the gathering. Tonight was no different. The clan elder who was acting as host, Omar Elmi Dihoud, normally had two armed militiamen with him, but Hassan had ordered Dihoud's security detail to retire elsewhere for the night. This was solid ICU territory. They had little to worry about here.

Mahmoud and Jama stood in silence. The Sheikh was an austere personality who did not appreciate small talk. They had learned to keep to themselves for the most part, even in their master's absence. Mahmoud began to pace back and forth in a small square. They had not been told how long the meeting would last, just that it would finish before the *isha*, the nighttime prayers.

Whoop whoop.

It was faint but still couldn't be missed. Not with how quiet it was on the outskirts of the village.

Whoop whoop.

Mahmoud cocked his head upwards and listened. There was definitely something out there.

He turned to his left to Jama, who was now also looking skywards. "Do you hear that?"

Whoop whoop.

———

From his place on the starboard side of the modified Sikorsky HH-60U Black Hawk helicopter, commonly referred to as a Ghost Hawk, Commander John Clark of the Naval Special Warfare Development Group, also known as DEVGRU or Seal Team Six, surveyed the landscape below. As the Ghost Hawk neared its destination, the target building became clearer through Clark's night-vision goggles. The mud-walled compound was surrounded by the Somali desert, with a single dirt road leading to it. It was practically an island unto itself, with the sleepy village of Dhayo almost a kilometer away. Clark thought of the famous raid to kill Osama bin Laden, which took place in a Pakistani mountain resort town. The DEVGRU operators on that mission had to contend with an urban environment and curious locals awakened by the sounds of the operation. These conditions were much more favorable, meaning Clark expected a smooth in-and-out. No hiccups. No surprises.

He shared the space on the helicopter, Super Six-1, with six other operators and a Belgian Malinois Ronin, who had been trained to detect explosive boobytraps. This was Alpha Team. Another Ghost Hawk, Super Six-2, flying adjacent just 50 feet away, carried seven more of his teammates, those on Bravo Team. The DEVGRU unit had lifted off from the USS Carl Vinson in the Indian Ocean at dusk and traveled into Somali airspace several kilometers south of the coastal city of Baraawe. They were coming to kill Mohammed Said Hassan, a member of the ICU senior leadership. So far as Clark knew, this was to be the first such kill mission since US Special Operations had come back to Somalia. The previous foray had been in the early '90s and culminated in the infamous "Black Hawk Down" incident. In the initial briefing, Clark and his team had learned that Hassan was a key figure in the ICU, but what most interested the US military was his background as a chemical engineer and his education obtained in Europe. It was reported that, on top of leadership duties, Hassan was guiding his militants in bomb making, which the ICU had thus far been using to devastating effect via suicide and truck-bomb attacks.

The intelligence that set up the night's operation had come from a CIA asset deep in Hassan's inner circle: an aide-de-camp who was once a student of Hassan's at the University of Mogadishu, an establishment that, in a tragic twist of irony, Hassan had subsequently directed attacks against. The asset could not provide detailed information; Hassan and the ICU hierarchy were obsessively secretive and acted or released information on a strict need-to-know. The asset could only say with certainty that his boss was having a sit-down at this compound, the home of an area clan leader. Who with, or what about, could not be ascertained. Clark and his team were told that security should be light, a hallmark of Hassan's, but the total number of people who would be present in the building was unknown.

The Somali central government had long been little more than an idea in southern Somalia, and now it was firmly under the sway of the ICU. Hassan moved freely in this area but also at random, often with little to no notice of his next destination. He may have been sure of his personal safety in ICU territory, that there was minimal threat on the ground, but this did not eliminate the paranoia that US drone capabilities could instill in even the most confident militants. This was the first occasion since the CIA had established the bona fides of the asset that they had information on Hassan's whereabouts with sufficient lead time. This was DEVGRU's chance.

As they had approached, Super 6-2 broke north so Bravo Team could land on the north side of the compound, the rear side. Clark's Ghost Hawk would set down on the south side, facing the main gate into the compound. Two guards were supposed to be stationed at that gate, and that was reportedly the only security outside the building.

The Ghost Hawk was traveling east to west, so Clark's side of the craft faced the compound entrance. The chopper began its descent, and Clark did a quick scan of his teammates around him and Ronin, all sitting perfectly still. Clark nodded twice to himself, anticipating what was about to come. They touched down about three hundred yards from the building.

Show Time.

The SEALs flanking him on either side, the unit's two sharpshooters, Chief Petty Officers Mike McCabe and Jason Smith, disembarked ahead of Clark. Ronin and Ronin's handler, CPO Pat Krol, followed. The rest of the Alpha Team alighted on the other side of the aircraft. McCabe and Smith darted into the night and settled into firing positions on the desert floor, aiming their silenced SEAL RECON weapons towards the two guards at the entrance.

Whoop whoop.

Jama looked back at Mahmoud. "Yes, sounds like it is coming from straight ahead. It's so dark out here I can't see anything."

Mahmoud shifted his weapon and took a step forward. "Stay here, I'll go—"

He never got to finish the sentence. His head snapped back, and blood spattered the compound wall behind him. Jama had no time to show surprise, as a moment later, he joined his partner splayed on the ground, instantly dead.

———————

McCabe and Smith simultaneously spoke into their comms.

"Tango down."

"Tango down."

Commander Clark peered through the scope of his HK416 assault rifle towards the gate and looked over the two dead militants on the ground, dust still settling around them.

Smith spoke once again, "Main gate is clear."

Clark signaled to the rest of the team to move forward towards the target and radioed to Bravo Team, which had touched down on the north side of the building.

"Bravo Team, copy."

The Bravo Team lead, CPO Ben Macelar, came in over the radio, "Copy, over."

"Entryway sentries have been eliminated. Alpha Team moving towards target, over."

Macelar responded, "Bravo Team advancing on target, over."

Clark's team of operators stacked up on either side of the gate. Clark gave a shove to one side of the two-sided gate, wide enough for a vehicle, and it creaked open. At the same moment, Bravo Team on the north side were scaling the six-foot-high mud wall surrounding the compound. McCabe and Smith crouched on either side of the gate and faced the desert expanse towards Dhayo. If any enemy combatants nearby became alerted and rushed the compound, they'd be the first to receive them. Clark stepped into the opening and led the way in. The rest of Alpha Team followed his lead, silenced HK416s drawn.

The DEVGRU commandos, moving in an inverted V shape, entered the courtyard and approached the two-story concrete home that was crowned with ornate accents. A large balcony jutted out from the second floor and stretched the entire width of the building. No light shone from the windows on either floor. The whirr of a generator resonated from somewhere to the left. Four Japanese SUVs of varying age and quality sat in a semi-circular dirt driveway that curved in front of the house. Clark moved to pass in front of the pick-up truck at the head of the caravan. He glanced to his left and saw, a few yards away, a wide lean-to constructed out of corrugated metal. Underneath it, several camels lay on haunches, their heads following the operators' advance. A step-up concrete pad porch, about six feet in depth, led to the large, wooden front door. It was surrounded by a colorful balustrade. Clark crouched against the balustrade where it met the step. Krol, with Ronin tight to his side, settled behind Clark, and another commando, Petty Officer Warren Castello, crouched behind them. The remaining two members of Alpha Team, Petty Officers Chris Dejuiste and Bryan Roccia, knelt down in the path leading to the front step, their assault rifles pointed at the front door. No noise or stirring had come from inside thus far.

Clark gave a hand signal to Roccia: thermal.

Roccia set down his backpack and removed a tablet-like device, then crept towards the front door. The device was a scanner that would show heat signals, such as those thrown off by a human or animal, up to a certain distance beyond an obstruction, like an exterior wall or doorway. He pointed the scanner at the front door and studied the screen.

After a moment, he crept back next to Clark and whispered, "No signals."

It meant there wasn't anyone within the vicinity of the front door. Clark and his team were in the dark as to the layout of the home, so it was possible that Hassan's meeting was happening more towards the rear of the home, or even upstairs.

CPO Macelar led his team towards the rear of the house, roughly thirty yards from the compound back wall. Two neatly stacked piles of construction materials—roofing tiles or brick pavers, covered by tarp—lay in front of the approaching commandos. Macelar crouched behind one pile and looked towards the house. He noted a back door and two sets of windows on either side. Light poured out from the windows to the right of the door.

He spoke into his comms, "Alpha Team, copy."

"Copy."

"Rear door flanked by windows. Light in windows on west side. Will hit with thermal. Over."

"Copy. Over."

Macelar, back to the pile of materials, leaned over and looked to his teammate, Petty Officer Steven Brower, a few yards away behind the other pile.

In a hushed tone, he ordered, "See if you can get anything through that window."

Brower nodded and crouch-walked to get beneath the window to the right of the door. He could hear the thrum of the generator just around the corner. He positioned himself at the edge of the window, the bottom of which was about four feet from the ground, and lifted his night-vision equipment to his forehead. Slowly rising, keeping himself to the side and out of sight as best he could, he peered through the window. He gave a slight shake of his head, crouched back down, and headed over to Macelar.

"Window has one of those frosting films over it. No view to the inside, all blurred."

Macelar nodded. "Alright, let's put some thermal on it."

"Roger."

Brower removed the thermal imaging device from his kit and crept over to the back door. He scanned the door and the walls to either side, studying what came up on his device. After a few moments, he made his way back to Macelar's side.

"Sir, beyond the wall to the west side of the door, I think I might have hit a jackpot. Picking up at least four signatures, looks like they are seated at a table."

Macelar didn't respond immediately, thinking for a beat. Four bodies.

That sure seemed like a meeting. If that, indeed, was Hassan's get-together, then one of the three others was likely his lieutenant, which the CIA officer on the ship had mentioned. Another of the grouping should be the asset who had provided all the intel. The fourth body was the unknown, someone Hassan felt the need to see in person. Whoever it was, if they were armed, they would get the same treatment intended for Hassan and the lieutenant. The SEALs could not be going in with guns blazing, however. They were there to terminate Hassan but also needed to extract the asset.

He nodded at Brower and spoke into his comms, "Alpha Team lead, copy."

"Copy, over."

"Picking up four thermal signatures in a back room, west side of the building. Subjects all appear to be seated. Looks like a meeting. Requesting permission to breach and engage, over."

"Granted. Alpha Team will be coming through the front door. Check your fire. See you on the other side, over."

"Copy, over."

Macelar looked at Brower and said, "Prepare to breach."

Brower turned around and whispered to the rest of the squad, "Prepare to breach, let's go."

The commandos made their way to the back door.

Silence hung over the room as Mohammad Said Hassan studied the photographs arrayed in front of him on the wooden dining table, slowly stroking his light salt-and-pepper beard. The two men seated across from him, the ones who had requested this meeting, both sat with their hands folded and arms on the table, looking in his direction but not directly at him. His young assistant, Fahad, sat to his right, nervously bouncing one of his legs and looking around the room. At what? Hassan did not know. Fahad wasn't like most of his peers in the militant group who wore their religious fervor and capacity for violence conspicuously. With his small frame and almost gentle features, he could still be mistaken for a shy, quiet schoolboy. Oftentimes, it was easy to forget his presence. For some reason, however, he was unusually fidgety tonight. *Perhaps just anxious for a smooth meeting*, Hassan thought. It wasn't often they had foreign visitors. Hassan's lieutenant and Chief of Security, Ahmed, sat slightly slouched in a chair against the wall behind Hassan, an AKSU submachine laid across his lap, combat-booted feet crossed at the ankles in front of him.

On the other hand, the two guests on the other side of the table had become a bit more relaxed since their arrival. When they had arrived and first stepped out of their vehicle, Hassan could see fear on their faces. This meeting was their idea, but still, some things were unavoidable. Not only was Somalia one of the most dangerous places in the world, but Hassan and his organization also made for intimidating interlocutors. But, despite the violence that had come to characterize his life, Hassan knew how to be diplomatic, and he had not completely lost his Somali sense of hospitality. He had greeted the two visitors warmly, letting them know his military fatigues were just his everyday attire. He had even let one light up a cigarette and have a smoke before entering the house, despite the ICU's ban of the practice in its territory. They were his guests, and they should be afforded some small accommodations. He wanted them to feel at ease, for the word was they had something very important that he needed to hear.

They had introduced themselves as Wu Laichang and Jiang Hongbo, principal geological engineers at San Lang Mining Corporation. Both spoke passable English, Jiang with a heavy accent, but Hassan had no trouble understanding. His own English was near perfect from years of living abroad.

Wu and Jiang's associates had found an ICU middleman in Mombasa, Kenya, someone the group used to facilitate business transactions and recruitment outside the country. The middleman was one of the few people inside and outside Somalia who could reach Hassan. He helped the Chinese establish contact with Hassan and eventually set this meeting. The connection in Mombasa seemed convinced that this was a sit-down worth taking, and after some back and forth, Hassan agreed. Now, having heard the initial pitch himself and looking at the photographs Wu and Jiang had provided, he was beginning to think so himself. The ICU was going to need more resources. He sensed that American involvement would soon turn the tide of the war. The large loss of weapons and munitions less than ten days prior, thanks to a US air strike, still aggravated him.

He looked up at the two men and spoke. "What you have here interests me greatly. And I do agree, we may have a situation that can be of mutual benefit to your company and the Courts Union, and therefore my Somalia. I appreciate you having brought this to my attention. However, I have a curious mind, and I must ask...is China now operating drones in my country? How were you able to obtain these images?"

The two Chinese men threw a nervous glance at each other. Hassan was surprised at their anxious reaction. They must have known the question would come up. Someone could not give him a stack of photographs showing Somali countryside, an area not far from where they sat, that demonstrated some of the most state-of-the-art drone and imaging technology, and not expect him to wonder how they had come by it. It was interesting too, Hassan had thought, that none of the photographs featured any Chinese characters. He was no expert in linguistics, but everyone knew what Chinese script looked like, and there was none to be found on what these two Chinese nationals were showing him.

It was Wu, with the better command of English, who spoke up, "Mr. Hassan, I am sure you know, the world of rare earth mining is very competitive, particularly for minerals that are now so critical to daily life, such as lithium, cobalt, and coltan. And China—" He stopped himself there, realizing his little slip of the tongue. "San Lang must always be on the cutting edge and use its advantages to stay ahead of competitors."

"I appreciate that fact, Mr. Wu, but it doesn't really answer my question. I did not realize China was in the business of operating drones here in Africa—"

Before he could complete his thought, a small explosion rocked the room.

Having found the back door locked, Bravo Team, stacked on either side, had set explosive charges and blew the door off its hinges. Macelar led the way in, HK416 at the ready. As he heard the sound of the front door being breached by Alpha Team, he came to a doorway to his right and swiftly turned in, trigger finger poised.

A young girl, around 10 or 11, wearing a colorful dress that also covered her head, stared wide eyed at Macelar. She was turned around, sitting at a small dining table with her back to the doorway. Seated to her left was a young man in a white shirt and checkered skirt, traditional Somali menswear, and next to him, at the end of the table opposite the door, was an older man with a full white beard in a similar outfit. The final seat to the girl's right was occupied by a woman in a dress like the one worn by the girl, only black. All of them looked back at Macelar with expressions somewhere between terror and confusion. Half-eaten meals crowded the table. He lowered his weapon and said, "Fuck."

Two of his teammates had broken to the left of the back door and went to clear the room opposite the one he stood. He held up a fist to Brower who came up alongside him. He could hear Alpha Team to his left. He turned in that direction to look down a darkened hallway leading towards the front door, flipping his night-vision equipment back down over his eyes. Midway down the hall, faint light poured into the space from a stairwell. Someone was pounding down those stairs.

Commander Clark moved into the hall at the front of the home, his rifle aimed forward. Since the thermal device picked up no signatures in this space, he felt confident moving in directly and letting Roccia and Castello clear the two rooms on either side of the hall. He saw CPO Macelar facing him at the end of the hall, next to a lit doorway, Brower at his side. Something had given them pause. He expected them to be engaged. He heard movement coming from ahead from a stairwell leading into the middle of the hallway. In that moment, a tall male leapt from the stairwell into the hall and turned to the back of the home, towards Macelar and Bravo team. It was happening fast, but Clark could make out that the individual was holding a weapon, an AK variant of some kind, and he let off three quick rounds into the man's back center mass without hesitation. Dark red spots blossomed in the man's camouflage fatigues, and he crashed face first onto the floor, his weapon clattering towards Bravo Team. Clark moved toward the body quickly and, standing over the corpse, placed two more rounds into it.

Macelar hustled over to Clark and said, "It wasn't the meeting, it's the fucking family that lives here. Must be."

A shout came from the up the stairwell, "Ahmed! Ahmed!" followed by a stream of Somali.

Behind Macelar, the older Somali man and the local clan leader who owned the home, Omar Dihoud, had stepped from the dining room and shouted something in Somali.

Clark looked in his direction and directed the two commandos standing near the man. "Shut his ass up!"

They grabbed Dihoud and dragged him back into the dining area.

Clark turned back to Macelar and said, "That must have been Hassan we just heard from up there. If he's got a cell, he'll be calling in the cavalry, I'm sure. We gotta move on him now. There were no lights from the windows up top so there must be a landing or something right above us. Get up there and hit it with some flashes."

Macelar nodded, turned, and motioned to Brower to come join him at the bottom of the stairs.

Macelar and Brower had both removed flashbang grenades from clips on their tactical vests and moved swiftly up the stairwell. Near the top of stairs, the wall tailed down to a half wall, and they both threw their grenades over and into the space beyond.

———————

Hassan heard something hit the floor downstairs moments after Ahmed had jumped up and charged down the stairs. Was that the muffled report of a silenced weapon? Hassan called to Ahmed but received no response. A few moments later he heard the shouts from Omar that Americans were here. Wu and Jiang had both stood up and were now frantically asking him what was going on. He didn't have time to deal with them.

He turned to Fahad, who had also stood up and backed away from the table, and said in Somali, "Fahad, get to a bedroom."

At the same moment, he took his cell phone from the breast pocket of his fatigues and moved towards Omar's master bedroom overlooking the front courtyard of the home. He went to dial his security detail in Dhayo.

Then the room went white.

BANG.

BANG.

A second after the reports from their flashbangs, Macelar and Brower bounded up the rest of the stairs, Clark and Roccia behind them. They came into an upstairs living room with a long rectangular table in the middle. Macelar took the right along the half wall, while Brower moved toward the center. He first registered a younger Somali man slumped in the corner at the back of the room, hands cupping his ears, no weapon visible, and immediately realized that it must be the CIA asset. In the center of the room, a man in military fatigues was straightening himself from being bent at the waist. As the man righted himself, Brower recognized him from intel photos as their target—Mohammed Said Hassan.

A pistol sat in a holster on Hassan's hip, not a direct threat, but it was of no consequence—the DEVGRU team had not come here to take Hassan with them.

Brower fired three rounds from his HK416 into Hassan's chest. Hassan fell backwards heavily, as if shoved with two hands. He was dead before his body met the floor.

Brower moved onto Hassan's lifeless body and put two more rounds into the chest area.

He then spoke into his comms, "Cochise," using the code word assigned to Hassan, "Enemy KIA."

Commander Clark appeared beside him and took a small digital camera from his chest rig, ready to photograph Hassan's face as evidence of a successful mission.

Before he could do so, he heard Macelar from his right. "What the fuck?"

Clark turned towards him. Macelar had lowered his weapon and was looking down. Macelar was on the other side of the table, which partially obscured Clark's view, but he could see the top of two heads just breaking the plane of the table, and those appeared to be what had Macelar's attention. Clark handed the camera to Brower but motioned with his head towards the two bedrooms doors, both ajar and showing darkened rooms.

"Make sure those are clear, then take the pics."

When Clark walked around the table from the other side, such that he was facing Macelar, and looked down, he found himself staring at two shell-shocked Asian men seated on the floor.

Macelar said, "Commander, who in the hell are these two?"

Clark took a moment before saying, "I have no clue."

Clark crouched down to bring himself eye level with the two men. They were still shaky from the shock of the flashbangs but seemed aware. He assumed one or both of them must speak English. Chances that Hassan spoke an Asian language of any sort were near zero, the same for the young Somali at the other end of the room that he imagined was the CIA asset.

He spoke to both men, who were now looking at him, "Who are you? What are you doing here?"

They both stared at him. No response.

Roccia made his way over and spoke from the other side of the table, speaking to Clark. "Sir, confirmed the other individual here is the asset. I asked if Hassan was able to get off a phone call and he says no—" He stopped himself when he made it to the table's edge and saw the two seated men. "What the fuck?"

Clark shifted his weight in his crouched stance and again asked the men, "Who are you?"

Still no answer. They were probably terrified, having just been double flash-banged and now sharing a room with a dead body and four heavily armed commandos. Oftentimes, in such a state, individuals would respond to questions without hesitation as their minds race, and the best they could conjure would be the truth. But these two remained silent.

Clark rose from his crouch and looked at the paperwork that was spread out on the table then said to Macelar and Roccia, "Alright, check this stuff out here really quick."

He then turned his attention to a briefcase on the floor that he had stepped over when coming around the table.

He picked it up, causing one of the Asian men to shoot up into a standing position, concern visible on his face, and shout, "Hey!"

Just as the man stood, Clark shot his hand out, palm forward, the universal sign for *stop*. The man didn't move. He was in no position to object.

Clark set the briefcase on the table and popped it open. There were a couple of black folders embossed with an emblem that showed three wolf heads, and surrounding that logo, the name *San Lang Mining Corp* in English and what appeared to be Chinese characters. The top portion of the briefcase had a sheath in which were tucked two passports. He pulled them out. Both were from the same country—People's Republic of China.

He looked over at the two Chinese men, both of whom were now standing facing him.

The one who had objected to his handling the briefcase said to him, "That is our property. You give that back."

Clark ignored him as Macelar was now speaking. "Sir, this looks like our stuff."

Clark tossed the passports back in the briefcase and removed one of the folders. He went to the other side of the table to where Macelar presented him with a couple of oversized photographs that had been on the table. They were aerial images, the type a drone might capture. He wasn't entirely sure what they showed, but the landscape certainly seemed like Somalia, and that would make the most sense. One thing he was nearly certain of, though, was that they were from an American aircraft. The data on the bottom left of each of the images indicated as much.

He looked back at the Chinese men. "What is this? How did you get these?"

Silence. Blank stares. A moment passed while Clark considered the situation. The two were clamming up, and Clark didn't want to linger longer than necessary while he tried to extract information from them.

He spoke to Macelar, "Gather this stuff up quick, then we are moving." Then he said to the room, "Time to boogie. I don't care if Hassan didn't get a chance to call in help. No hanging around. We are heading to extract."

Brower, now standing with the CIA asset, his hand on the young man's shoulder, coaxed him towards the stairs and began heading down.

Macelar nodded towards the Chinese men and said to Clark, "Sir, what about these two?"

"I hope for their sake they have keys to one of those Toyotas out front. Let's move."

Clark spoke into his comms, "Super Six-1, Super Six-2, do you copy? Over."

The two pilots, their crafts in a holding a pattern over the compound, both came back.

"Super Six-1, copy, over."

"Super Six-2, copy, over."

Clark replied, "Asset secured. Alpha and Bravo teams moving to primary exfil, over."

"Roger that, see you on the ground, over."

Clark took one last look at the two Chinese men. Neither had moved. They continued to stare back at him. He said nothing and made his way down the stairs.

As Commander Clark came to the bottom of the stairs, two commandos from Bravo Team passed in front of him, heading towards the front door. The main designated extraction point was in front of the compound, where Alpha Team had disembarked. He looked to his right and saw Bravo Team member Petty Officer David Ross standing, facing the doorway into the dining area, keeping watch over the family of the home.

Clark called over to him, "Ross, let's go."

Ross turned and jogged passed him. Clark followed him, gripping the folder labeled *San Lang Mining Corp* in one of his tactical-gloved hands; he was the last of the DEVGRU raiders out the door. They all moved through the compound gate at a light jog, in something like single file. All had night vision down over their eyes and scanned their surroundings with weapons at the ready. Brower escorted the asset, gripping his arm, the Somali man working to keep up. The DEVGRU team exited through the main gate, passing the bodies of what used to be Mohammed Said Hassan's security detail. As they reached the extraction point, the now fifteen men and a dog fanned out and took up positions, awaiting the arrival of the two Ghost

Hawks. The faint *whoop whoop* of the chopper blades was already audible and getting closer. Dhayo, covered in darkness, seemed quiet. No discernable activity from ICU units billeted there. It looked like the DEVGRU men were going to exfiltrate without much of a fight.

Within thirty seconds, the two helicopters touched down on the sandy landscape in front of the assembled men, all waiting crouched on one knee, alert to any potential dangers. As soon as the Ghost Hawks were in position, the commandos, Somali asset, and Ronin all made their way onto the two aircraft. Commander Clark was the last on to Super Six-1, taking up a position in the open doorway. As the helicopter ascended, he looked through his night-vision gear down towards the compound, perplexed by what had transpired in the home.

What in the hell did we walk into?

4

October 17, 2025. 02:07 hours local time.
Chaoyang District, Beijing, China.

Ma Qianli kept glancing down at the smartphone resting on the side table next to his plush recliner, anxious for the large screen to light up with a call.

They should be done by now, he thought.

He picked up the highball glass that sat next to the phone, leaving a ring of moisture on the table, and finished what remained of the now ice-diluted bourbon in one pull. He contemplated pouring another finger to soothe his nerves. Ma sat in the darkened living of his luxury apartment in Beijing's Central Business District, looking out the row of tall windows at the city some twenty floors below. Despite being home to twenty plus million people, Beijing was mainly still at this hour. Few lights were on in the glass and steel skyscrapers surrounding his building, and only occasional headlights flashed by on the normally traffic-choked roads.

Ma had told his wife it would be a late night for him, that he was waiting on an important call. It was already after two in the morning, and he had a meeting with the company board in less than six hours. Ma let out a sigh as he thought of having to attend an important gathering while running on what was sure to be very little sleep but looked forward to delivering the good news that he anticipated the phone call would bring. Fortunately, San Lang Mining's headquarters were just around the corner from his building, only a five-minute walk away.

It had taken him a while to work his way to his newfound position at the company, Chief Operating Officer, since he lacked many of the Communist Party and Politburo connections that most of his peers could rely on to land high ranking jobs in key industries. Now, at fifty-three, he had made it, and he wanted to show his contemporaries that they were right to put their faith in him. He was about to cement San Lang's first major foreign deal since taking over from his predecessor, who had been caught up in one of the government's recurring and sweeping "anti-corruption" campaigns. Ma had heard the man was now breaking rocks in a quarry in southwest China. The problem, he knew, was that nearly everyone was corrupt. You just had to show your worth, to make yourself too important to exile or face the firing squad. The Somalia business would be him doing just that. While he didn't have friends in the highest places, he still had useful connections, and he had leaned on those to bring this Africa opportunity to light.

He was still staring out the window contemplating all of this when the phone buzzed, and the darkness of the room was broken by the white glow of the phone screen. He looked down. It was the call he was expecting.

He answered, "Hongbo. What do you have?"

The voice of his engineer sounded shaken. He stammered for a moment before responding. Something was wrong.

"Sir, we...uh...we..."

"Fuck, Hongbo, get it out. What's going on?"

"It's all gone wrong. Americans came. Commandos. They raided the building and killed Hassan."

Ma was silent as he processed what he'd just heard. This was something he had not prepared for. Sure, Somalia was an active combat zone, and the Americans, as always, had now meddled, but the information he had been given indicated ICU leadership were adept at avoiding danger. Obviously, there was always risk. The same was true when, as a lower-level manager at San Lang, he was party to deals with the Taliban to mine some of

Afghanistan's huge lithium deposits. That was at the height of the Ameri-can-led occupation of that country. San Lang couldn't help the fact that oceans of resources were often found under the soil of shattered countries. Still, what were the chances?

"What..." Ma had to clear to his throat, "...what happened?"

"It happened incredibly fast, sir. We were partway through talking with Hassan when a commotion came from downstairs. Maybe a minute later, the commandos used stun grenades on our room. When I came to, Hassan was dead. Four or five Americans were in the room with us"

"And Laichang? Where is he?"

"He's here with me, sir. We are both unharmed. The fixer is on his way to the meeting place to retrieve us. He had left to stay in a nearby village while we met with Hassan."

"What of the Americans? What did they say to you?"

"They left as quickly as they came. They tried asking us who we were, what we were doing there...but neither of us said anything."

"Good. That's good."

"Sir...you should know that...when the commandos came in, the photographs we brought to show Hassan were all on the table. They noticed and took all of the material. They asked where we got them, but we remained silent...Still, they left with the pictures."

Ma could feel heat rise from his chest and his face flush. The killing of Hassan, even in the presence of his two engineers, could be worked around. But the Americans seeing those images and confiscating them...that was a complicating factor. Real damage control might be required.

"Fuck," was all he could muster in response.

"I'm sorry, sir, we—"

"No, it's OK, Hongbo. Nothing you could do."

He paused for a second. His mind was already moving to what needed to happen next.

He continued, "I'll handle this. Listen, I have to make some calls now. This cannot wait. Let me know when you are back in Kenya."

"Yes, sir, I—"

Ma killed the call and immediately went to his contacts to make another.

A half hour later, Ma found himself sitting in the driver's seat of his Mercedes-Benz sedan in the underground parking garage of his building. Given the time, even in a city of Beijing's size, there were few open options for a meeting, and this was not a discussion he wanted to have over the phone.

"I'll come to you," the man he called after hanging up with Jiang had said, "Wait in your car in the garage."

The man's voice always unnerved him. Not only was it laden with the famously harsh accent of northern China, but the man's vocal cords had also been ruined by years of chain-smoking. Ma thought of rusted train wheels passing over steel rails whenever he heard it.

He continued to ponder how he would deliver the news of the Americans coming upon the Hassan meeting. Had he been reckless by rushing into talks with someone on America's kill list?

His thinking was interrupted by the sound of the passenger door opening up, causing him to startle. The large, squat frame of Zhang Hudao entered the vehicle and settled into the passenger seat, shutting the door as he did.

Zhang had the intimidating look to accompany his disconcerting voice. He was heavy-set and broad-shouldered, with a close-cropped haircut, gray stubble taking over on the temples. His hands could have belonged to a bricklayer, and he had a thick scar that ran from the top of his left eyebrow to his cheekbone. Ma had never asked about its origin.

Zhang worked for the Ministry of State Security, China's foil to America's CIA. Foreign intelligence was nominally his area of expertise, with the occasional foray into industrial espionage. It was he who had given Ma the drone imagery that Jiang and Wu brought to show Hassan. Ma had studied geological engineering with Zhang's younger brother during their university days, often helping with assignments and studies. He was still in touch with the younger Zhang, who had gone on to leave the industry and become a bureaucrat. Though Hudao was far from the sentimental type, he apparently had not forgotten the kindness Ma had shown his brother.

"What is it?" Zhang said to him, by way of greeting.

Despite the curtness, Ma didn't get the sense that Zhang was perturbed by their meeting at such an unseemly hour. He had answered on the first ring when Ma had called. Ma wasn't sure if the man ever actually slept.

"The imagery you provided...the suspected mineral deposits in Somalia. The Americans...they know we have it..."

Ma braced for the upbraiding that was sure to come after delivering that piece of information.

Zhang continued to look ahead out the windshield at the concrete all around them. He grunted. "How did that happen?"

"Two of my engineers were meeting tonight in Somalia with one of the heads of the Islamic Courts Union, the militant organization that—"

"I know what it is."

"The ICU controls the territory where those deposits are. They were having an initial meeting to discuss an agreement to mine the area. In the middle of the meeting, American commandos showed up and killed the ICU man. My men were unharmed, but the Americans saw the material and took it with them.

Zhang sat motionless. Ma shifted in his seat, unsettled by the silence in the car.

Zhang finally spoke, "Is that it?"

"Yes, I thought you should know."

Zhang nodded, more to himself, and said, "OK," then began to get out of the vehicle.

"Wait," Ma said hurriedly, "That's it? I...what should we do?"

"Nothing for now."

"I am meeting my board in just a few hours. What do I say?"

"I'm sure you'll figure something out."

Zhang opened the door and got out. Before walking away, he leaned down and into the car, facing Ma.

"Go to bed. I'll be in touch."

He quietly closed the door and slipped into the darkness of the garage.

5

October 16, 2025. 22:55 hours local time.
Aboard the USS Carl Vinson. Five kilometers off of the Somalia coast.

Commander Clark was seated at a metal table in the small Special Program Access Facility (SPAF), an area similar to a SCIF but with even greater restrictions, deep below deck on the Carl Vinson. A paper cup of coffee, steam wafting out, sat by his folded hands on the table. The folder he had taken from the two Chinese men, filled with the aerial imagery his team had confiscated, lay next to the coffee.

It was an austere room, with just the small metal conference table, a bank of computers along one wall, and one large LCD monitor on another. All the screens were darkened. It was the ship's facility for classified meetings and mission debriefings, the latter the reason Clark sat in wait.

The heavy steel door, reminiscent of those separating compartments on submarines, groaned open, and Clark's DEVGRU superior, Captain Elliot Farr, stepped in. A tall, thin man wearing a simple gray t-shirt and jeans followed behind him. This was the CIA liaison who had handled the asset and intel for the mission. Everyone knew him only as Mike.

Captain Farr nodded at Clark as they made their way to take the seats opposite him.

"John, good work tonight. Glad you and the team are back safe and sound. As always."

Clark nodded back. "Thank you, sir. It was...mostly straightforward."

Mike sat down next to Farr without uttering or motioning any greeting.

Clark looked at him and asked, "How is your asset?"

"He's good. Little shaken up, but he'll be fine. Has a cozy apartment in Minneapolis waiting for him when he's done going through the motions. Nice work tonight."

Clark nodded a thanks.

Farr got right down to business. "So, after action report. What can you tell us? We learn anything about this gang?"

"Well sir...again, fairly straightforward. Security was light, as expected. Minimal resistance, really. Civilians were on the scene, Somali family that lived in the target building, I imagine, but no collateral damage. There were also...two Chinese males. Middle aged, civilians. They were in the room with Cochise. Appeared to be meeting with him."

Mike, who had been looking down at the table while Clark spoke, looked up at that last statement, concern evident on his face. "Chinese?" He asked.

"Yea. PRC nationals. They had a briefcase with them containing their passports. Not diplomatic, though. They—"

"Did you get anything out of them? What were they doing there?" Mike cut him off.

"They wouldn't say a word. I only could get a couple questions across. I didn't want to wait around to see if ICU fighters in Dhayo were notified or heard any commotion. The two Chinese guys had also been flash banged and were still coming to."

Mike leaned back in his chair, digesting what he had just heard.

He said, almost to himself rather than either Farr or Clark, "The Chinese aren't the most discerning when it comes to who they will do business with. Mining deals with the Taliban come to mind. But what in the hell would they want with the ICU?"

Clark responded, "Well, we might have some idea." He pushed the folder in front of him across the table towards the other two. "Took these from the mission site. The Chinese guys had brought them as part of a presentation, or so it appeared."

Mike picked up the folder and opened it to reveal the contents, not noticing the company logo on the front. He pulled out the sheaf of photographs and spread them on the table in front of Captain Farr and himself. Both men took a minute looking through the images.

It was Farr who broke the silence, "These are from one of our birds."

Clark nodded at that.

Farr continued, "Clearly a BDA. My guess is the munitions depot we struck not long ago. Timestamps on these seem to line up with that. I was in one of the briefings about the strike. AFSOC did the targeting. These two Chinese guys had all of these on them?"

Clark nodded again and said, "Yeah, looks that way. Given the arrangement on the table, safe to assume these were being presented to Cochise, and he was studying them before we broke up the meeting."

Mike, holding one of the images, spoke to Clark without looking up, "These yellow lines shown on the surrounding landscape here—"

This time Commander Clark cut him off. "Yea, that is why I say maybe we can put two and two together and hazard a guess as to what those two were doing there. Check out the folder. I nipped that out of their briefcase."

Both Farr and Mike looked down at the folder. It still lay in the open position, so Mike flipped it closed to see the front.

He read out loud, "San Lang Mining Corp."

Clark nodded. "Yea, they had that look to them, like engineers or paper pushers. Do you know anything about that company?"

Mike shook his head. "No, East Asia isn't my wheelhouse. I can definitely make the inquiries, though. If the individuals were from this mining firm, then these line overlays here must represent something that piqued their interest. Otherwise, I can't see how this BDA would mean anything to them."

Clark once again nodded. "That's my theory. The thing that gets me is, I'm no technical expert, but those seem like they are embedded in the imagery. I don't think the Chinese could have manipulated the imagery to create that overlay. That must have been done on our end, but now we are getting above my pay grade."

Captain Farr chimed in, "Of course, the 800-pound gorilla in the room here is, how in the hell did two guys from a Chinese mining company end up with these?"

That was met with silence from the other two.

After a moment, it was Mike who spoke, "Do either of you know what our Air Force brethren have going on in-country? Can we find out about the aircraft that produced these photos?"

Farr responded, "I've been in regular contact with AFSOC throughout this mission. They've got a small fleet of drones supporting their activities. I am pretty sure drone flights are being handled out of Creech."

Mike considered that and, after a few seconds, said, "I think we need to set something up with the good folks in Nevada then."

6

October 17, 2025. 12:22 hours local time.
Air Force Office of Special Investigations Headquarters, Quantico, Virginia.

The smell of cordite lingered in the air as Special Agent Henry Purcel stood waiting for his paper target to pull up to him. He watched as the sheet, featuring the silhouette of the upper part of a human form, slowly drew forward along the cable of the firing range's target retrieval system. As the target came to a stop in front of his firing booth, he took off his ear protection and placed it next to his service weapon on the booth counter. He reached up and unclipped the target, pulling it down to inspect his handiwork. He'd fired a whole clip, aiming all but the last two shots for the center mass. The final two bullets he'd aimed for the head of the target, with one finding purchase and the other hitting the throat of the silhouette. He was happy to see most of the shots in the chest area were packed quite tightly.

He continued to look at the target in his hands, though his mind began to drift, the image of Hani Khatib writhing on the cafeteria floor momentarily flashing before his eyes. He shook his head to get rid of the thought. He did not hear the approaching footsteps.

"Still shooting pretty tight rounds, Special Agent?"

Purcel startled slightly and turned to see Master Sergeant Gene Surprenant, the Range Supervisor, standing behind him.

Noticing Purcel's reaction, Suprenant threw up both hands in a "my bad" gesture. "Sorry Special Agent, didn't mean to sneak up on you."

Purcel did not say anything for a brief moment. He had noticed that, since the Jordan incident, he'd been jumpier and more easily taken by surprise.

"No, no worries. Just a bit lost in thought is all."

"Figured I'd come see how you did."

The Master Sergeant turned his head to both sides, in a show of scanning the building. "It's quiet around here this time of day. Pretty odd way to spend the lunch hour."

Purcel offered him a half smile. "Yea. Slow day today. Figured I could squeeze in a session. I tend to get through my lunch pretty quickly anyway."

"Reed going to unchain you from the desk pretty soon?"

He was referring to Lieutenant Colonel Al Reed, Purcel's commanding officer.

"Not that I've heard, no."

Surprenant nodded in a knowing way. The Master Sergeant was what many of the agents at AFOSI referred to as *the old battle axe*, as he had over thirty years at the agency. His face was etched with deep wrinkles, and despite living in Virginia for so long, he never did shake his heavy Boston accent. Surprenant had helped Purcel hone his shooting skills when Purcel joined the agency nearly two decades ago, and the two became close over the years, as the fastidious Purcel made it routine to visit the range to stay sharp. Surprenant knew how Purcel was and that being kept out of the field was killing him.

Surprenant motioned with his chin towards the target that Purcel still held. "How'd you do?"

Purcel shrugged and passed the target over.

The Master Sergeant held it in front of himself and, after a moment, pursed his lips in satisfaction and nodded. "I'd say you still got it, Special Agent. This is not a bad grouping."

Purcel gave his characteristic half smile once more and shrugged. "Yea, not bad."

When Purcel added nothing more, the two men stood awkwardly for a second.

The Master Sergeant put his arms down by his side, one hand still holding the target, and asked, "How's the arm?"

Purcel reflexively flexed his hand open and closed. Looking down at his arm, he said, "Getting there. Odd jolt of pain now and then. Surgeons said that'll happen, part and parcel with nerve damage. Didn't bother me just now and doesn't with other activities."

Suprenant nodded and said, "Good."

When Purcel had nothing more to say again, Surprenant added, "Give it some more time. That was no small thing that shook down in Jordan. You're lucky to have come home. You'll be back at it soon enough, Henry."

Purcel brought his gaze back up and looked straight at Surprenant. "I sure hope so."

7

October 18, 2025. 19:30 hours local time.
Aboard the USS Carl Vinson, off the coast of Salalah, Oman.

Captain Farr, Commander Clark, and Mike sat silently in the Vinson's SPAF. This time, all three men were on the same side of the metal conference table, facing the LCD display that dominated the room's far wall, waiting for it to come to life. An intelligence analyst from the Vinson's crew who had been assigned to the meeting sat off to their right at the bank of computers, working away, his clicking and typing the only sounds in the room.

Finally, he said, "Should be coming online now, Captain."

Farr simply clicked his pen in response. After a moment, the LCD screen lit up, and within a few seconds, the three men were looking at four others, three in Operational Camouflage Pattern uniforms, or OCPs, and another in a collared dress shirt, sharing a conference table thousands of miles away in a SPAF of their own.

Captain Farr was the first to speak, "Colonel Chavez, can you hear me OK?"

Chavez's voice came clear over the channel, "Yes captain, we can hear you just fine."

"Great. Thank you for making time for this."

"Glad to. I have here with me Lieutenants Moore and Gajewski." He moved his hands from their folded position in front him to indicate the two young men to his right, stating, "They are the leads for our drone operations here at Creech."

With his left hand, he motioned to the other man, who appeared to be in his upper forties or mid-fifties.

Chavez said, "I've also asked our liaison with the NSA, Steve Giresi, to join us. Given the matter you indicated in your communication, I thought his presence might be warranted."

Captain Farr nodded at that. "Very well. Thank you again, sir. I have with me Commander Clark from my DEVGRU team, and this," Farr said, motioning with his head to his right, "is Mike, from the Agency. He's been doing a lot of the intel work aiding Eastern Promises. It was his asset that provided the intel for our op the other night, eliminating the ICU principal, which I'm sure you are aware of."

Four nods came from the screen.

He continued, "I'll get right to it then. Colonel, as I alluded to, during the op, Commander Clark's team recovered some material that I believe belongs to us, and specifically from one of our reconnaissance aircraft. Commander, if you would."

Clark cleared his throat and said, "Yes, sir. Colonel Chavez, the target was in the middle of a meeting when we engaged. That meeting was with two men, Chinese nationals. They were the ones in possession of the imagery in question. Obviously, things were a little helter skelter in that room, but I don't think it requires a leap of faith to assume it was these two individuals who had the photos and were showing them to the ICU principal."

No one spoke for a moment.

Finally, Colonel Chavez said, "Chinese nationals? How were they identified?"

"We found their passports among their belongings. Also, some other documentation backed that up. Looks like they were representatives from a Chinese mining consortium or firm."

Upon hearing that last part, Giresi, the NSA agent who had been sitting back in his chair, now leaned forward and put his arms on the conference table, suddenly more engaged but remaining silent.

Colonel Chavez responded, "I see."

Captain Farr said, "Right. We have obviously walked into something that raises all kinds of questions. I'd like for you gentlemen to take a look at what Clark's team brought back. LT, let's get those up."

The intel analyst responded, "Yes sir." After a few clicks on his screen, he said, "Colonel Chavez, sharing with you now, please confirm you see on your end."

"We see it."

The intel analyst slowly clicked through scans of the drone photographs he was sharing, giving the men on the other side of the world a moment to study each one.

The NSA analyst had an ashen look on his face as the imagery passed in front of them. Colonel Chavez ran a hand over his face but said nothing, nor did any of the others with him.

It was Clark who broke the silence. "Colonel, I take it you recognize what we have here?"

"Yes, this is from one of our birds. If I'm not mistaken, Lieutenant Moore, this is your Ocelot drone?"

Moore nodded. "Yes, sir, this is from the BDA on the ICU munitions storage, the camel slaughterhouse."

Chavez spoke to the men on the Vinson, "You're saying all these print-outs were found during your raid in the possession of these presumed Chinese nationals?"

Clark responded, "Yes, sir. Mostly scattered on the table where their sit-down was happening. Again, it only makes sense the Chinese men were the ones who brought them."

Chavez looked over at Giresi, who could only shake his head. Moore and Gajewski both looked shaken.

Mike spoke, "Before we get into how these pictures came to be in the hands of these PRC nationals, I would like to know what is represented by these yellow lines that overlay some of the images. I haven't seen those before on any drone captures. Are those ours?"

Lieutenant Moore looked over at Colonel Chavez. who gave him a nod and said, "It's alright, they're read in."

Moore cleared his throat. "Sir, those lines represent possible deposits of certain minerals, namely cobalt, coltan, and lithium."

Now, it was the men in the Carl Vinson's SPAF who were silent. Mike had raised his eyebrows.

After a moment he finally spoke, "I don't understand. You're saying the drone was able to...identify those and add the overlay onto the imagery?"

Moore responded, "That's correct sir, yes."

"How...how is such a function being performed?"

Moore moved to respond, but Giresi cut him off. "This was part of a highly compartmentalized program, a collaboration between my agency, the US Geological Survey, and the Air Force: designing a system that can identify, from the air, potential deposits of specific rare-earth minerals that are critical to national security, not to mention daily life."

"How is that even possible?"

"My expertise is in signals intelligence, not the science of this technology, but it pertains to reading the radioactive signatures—however minute they may be, in many cases—of the minerals, even when deep underground. The built-in technology maps out the locations of the signatures in real time, thus showing potential veins."

Mike leaned back in his chair. "Jesus Christ," he said.

The NSA man continued, "It has only just recently been deployed. To my knowledge, Lieutenant Moore's Ocelot is the only drone currently in operation that carries it. The principle behind all of this is: if we are going to be engaging in military operations in countries with the permission, or even at the request, of local governments, we should be using that as an opportunity to identify sources of select rare earths. It's an area that is becoming more and more salient, and Mike, as I'm sure as you know, China currently maintains a significant advantage over us. *Significant* is probably not a strong enough word. More accurate to say the Chinese are eating our lunch on this."

Mike nodded at that last part. "Yes, they have turned eastern Democratic Republic of the Congo, where so much of this stuff is found, into a veritable fief. They practically own the supply chain."

"Correct. This is just one move in our efforts to gain more of our own foothold in the rare earths industry."

"I'll be damned."

Giresi continued, "Again, this is highly compartmentalized work. Only a few outside of this call are currently aware of this technology."

Mike said, "Except for who-knows-how-many members of the Chinese military-industrial complex, or so it would appear."

"We don't know for sure how they were interpreting this intel. We haven't ascertained the level of knowledge on that side."

Mike spoke to Colonel Chavez, "Colonel, if I may, could we excuse the lieutenants?"

Chavez looked over at his two subordinates and said, "Thank you, gentlemen. You can step out. I'll see you back at your station."

Moore and Gajewski thanked the colonel, acknowledged the Navy men on the call, and stepped out of the SPAF.

When they were gone, Mike said to the colonel, "Sir, I think it is safe to assume the two Chinese nationals knew exactly what these drone images portrayed—"

Giresi cut him off, "Listen, we can't jump to conclusions like that, not at this juncture. It certainly doesn't look good. But it is possible they were fishing."

"No, no we absolutely can. You do not expend the resources and energy to find and set a meeting with someone like Hassan and meet him on his turf in the middle of an active war zone just on a hunch. These men knew what they had, and they went to broker a deal. With all due respect, assuming otherwise is wishful thinking, Now, the captain, commander, and I were all perplexed as to what these overlays could have represented, and we needed this phone call to find that out. Not only did the Chinese end up with these images, but they also knew how to interpret them."

He let that notion hang in the air. No one had any response.

After a moment, he asked Chavez, "Colonel, your two lieutenants, if I may be somewhat blunt here...what is your level of trust in these men?"

"I don't think I like your implication, Mike."

Mike held up his hands in a placating manner. He said, "They're pretty young guys to be handling such high-level intel. From what it sounds like, they are the only airmen who have the inside track on this technology. We start somewhere."

The Colonel gave a nod, ceding the point. He then said, "Young but mature. Been in my unit a long time. They undergo the regular background checks and interviews. I knew Moore's father when we were young airmen and based together at Griffiss in upstate New York. Good family. Gajewski's upstanding as well. No qualms about either. We will do the necessary debriefs and follow up on any outside communications they may be having, but I have complete confidence in both."

Mike nodded.

Captain Farr spoke up, "Colonel, we've done our part here. We have made you aware of what we found. In this part of the world, we blow open doors and shoot the bad guys. What happens now?"

Giresi was the one to answer, "I'll get in touch with the AFOSI and the FBI, immediately. This is now an urgent investigation, and it will start there."

Mike said, "I should be back stateside in a few days. I'll make sure my agency's resources are available, should they be needed. The Near East is my wheelhouse, but I know some people in the China shop. I'll set up a line of communication."

Giresi nodded and said, "Appreciate that."

No one had anything further to add.

After a few seconds of silence, Mike finally said, "There's a leak somewhere, and we have to put a plug in it."

8

October 18, 2025. 12:16 hours local time.
Chinatown, Manhattan, New York.

Pedestrians, mainly elderly Chinese men taking a stroll or making their way to watch friends compete at stone tables etched with chess boards, strode past Bao Jiaotong. He stood next to the statue of Sun Yat-Sen in the eponymous plaza, looking down at his phone. Some shouting, a mix of English and Cantonese, and the sounds of balls being dribbled and sneakers scuffing emanated from the basketball courts at the adjacent Columbus Park. The obnoxious beeping of a food delivery truck backing up came from behind him, somewhere on Mulberry Street. But Bao was oblivious to the cacophony that characterized this cramped, humanity-dense part of the world. His attention was completely taken by what he saw on his screen, a message that had been left in the Drafts folder of an email account.

We have a potential problem. The Americans found images in our possession from the drones we have been accessing. They have no knowledge of how we came to have these, but I wanted to make you aware. I am sure they will be starting an internal investigation into the matter. What level of confidence do you have in the asset? Do we need to worry about an investigation finding its way to them?

Bao had stepped out from his tiny office above a restaurant in Manhattan's Chinatown where he helped run a small travel agency, primarily serving locals looking to visit family in mainland China or Hong Kong. A few minutes before, at his work desk, he received a message in his business email account from someone addressing themselves as his cousin back in China. They were checking in, asking how things were, and mentioning the weather back home. It was the reference to the weather that prompted Bao to leave the office, as it was a signal to shift to his real role, what he had been doing for years in New York: spying for the People's Republic of China.

He was what those in his line of work referred to as a *non-official cover*, or NOC. The intelligence services for a given country oftentimes embedded agents in jobs at their embassies abroad, an *official cover*. By day, they were consular officers performing the associated duties, such as solving passport issues or responding to requests for assistance. By night, they plied their spy craft. Should something go wrong, namely the true nature of their work being discovered by the host country, they may be afforded some diplomatic protections. This was not the case for Bao. Being a NOC provided him more opportunities to gather intelligence and turn assets, as he was not sequestered to a diplomatic compound or burdened with keeping the pretense of an official cover. But should the Americans find out he was a spy, he would be on his own.

Communication with his "cousin"—his contact at the Ministry of State Security—was rare. When he saw the email prompt on his office desktop, he'd hoped it was fresh tasking, but the opening line of the draft message quickly extinguished that notion.

Eventually, he looked up from his phone and scanned the plaza around him. No one paid him any attention, all going about their afternoon. The bliss of a simple, complication-free life. He let a few seconds pass, and the anxiety that initially plumed in his chest like a mushroom cloud and made his throat constrict began to subside. He exhaled to calm himself. It took him a moment, but he realized he need not panic. Not yet.

What could the immediate implications of this be? He thought to himself.

Not much, really.

Nothing would happen right away. The work his asset had performed was, by design, difficult to connect back to them. The Americans would really have to pull this thread and work it, and even then, it may not yield anything. This news certainly wasn't ideal, but for now, it was far from catastrophic. There was no need to sound alarm bells just yet. He nodded to himself as he thought of all this, as if agreeing with his inner monologue. He looked back to his phone, deleted the draft, and began to type another.

———————

October 19, 2025. 01:24 hours local time.
Dongcheng District, Beijing, China.

A rustling came from somewhere within the assortment of buckets, bicycles, tools, and other odds-and-ends of life that lined the wall across the street from where Zhang Hudao sat on his plastic stool, low to the ground. He peered through the smoke of the cigarette he let dangle from his mouth, waiting for the source of the sound to emerge. He knew what it was, for it was part of a nightly ritual.

Zhang was sitting outside the entrance way to his small two-bedroom abode in one of Beijing's last remaining *hutongs*: the narrow streets or alleys filled with traditional homes crammed next to one another. Many of the *hutongs* that once covered much of the city had been razed to make way for hotels, restaurants, or apartment blocks. Progress, the city officials called it. Zhang wasn't sure how eliminating part of your history represented progress, but like so many things, it wasn't his place to say. Most of his colleagues in state security went home to large apartments in the newer districts that cropped up as China's capital sprawled, or even to modern farmhouses more than an hour outside the city. Not Zhang. He opted for this hovel, as his brother liked to call it, that he had inherited from their father, a lifelong member of the Communist Party. It was within touching distance of the city's most famous landmarks, the center of political power, and so much of the history that made him proud to be Chinese.

The rustling continued, and soon, through the faint moonlight—the sole source of lighting in the alley at this hour—he made out a gray silhouette slinking along the ground towards him. The mangy black cat rubbed itself against his leg, emitting a faint purr. One night, like now, during one of Zhang's frequent bouts of insomnia, the cat had shown up, and Zhang had given it a small bowl of rice. Ever since, the stray came back nearly every night expecting some sustenance. Zhang called him—at least he thought it was a him—*XiaoGui*. Little Ghost.

He flicked his cigarette butt out into the street and made to stand to get something for the cat when his phone dinged. An email. He opened up his email app to find one new message in the inbox. It was a response to an email he had sent a little earlier in the night.

Subject: *RE: How Are You?*

Hi Cousin,

Thanks for your message. Things are well here in New York. Business has been good. I look forward to many bookings soon, as the New Year approaches. It has been raining a lot recently, more than usual for this time of year. Hope things are well back home.

There was the reference to the weather he was hoping for.

After the previous night's emergency meeting with Ma Qianli in Ma's parking garage, Zhang had held off on immediately messaging Bao or informing him of Ma's news. He first wanted to ruminate on the matter and not act hastily. Zhang's initial thought was to do nothing with the information, to simply see if the matter developed any further, if at all. Keep it between himself and Ma and the two engineers. He understood Ma being practically distraught over the situation, but he was a civilian. Soft. Driving back from Chaoyang to the *hutong*, he had decided, for now, it wasn't anything requiring drastic measures. Protocol would be to inform his superior at the ministry, but that could wait. After a few hours' sleep, however, he figured it was best to at least let Bao know what had happened. It only seemed right. Most likely, Bao would be the first one to suffer any consequences.

Zhang went inside and sat at a small wooden table to the right of his entry. He kept an old laptop there, which he booted up and, after giving it a few moments to come alive, used to open an internet browser and access a Gmail account. He went to the Drafts folder, where he found an email typed up:

Understood. It is unfortunate, but I would not worry. I will make the asset

aware of this development, and I have confidence in their abilities and confiden-
tiality. I also think an investigation leading to our source is highly unlikely. It
would require an incredible leap of faith on their part. At the very least, it will take
an inordinate amount of time for them to reach such a conclusion. I think we are
safe for some time.

Zhang leaned back in his chair, glad to see that Bao shared his feelings. The Americans finding out that his country was spying on them did not worry him at all, really. Even if they eventually found out exactly what was happening, it would not be the end of the world. After all, it was expected on both sides that the other was engaging in espionage. There might be stern words in public, maybe a sanction or two or some minor economic action, the inevitable "tough talk" with someone high up in China's diplomatic core, but that would be all. Zhang was not completely sanguine about the matter, however.

Timing. Timing did worry him. That is, the Americans unearthing the source and putting a premature end to the intelligence leaks. As it stood, the source *was* critical. Zhang's agency *needed* the information being gleaned from this particular operation. While it seemed unlikely that the Americans would find anything soon, he was nevertheless aware of the potential danger. He still needed time.

Zhang erased the draft message and typed up another:

Good. Leave it be. Do not say anything to the asset. I do not want to instill panic and perhaps cause them to change their behavior. Carry on as you have. I will keep you apprised of any developments from my end.

He picked up his phone off the table and opened up the email app once more, replying to his "cousin" with a short message stating that he and his parents were well and that he looked forward to some cooler weather.

Clicking his phone off, he sat in the darkness of his tiny dining space, considering the situation at hand.

Let's see how good the Americans are.

9

October 20, 2025. 07:57 hours local time.
Air Force Office of Special Investigations Headquarters, Quantico, Virginia.

Seated in his oversized office chair, behind his equally oversized desk, Lieutenant Colonel Al Reed stared at his closed door, waiting for the knock that should be coming any moment. He thought about the phone call he'd just had moments before.

We want your best agent on this, Lieutenant Colonel.

What "this" was, the caller would not even say, just that it was about as high level as anything could be. What confused Reed, somewhat, was that the caller identified his agency as the NSA, but he was phoning from the Center for Intelligence, the headquarters of the CIA. It was obvious that Reed was not going to be privy to any details. All he needed to know was one of his agents was required, and the best, at that.

Normally, if that was the prompt, then the lieutenant colonel need not hesitate. Special Agent Henry Purcel was who he would put forward. But, given all that Purcel had been through in recent months, *was* he ready for a bigger case?

Reed knew what Purcel's answer would be. But it wasn't up to his star special agent. It was his call to make, and his alone. After setting down the phone receiver, he'd leaned back in his chair and considered the conversation. It had been years since Reed himself served as an agent in the field, but an investigator's skills never leave entirely. While the caller gave nothing away about whatever his pressing matter was, Reed could still detect urgency within the caller's words.

What the lieutenant colonel also couldn't see beyond was the fact that it was very rare, he would say extremely rare, that agencies within the national intelligence apparatus reached out to his unit for assistance. That alone made him consider the weight of the situation. Maybe this was the moment that he needed to release Purcel to do what he did best.

A knock came on the door.

"Come in."

The door opened, and in stepped the tall frame of Special Agent Henry Purcel. "The secretary said you wanted see me, sir?"

Purcel made no move to take one of Reed's guest chairs at the desk, and Reed didn't prompt him to do so. His agent would not be there very long.

Reed skipped any pleasantries. "Purcel. I need you to head over to Langley, straight away."

"Langley...um, OK, sir. Can you say what this is regarding? That's a two-and-a-half hour drive I wasn't counting on today."

"No, no. Not Langley AFB. Langley. Fairfax. CIA headquarters."

Purcel paused for a second. Wanted at CIA headquarters? That was... different.

"CIA, sir?"

"Yes, just got a call on the secure line from some spook over there. Actually, the guy said he was NSA, Giresi is the name, but he's at the CIA. All he said was they needed one of my best agents, and it seems like they wanted him yesterday. Whatever it is, it must have them wrapped around the axle, and I figure you're good to catch some field work again, so I'm giving it to you."

Purcel didn't say anything for a moment. He shifted his stance in a subtle display of building excitement. This sounded like it might have promise. He thought about his current cases. One involved an Air Force officer picking up his second DUI.

Whatever the Agency has going on, it's gotta be better than that bullshit, he thought.

"And my current caseload, sir?"

"Don't worry about it. I'll pass it off to Davis or Koch. They could use something to do. Pretty sure when I walked by his desk this morning, I saw Koch shooting balled-up paper into his garbage."

"Um...OK, great, I'll get going right now. Thank you, sir."

"Purcel?"

"Sir?"

"Am I right about that? You ready to get back out there? How's the arm?"

Purcel looked down at his afflicted appendage and reflexively flexed his hand. "I'm good, sir. Still feel the odd bolt of pain, but it subsides pretty quickly. I'm ready for something else."

"I figured. Good luck, with whatever it is. Now get going."

"Yes sir."

––––––––––

10

09:33 hours local time.
George Bush Center for Intelligence, Langley, Virginia.

Purcel fiddled with the Central Intelligence Agency visitor badge that hung from the breast pocket of his shirt. He looked around the secure briefing room. He was seated at the end of a large conference table, facing the entrance, as always. Besides the table and accompanying half dozen or so chairs, the room was sparse. On the wall to his right, a large LCD screen hung, while in the corner to the left of the door was an American flag on a pedestal. Along the same wall were four clocks showing four time zones: local, Greenwich Mean, Moscow, and Beijing. This is what he had to keep his mind occupied while he waited what was now approaching fifteen minutes. Upon entering the building, per agency protocol, he was temporarily relieved of anything that could be used to write or record: his phone, Apple watch, briefcase (containing his notepad and pen), even his car key fob. All of these items sat in a locker somewhere off the main lobby. Henry Purcel had every clearance imaginable, but everyone short of the president himself had to give up their phones and laptops when they were here. No chances were taken.

After checking him in, an agency secretary had ushered Purcel into the room and said, "They'll be with you shortly," telling him to hang tight while not giving any indication as to who *they* were or why *they* had called him up here. He had been given no briefing folder, nothing. She had offered coffee or water, which he declined. Now, he wished he had the water to at least give himself something to do.

After a few more minutes, the door finally opened and two men came in, one in a suit and tie and the other in khakis and a dress shirt but no tie.

Purcel stood as they entered, waiting for an introduction.

The one in the suit made his way around the left side of the table to Purcel, hand extended. "Special Agent Purcel, I'm Steve Giresi with the NSA. Appreciate you coming out."

"You can call me Henry," Purcel said as they shook hands. He turned to the other man who had come around the other side of the conference table, smiling and also ready to shake.

"Henry, I'm Chris, with the agency here," the man said.

Purcel nodded as they shook.

Giresi pulled out a chair, indicating that Purcel should sit back down. Once they were all seated, Purcel now flanked on either side by his interlocutors, Giresi began. "Again, thanks for coming on such short notice. I just landed at Reagan this morning from Nevada, Creech Air Base, and wanted to have this sit-down ASAP. You'll see what we have to talk about is more an NSA matter, but Langley made for a more convenient meeting point, and I know it was closer for you as well. Anyway, I read your profile on the flight over, very impressive resume."

Purcel nodded and gave a small smile.

Giresi continued, "This incident in Jordan...I'm glad you're OK."

This got another nod. "I appreciate it..."

Purcel thought about adding something, but what? How it could have gone very differently? How he was lucky to be here having this conversation? He had known these guys for all of two minutes.

There was a brief pregnant pause.

When Giresi realized Purcel had nothing else to say on that matter, he moved on. "I see you caught the Texeira case. Ukraine War intel fiasco."

He was referring to an incident in 2022 when a young air national guardsman from Massachusetts leaked, over a video game server, classified information pertaining to Ukraine's fight against Russia's invasion.

"Yea, that was more navigating media attention than anything. That kid made it easy for us, really. He shared the intel online to impress his buddies." Purcel shook his head at the memory.

"Still, you made quick work of it. We are hoping you can do similar here."

"Absolutely."

Purcel was eager to hear what was coming. AFOSI interfacing with other federal agencies was commonplace, but it usually involved the FBI, DEA, ATF, the more domestically focused outfits. Getting a call directly from an intelligence agency was rare. He also noticed that neither Giresi nor Chris carried any documents or folders, which was odd. He expected to have some materials to look through.

"I'll get right down to it. We have what we believe is a leak of sensitive, and I mean the most sensitive, intelligence" Giresi said.

As if reading Purcel's mind, he waved his hand between himself and Chris across the table and said, "You'll notice we don't have any briefing docs for you. No detail of this operation is going on paper unless it absolutely has to. What you're about to hear is strictly need-to-know, and the number of people that are read up on this is extremely limited. Or at least, that was the idea until this breach."

Purcel leaned forward and folded his hands on the table. Engaged.

Giresi took this as a cue to continue. "The NSA has collaborated with the Air Force and the Geological Survey to develop technology to identify, from the sky, potential deposits of rare earth minerals. This capability was designed specifically to be placed on UAVs. It has been in the works for some time, but we've only just recently put one of these UAVs into action, and that's been in Somalia."

The NSA man paused for a moment. Purcel didn't move or have any reaction, but he knew what he had just heard was a big deal. He couldn't speak to Air Force capabilities in depth, but given his work, he did his best to stay apprised of developments in technology. And even from that basic level of understanding, he recognized that what Giresi had just described was remarkable.

"Just under seventy-two hours ago, it came to light that photographs from that UAV in Somalia were in the possession of Chinese nationals."

Purcel raised his eyebrows upon hearing that. He leaned back in his chair and continued to look at Giresi. He thought for a moment and said, "Chinese nationals? Here?"

Giresi shook his head, but it was Chris, finally entering the conversation, who responded. "Three nights ago, a Navy SEAL unit conducted a raid in Somalia to kill a high-value target. You may have seen this on the news?"

Purcel nodded, saying, "Someone high up within their version of the Taliban or something. Yes, I did catch that."

"Apparently, the target was meeting with two individuals from the People's Republic. Engineers from a Chinese mining firm. The SEAL team just happened upon the meeting and found the drone photos with the Chinese. They recognized the images as having come from an Air Force bird and confiscated them. A colleague of mine in the Near East office helped put that raid together, and he was in the debriefing when the SEAL lead revealed their findings. I work in the China shop, so he reached out and put me in touch with Steve here."

Giresi cut in, "As I indicated before, this is an NSA and Air Force matter, which is why we contacted your office to help. Given Chris's area of expertise, he can be used as a resource if need be."

Purcel shifted in his seat, his excitement now starting to build. This is what he was talking about; this was his wheelhouse. Someone else at Quantico could take the exam-cheating scandals.

"I see. And I take it you have no idea how the Chinese nationals got a hold of the drone shots?"

Both shook their heads.

It was Giresi who said, "None at all. Again, this is compartmentalized at the highest level. The number of individuals read-in on this is very tight. Bringing in you and Chris represented a significant percentage increase. The two airmen, the only two, that handled these drones are young, but I don't think we have another Texeira situation. I spoke to them myself and got a good impression, though reading people isn't quite my thing. Their commanding officer thinks highly of them. I imagine it would be a place to start."

"I guess they are at Creech?"

Giresi nodded.

Purcel didn't say anything for a moment. He looked at Chris and then to Giresi. He peeked at his wrist for the time, forgetting he didn't have his watch, so he checked the bank of clocks on the wall across from him. He thought of the overnight bag with a couple changes of clothes he always kept in his car. He hadn't needed it for a while, but it was always best to be prepared at a moment's notice.

He looked back to Chris and said, "Can your secretary here pull up the next flight to Vegas

from Reagan?"

11

October 21, 2025. 10:37 hours local time.
Creech Air Force Base, Indian Springs, Nevada.

Henry Purcel studied Lieutenant Moore from across a small conference table. The young airman sat ramrod straight and looked at Purcel as he spoke, making eye contact. He showed none of the telltale signs of nervousness nor little cues that betrayed a guilty conscience, and he spoke without hesitation when answering Purcel's questions.

"Yes, sir, that is correct. Only Lieutenant Gajewski and myself use those machines on the regular. Colonel Chavez and Major Decker are the only other ones that currently have access to that particular SCIF. We each have our own code for the door, and only our access cards work for the computers."

Major Decker was Major Maya Decker, Purcel knew. They had met briefly when he first made it to Creech and had a quick meeting with Colonel Chavez. She was the only other principal involved in the Ocelot program at the air base, serving as a technical lead, given her background in computer engineering. He would be speaking more with her later.

He and the lieutenant were seated in a SPAF that had a small conference room specifically for secret-or-higher-level briefings. A necessity, given the subject matter of the conversation Purcel and Moore were having. Not only did any notes Purcel take automatically become classified material, but he also had to be careful about how he asked questions and what subjects he broached. The NSA man Giresi and Colonel Chavez had both instructed him to avoid written notes regarding the Ocelot's rare-earth capabilities.

Purcel had shown up to Creech unannounced. He didn't want anyone who could have been involved in the leak, including Chavez, to have any time to prepare for an interview. Before Purcel left Langley, Giresi had told him that none of the personnel at Creech linked to the Ocelots would have betrayed their country, particularly Chavez, whom he had known for some time. Purcel was inclined to believe him but, as an investigator, took nothing for granted. Upon Purcel's arrival at the base, Chavez told him that he had free reign and the full cooperation of the Ocelot team and the security personnel at Creech. The two Lieutenants seemed like the most obvious place to start, considering they had first access to the leaked material.

He asked Moore, "And I assume the entrance to your SCIF is under video surveillance around the clock?"

"Correct, sir. There's a camera mounted above the entrance itself and also another on an adjacent light pole. Only one way in and out."

Purcel took down some notes as Moore spoke.

The Lieutenant continued, "It is a very secure environment, sir. Before accessing that part of the base, we have to leave any phones, thumb drives, backpacks, briefcases, *et cetera* in a locker room and pass through a scanner. Even if someone got it through, a thumb drive in one of the ports would immediately be flagged, and you'd be locked out of the computer. Hell, we can't even print from those machines. That function has been blocked."

Henry looked up from his notes after hearing the last part. "You can't print?"

"No, sir, we cannot. Given the nature of the work, and with recent events like the Ukraine doc leak, which I'm sure you know about."

"Yes, I caught the case actually."

Moore's eyes widened. "No kidding?"

"Yes, I was the main investigator for AFOSI. The first to interview the suspect. Anyway, you were saying?"

"Right. In the wake of that incident, new policy was implemented for certain classified programs, and part of that was limiting printing capabilities. I suppose you're well aware it was printed material Texeira took and leaked."

"What if you needed to print imagery from a drone for further analysis or a briefing?"

"We have to obtain permission from up the chain, then we are provided with a unique one-time code that overrides the blocking function, allowing for a physical print. One of the guys on the base software security team provides the code."

Purcel nodded as he listened then asked, "And none of those individuals, those from the computer security team, have access to the SCIF or your and Lieutenant Gajewski's machines?"

"Correct. Again, only the four of us can. Our access cards and our unique pins are the only ones able to get through the door, and the same goes for logging onto the machines."

"What about SIPRNet access?"

He was referring to what was, essentially, the Department of Defense's own private internet. A secure space for sharing sensitive information over a network.

"The machines in the SCIF are connected, yes."

"So—and I understand I'm implying a potential massive oversight here —is it possible to send material outside the SCIF over SIPRNet, say, as an attachment?"

"That's a good point, sir, but no, that was taken into account as well. We can send messages via our SIPR accounts, but attachments are disabled."

Purcel nodded at that. He then said, "Even so, you understand that I am going to request of Colonel Chavez that he authorize a forensic of Lieutenant Gajewski's and your SIPR activity, yes?"

"Yes, sir, I do. I am all for it. I want to get to the bottom of this situation as much as you do."

"So, Agent Purcel, what do you think so far?"

Colonel Chavez now sat in the same seat that Lieutenants Moore and Gajewski had while being interviewed by Purcel. After a quick break for lunch in the base canteen, Purcel had then spoken with the base's cybersecurity people. He next contacted the colonel again for a follow-up.

"Well, sir, it almost feels like a Poirot story. A murder is discovered in a room where the doors and windows are locked from the inside, that kinda thing."

Chavez chuckled, "Meaning what, exactly?"

Purcel paused as he considered how to phrase his answer. "Most times, sir, with incidents like this, there is a human in the loop, either acting nefariously or in error. With this particular case, it's almost a dream setup for an investigator like myself. It is a very small circle I have to deal with, given the limited number of people who could have had access to that imagery or the computers that the drones talk to. And, as you conveyed yourself, my initial takeaway from talking to your two airmen is there are no red flags. Both have been very cooperative and forthright. Of course, I am going to need to look into their backgrounds a bit more to make sure nothing is going on outside of the workplace that may make them susceptible to blackmail, *et cetera*. Also, from what I am understanding of the environment here, it seems secure. The protocols in place to ensure that no sensitive information is leaked via human action seem airtight."

The Colonel nodded at the last statement. "I'm sure you've encountered some pretty wild stuff in your time at AFOSI, and by that, I mean gross levels of incompetence and negligence. Poor OPSEC. I've been in the service a long time, Agent Purcel, and trust me when I say I've seen some real shit. But we have really tried to button things up around here over the last couple of years. Exercise real diligence and good solid OPSEC. I like to think we are executing well, even more so since we were given responsibility for these particular Ocelot drones."

"Of course, we are only just over twenty-four hours since I caught this case, but my initial investigation indicates that nothing untoward happened from here. I suspect an analysis of video recordings of the drone SCIF and of your team members' communications will affirm that. There are still other avenues that will need some exploration to rule out a leak from our end. I also still need to talk to Major Decker."

"I figured. She's on her way. Should be here momentarily."

The phone in the middle of the conference table rang. Colonel Chavez reached over and picked it up. "Colonel Chavez." After listening for a second, he added, "Send her in, thank you."

He set down the phone and with a smile said, "Speak of the devil and she shall appear."

12

October 21, 2025. 19:01 hours local time.
Utica, New York.

Edward Voss, "Eddie" to most of his acquaintances, looked down at his watch. One minute after seven. The person he was meeting was only a minute late, but he was anxious to see what this was all about.

It's alright. I'll give him till ten after before trying to call.

Calling was a big deal. He and "Tony," as he knew this interlocutor, never spoke over the phone. That was strictly for emergencies only. In person or by email was how they communicated. Keeping off the phones as much as possible was best practice. This meeting was prompted by an email to his personal account from Tony, who, if one were to trust their innocuous email exchanges, ostensibly lived in Florida. Tony had asked if Eddie thought the Yankees would be making any big off-season moves. The reference to baseball was code for Eddie to check a throwaway Gmail account he and Tony shared and look at the Drafts folder, where a short email awaited him.

We need to meet. Usual spot.

It had been a while since he had communication of any kind from Tony.

A message so terse and seemingly urgent set off alarm bells in Eddie's head. It made him nervous. Something was up.

To occupy his hands, he took a sip of water from the glass the waitress had brought over when he'd first sat down. He ran a hand down his modest-length ginger beard, flecked in places with gray patches. A paunch hung over his belt, and his hairline was making an early retreat.

Eddie Voss had never been attractive in any conventional sense, but the ways in which stress could wreak havoc on one's body were making themselves evident each time he looked in the mirror.

He tried looking at the menu the waitress had left, but he couldn't concentrate. He wasn't feeling very hungry either. He peered out through the drizzle-flecked window onto the nearly empty parking lot.

He glanced at his watch again. 7:03 pm. Not only was he eager to find out what was so important, but he also didn't want to be gone for too long. Voss hated leaving his old mixed shepherd Layla alone for long periods. She got nervous when left alone. Home was an hour east in Schenectady, and having to come all this way for what was likely to be a very brief meeting wasn't ideal, but it was best to do it a safe distance from where Eddie lived. And worked.

After another moment, headlights reflected in the window, and a dark car pulled into the parking lot. He watched as an Asian man, Tony, stepped out of the vehicle into the harsh light let off by the neon Denny's sign, the collar of a long raincoat turned against the drizzle. Seconds later, Eddie looked towards the front door as the bell jingled. When Tony entered, he immediately saw Eddie facing him and made his way over to the booth.

Bao Jiaotong didn't bother to remove his raincoat as he slid into the booth opposite Eddie, giving only a curt nod as he did so. He didn't like sitting with his back to the entrance, but he doubted that Voss had chosen his seat out of some sense of operational security, and he wasn't going to make him swap places. That would look odd to anyone paying attention, although the restaurant was nearly dead. They wouldn't be here very long, anyway. It had been a long drive up from Manhattan, most of it through rain, and he would be turning around and heading straight back after this meeting. It was already an exhausting day, a lot of travel for such a short face-to-face, but he felt it was necessary to let Voss know what was going on. Zhang had told him specifically not to do this, to sit tight instead, but Voss was Bao's asset, and after a couple of restless nights ruminating on the matter in his Chinatown apartment, Bao made the decision to disobey orders and reached out to Voss.

Before either could say anything, the portly waitress, beaming with a smile, appeared by their tableside and placed a menu in front of Bao. "Good evening, welcome in. Can I get you something to drink?"

Bao picked up the menu and, handing it back to her, said, "I'll just be having a coffee. Black."

Eddie Voss gave her his menu as well and said, "Same for me."

She smiled and nodded. "Be right over with that."

"Thanks," the two men said in unison.

Once the waitress was a few steps away, Voss, hands on the table in front of him, lifted them up in a *what gives* gesture. He said, "Well? What's up? What's going on?"

Bao looked around the restaurant. Only one other table was occupied, a couple of construction workers by their look, and they were well out of earshot.

He leaned forward over the table, looking straight at Voss. "Listen to me. It is important you do not panic. Do you understand?"

Voss felt the panic well up in his throat. That was not the way to open a conversation with him. He swallowed and nodded.

Bao continued, "There is no cause for alarm. Not at this time. But I felt that you had a right to know. The Americans are aware they have a leak."

Voss blinked a few times, processing what he had just heard. He shifted nervously, the worn leather of the booth seat all of a sudden feeling uncomfortable.

"What? What happened? How?" It came out louder than he had intended.

Bao calmly told him to lower his voice. Before he continued, in his peripheral, he saw the waitress coming over, steaming coffee mugs in each hand. He paused and waited for her to set them down on the table.

"Here you are. Anything else, just flag me down."

Bao said thank you. Voss was silent. He stared at Bao, awaiting explanation.

"The circumstances are unimportant. Americans found materials that had been obtained via the Trojan in the possession of our nationals. It happened in another country, far, far from here."

"I don't understand. How did that happen? Is my government aware of where the leak is?"

"The less you know the better. Given the circumstances, yes, I believe it is safe to say they know it came from one of these aircraft."

Voss drew in a deep breath, his face flushing and filling with heat.

"Oh, Jesus Christ, Tony, what the fuck!?"

"Calm yourself. There is absolutely no need to panic. This only occurred within the last few days—"

"This happened DAYS ago?! And I'm only just hearing about it?!"

"You need to lower your voice, Eddie. I did not find out about it immediately either. I needed some time to consider the situation, and I will tell you that I am also disobeying orders even being here. I was instructed to retain this information so as to not instill panic. It appears that was an order I should have better heeded. Remain calm, Eddie. There is absolutely no need for you to be panicking."

"How? How can I not? Do you know what the word *treason* means?"

"You know better than anyone the way this all works. It is my understanding that the likelihood of a trace back to you or your company is extremely remote. Is that not the case, Eddie? You tell me."

Voss once again drew in a deep breath. He looked at the coffee mug, still untouched, next to his arm on the table. He sat silently for a few moments, thinking.

Without looking up he said, "I—I just don't know. I...I suppose, if anything, it would take a lot of digging to even get to me. But wha—" he stopped mid-sentence and looked out into the parking lot, his mind fogged with fear.

He looked up at Bao and asked, "What happens now?"

"For you? Nothing. It is imperative that you do not change your behaviors or routines. Anything of that nature will only arouse suspicions."

"No, no, I mean, what is the government doing? I'm sure they won't simply let this drop."

"I imagine an investigation is being opened. I cannot say what entities will be involved. FBI, perhaps. But I am confident they will only find dead ends. This initiative you are helping with was taken up specifically due to its difficulty in being detected."

"What about your...compatriots? The ones you say were found with the material. What if they talk?"

After his exchange with Zhang Hudao, Bao had seen the story of the American raid in Somalia on the news and put two and two together. In a subsequent email communication, Zhang provided him with more detail on what had actually occurred.

"They are not a problem. First, they had zero knowledge of where the material came from. Second, they were not even detained by the Americans. It is my understanding they hardly exchanged words."

Voss didn't say anything. He looked back out the window. His leg bounced rapid fire under the table.

Bao broke the silence.

"You should be happy to hear that your work is proving to be so useful. This all came about because of a rather unexpected trove of information received."

Voss looked back at him and held up a hand, indicating for him to stop.

"Listen, I don't want to hear that. I don't care what you and your friends get or don't get. We have our... arrangement, and that's all."

Bao nodded. He picked up his coffee for the first time, took a sip, and grimaced.

"My father was an intelligence agent in Vietnam for many years. He would sometimes bring Vietnamese coffee home. Coffee drinking is still not very popular in China, but I began it at an early age. I am not sure how people can drink shit like this."

Voss glared at him. His handler seemed far too relaxed about this whole situation.

Bao pulled out his wallet and removed a twenty, tossing it on the table. He looked around the restaurant, his eyes searching for the waitress.

"Go home and go about your business, Eddie. Everything will be fine."

13

October 21, 2025. 18:55 hours local time.
Las Vegas, Nevada.

Henry Purcel looked down through his fourth-floor hotel room window at the car headlights streaming along Durango Drive, the busy thoroughfare his room overlooked. Commuters heading home to Las Vegas's sprawling suburbs in the early dark of October. Behind him on the desk, his notepad lay open, an empty Carl's Jr container next to it. Purcel wasn't elated with having fast food for dinner, but the place was right next to his hotel, and he wasn't one to drive around looking for better options. Not when he had other matters on his mind.

He had booked a room at a Homewood Suites right on the northern edge of the city, geographically the nearest hotel to Creech. He reserved two nights but wasn't sure he would even need the second. Despite having only spent one day at the air base, he felt like the answer to this case was not to be found in the Nevada desert. He trusted his gut, but he tried to trust the facts even more, and that was what they indicated thus far. The federal government as a whole, and the Department of Defense in particular, were often characterized as lumbering bureaucracies beset by inefficiencies, but the situation at Creech appeared to be buttoned up tightly and well run.

Betrayal from someone on the Ocelot team wasn't what led to this leak, he was convinced. He had already called back to Quantico to request further background checks on all the relevant personnel, and it was possible follow-on interviews might be needed, but right now, Purcel thought his time would be better allocated elsewhere.

He watched the traffic moving below him but wasn't really seeing it. In his mind's eye, he replayed his final interview at the air base, his conversation with Major Maya Decker. He had been impressed by the major. Despite her relatively small stature—he guessed she couldn't have been over five foot three—she had her highlighted brown hair up in a tight bun and carried a takes-no-bullshit-from-anyone air: confident, straightforward, and in some ways, intimidating. She reminded him of the Ilsa Faust character in the more recent Mission Impossible films. Someone not to be messed with. The interview with her further solidified his feelings on the case.

"Major, it is my understanding there are currently only two Ocelots deployed that have the rare-earth identification capability?"

"Correct. Ocelot IIs, we call them, officially. This one that experienced the apparent leak and another at Camp Lemonnier in Djibouti that hasn't flown any missions yet. We've grounded both for now. We have a handful of Ocelot Is in operation, which, of course, lack that specific ability. Lockheed Martin also had a sale of some to Taiwan and South Korea approved, I believe."

Purcel knew the second piece of information; it was public record. *Defense News* published an article on Lockheed's sale to the two friendly countries a few months ago. He had come across it while doing background research during the flight to Nevada. Of course, the article just referred to them as Ocelot drones. Using Ocelot I would have suggested the existence of the super-secret Ocelot IIs.

"I am wondering about an intrusion right at the source, the drone itself. Are we aware of the technicians handling these in the field? Is it possible a memory card containing the photos was pulled and the content downloaded somewhere?" Purcel asked.

The major nodded as he spoke, seeing already where he was going.

"It's a good thought, but it just cannot be the case. Only USAF Spec Ops personnel maintain the drones in the field. For the particular Ocelot in question, Somali military are present, but the drones tend to be kept in an area accessed only by AFSOC operators, separate from the main base, and the Somalis don't have anywhere near the training or technical know-how to tamper with one. The drones have onboard encryption software, all of which is the latest NSA-certified stuff. The Ocelots don't even have a removable memory card. If one wanted to get the images from its internal card, they'd need to be physically next to it and connect a laptop which has encryption/decryption software, so the images are actually viewable. The only machines with that capability are in the SCIF here."

"I see. So, the internal memory card is encrypted?"

"Correct."

"But could that be hacked? Someone accesses the location and uses their own machine to hack into the card."

"Well, I suppose, in theory, if they were really skilled, but this was taken into consideration. First, the panel covering the memory card location is password protected with a keypad. There is one code per Ocelot and, for the ones with the geological surveying capability, only I and Lieutenants Moore and Gajewski have that code. There is no need for any of the personnel in the field to have it. Not at this time, at least. Actually, the spec ops guys on the ground aren't even aware of the mineral identification function on this Ocelot. As part of the anti-tamper protocols, if the incorrect code is input three times, the memory card will erase itself. Or, perhaps more likely, should the drone crash or be shot down and the panel damaged or pried open somehow, same thing happens."

Purcel leaned back in his chair, processing what he was hearing.

They really did cover their bases with this thing.

Major Decker interrupted his thoughts by adding, "I understand it is your job to question everything, as you should. But if you're still considering the possibility of someone with some official level of access to these drones acting on behalf of the Chinese, it would require multiple actors. And we are talking about individuals in highly specialized roles who have been serving or risking their lives for this country for a long time."

Purcel leaned forward, folding his hands on the table in front of him. He sensed a hint of defensiveness in the major's voice. He understood that.

In interviewing the major and her partners on the Ocelot team, and with his line of questioning, he was not-so-subtly treating them, and their brothers-in-arms in the field, as suspects.

"Major, I understand there are certain implications in my being here questioning you, the colonel, and the two lieutenants, but, frankly, in cases like this, human negligence or malfeasance are often at play. So, it is always where I begin and, still being frank, you four are the closest to this material—"

"I understand, Special Agent. My apologies, things have been a little tense around here in the last seventy-two hours."

"It's quite alright. I can appreciate that this is a trying time for your squad. Now, having said all of that, given what I have learned in these initial discussions and seeing the OPSEC around here, I am inclined to agree. A leak from the inside appears highly unlikely."

Major Decker nodded and said, "With everything that has happened in recent years...document leaks, mishandling of information, dis-info campaigns by Russian troll farms...we've really tried to tighten up, and the Ocelot II compartment is one of the more highly sensitive programs we've been involved with for a while. We're trying to do our best to keep the technology and information safe."

"Right. I gather that, even if two or more within the circle collaborated to leak this material, unlikely in and of itself, there are safety catches in place so that it couldn't go unnoticed."

The major allowed herself a slight smile.

"Well, I'm glad that we've made a good impression with someone."

Now, Henry Purcel found himself here, on the edge of the desert, considering the next move. He had come to the beating heart of the system that had somehow been breached and encountered only cooperative principals and layers of security specifically put in place to guard against data leaks. Upon returning to his room, he tried to game out on his notepad possible ways that security could have been contravened and couldn't come up with anything. Nothing plausible at least. Nothing that wouldn't require the involvement of several individuals at Creech. He was a big believer in Occam's razor. If the proposed answer appeared overly complicated, it probably wasn't the answer. An American service person acting on behalf of a foreign power was not unheard of. It was only a couple of months ago, he remembered, that two Navy corpsmen had been caught passing sensitive information to the Chinese in separate, unrelated incidents. But two or more from the same unit collaborating and going undetected in a place like Creech, that was stretching credibility.

He turned around from the window, moved to the desk, and looked down at his notepad. He tapped it a couple of times with the fore and middle fingers of his right hand, thinking. Something else about the case was bothering him. The turnaround time of it all. The time between when Lieutenant Moore's Ocelot had captured the imagery showing suspected mineral deposits and when the two Chinese engineers were encountered by the DEVGRU team was not even two weeks. It seemed far too quick in Purcel's mind. First, someone with access to the images would've had to somehow have gotten them from Moore's machine or the drone itself. He had confirmed with the Creech cybersecurity team what the Ocelot group had said about the inability to print materials from that SCIF or send out attachments over the internet. So, even if the images were somehow snuck out, it wouldn't have been immediate. Then there would have been the handing over of the images to the Chinese, who would have formulated some plan of action and eventually pursued the meeting with Sheikh Hassan, the Islamic Courts Union principal, which was not something that would happen overnight. No, that situation didn't add up, Purcel thought. It was almost as if the Chinese had ripped the drone imagery in real time.

He sat down at the desk, tapping a key on his laptop that had been sitting idle next to his notepad, bringing it to life.

"Let's get back to Quantico" he said aloud.

14

October 22, 2025. 03:23 hours local time.
Brooklyn, New York.

The homeless man cast a long shadow in the yellow glow offered by a streetlight as he shuffled between garbage cans on the sidewalk. He would stand over a container and peer in, giving only a halfhearted dig through the contents before moving on. He was the only one in Main Street Park at this dark hour, or so he thought. He had not yet noticed the man in a long raincoat, collar raised, seated on a bench along the pathway, just outside of the faint illumination of the streetlight. The orange flame of a cigarette was the only thing betraying the man's presence.

The vagrant arrived at the garbage can nearest the man sitting on the bench and once again rummaged momentarily, not encountering anything of interest. Main Street Park was busy during the day, a place for people to take a lunch break or stroll with a snack from a food truck, so some good leftovers usually found their way into the trash. This evening there wasn't much luck, however. Perhaps the wet weather was thinning the ranks of pedestrians. The homeless man swore under his breath and went to move on but, feeling that he might not be alone, looked to his left, in the direction of the occupied bench. With eyes adjusted to the dark, he saw the lone figure sitting there, smoking. He said nothing, his mind having to first process what the hell someone would be doing here at this hour. Someone who wasn't digging through the trash, at least.

After a moment, he finally said, "Hey man, got anything you can spare?"

Bao Jiaotong didn't respond, letting the homeless man's question hang in the air. He blew some smoke from his nostrils, dropped his half-smoked cigarette into the grass at his feet, and mashed it out with one of his sneakers. He rose from the bench, turned to his left, the direction of the Brooklyn Bridge, and started walking away, still ignoring the homeless man.

After a few steps he heard from behind him, "Aw, come on man."

Bao continued, walking on the grass, staying off the sidewalk and out of the streetlight. Late night walks were his antidote for restlessness, a common ailment for those in his line of work, but tonight he was not sure it would provide any relief. Despite the long day of driving to and from Upstate New York—he had only arrived back to his Chinatown apartment at near midnight—and the long walk from Manhattan into Brooklyn that followed, he still felt a red-hot coil of anxiety burning in his chest. Shortly after returning from his meeting with Eddie Voss, he could feel a sleepless night coming on. He had brought this on himself; he had to concede. He couldn't shake the thought that he had just made a major mistake.

Why had he felt the need to warn Voss? He had been working Voss for a long time; he should have known the man was a nervous wreck and would immediately go into panic stations. Why was it in the forty-eight hours after his exchange with Zhang that he decided it was best to let Voss know? With the discovery of the San Lang engineers by the American special forces, this mission had become delicate, and Bao had taken that delicate object and put it in the hands of a half-wit like Eddie Voss. He was beginning to doubt his own memory of what led him to this course of action. He certainly had no personal affection for Voss. He was a fat American with zero charisma or social skills, just a useful tool, someone whom Bao could exploit for his and his country's benefit. Bao wasn't going soft; he knew that. His father had raised him to never show empathy, for empathy could be used against you. Bao also didn't make it through the brutal physical and mental endurance training in the harsh Tibetan winter long ago, earning commendations and plaudits from his instructors, just to find himself showing grace towards one of his assets.

So, that wasn't it. As he stalked around the city, the best he could conjure was that he really had convinced himself that telling Voss was a form of preemption, that if an investigation found its way to Voss, he would already be steeled against it. And in the meantime, he would know to exercise extra caution and not take any risks that might draw attention. Instead, it had the opposite effect. Now, Bao was concerned the American would panic and, worst case scenario, turn himself over to American authorities and confess, potentially ruining the entire operation. Voss wouldn't know that the information from the drone that mapped mineral deposits was just a coincidental ancillary outcome, complete dumb luck. The real, true purpose of the mission was ongoing, and a premature loss of access to information could be disastrous. Now, Bao may have inadvertently set that in motion through his lapse in judgment.

Bao was furious with himself. His entire drive home from Utica he could only curse his, as he saw it now, blatant stupidity. Not only had he potentially put the mission at risk, he also did so by disobeying a direct order from Zhang, his superior. It did not help that he was afraid of Zhang. Bao was one of the People's Republic's most skilled agents in the field, but Zhang occupied a space of his own. Zhang had established something of a mythos amongst much of the Chinese intelligence community, earned by his ruthlessness, relentless drive, and penchant for violence. Bao's first overseas posting had been with Zhang, in the Democratic Republic of the Congo. Bao witnessed Zhang kill three local militiamen singlehandedly with a knife, moving with speed and agility that didn't seem possible for a man of his physical build. It wasn't lost on Bao that, should Voss do something to jeopardize the mission, it could also put him in peril.

Shortly after leaving the Denny's, Bao had, for a moment, considered turning around, following Voss back to his home, and killing him. At this stage, keeping the connection with Voss was simply looking ahead at future opportunities. As far as the current operation was concerned, he had outlived his usefulness. Bao decided, however, as tempting as it was in the moment, a dead body would risk further complications. He brushed aside the thought that he was finding excuses, because for *him,* it would be the first time taking a life over the course of his career. No, he could do it. If it were necessary.

He made his way to cross the Brooklyn Bridge back into Chinatown. He knew he wouldn't sleep tonight—his mind was still racing—but it was time to rest a little before the city came to life in a couple of hours. For now, he would just have to wait for what was to come.

15

November 5, 2025. 22:49 hours local time.
Camp Lemonnier, Djibouti.

"What the hell is that noise?"

Kurt Miller said this out loud to himself from his makeshift setup of a folding chair and a plastic card table, all placed beside the Ocelot II drone. He turned his head towards the back of the small hangar, in the direction of the sound. A combination of yipping and cackling. He stood up in the glow of his laptop, the only illumination in the hangar, and leaned backwards to stretch his lower back, now tight from a couple hours of sitting. A work light lay extinguished on the table. Its harsh light only made him feel more uncomfortable in the stifling desert heat, so he shut it off when he didn't need to be looking at the aircraft. He couldn't have done this work during the day, when the hangar might as well have been an oven. He had tried getting to work in the late morning the day before, his first full day in country, but found the conditions unbearable.

Miller turned and exited the hangar, walking out into an area roughly the size of a baseball diamond, surrounded by a tall chain-link fence topped with razor wire. In the weak light cast by the single floodlight in the northwest corner of the space, he stopped and listened. This was the

restricted area, accessible only to certain US personnel, where drones operating in East Africa were housed and brought for maintenance. He could
still make out the odd sounds, and they were definitely coming from
behind him. He walked around the back of the hangar, coming to the chain
link, and peered out into the vast desert that lay beyond the base.

About fifty yards from where he stood, a fire burned in a single oil
drum, providing light for three Djiboutian soldiers, AK-47s slung on their
backs. They took turns removing something, he couldn't quite make out
what, from a crate at their feet. Beyond them, several green circles levitated
in the darkness, and the laughter-like noise was clearer. Miller watched as
one of the soldiers made a throwing motion, and seconds later a dog-like
creature appeared in the light of the flame, snatching from the dirt whatever it was the soldier had thrown.

Miller heard footsteps behind him and turned to face Sergeant Gordon,
the intimidatingly tall African American Marine who was on guard duty
for the drone area that night. He must have caught sight of Miller making
his way towards the back and decided to join him.

As Gordon drew closer Miller said, "Are those…"

"Hyenas, yea."

"Uhhh."

Gordon chuckled at Miller's dismay.

"Yea, I know. Seems a little nuts. But once or twice a week some of our
hosts go out there with leftover meat from their canteen. Usually camel or
goat, I think."

"No shit?"

"I thought the same when I first saw it, but I asked one of the inter-
preters, and he said these guys aren't afraid of those things at all. They
think it brings them luck or something to feed the hyenas."

"Guess I'm not at Quantico anymore."

"No. They have a different relationship with nature out here. I respect it,
actually."

Miller had nothing to say in response and just turned back to the
tableau before them. He let out a sigh.

Gordon asked, "Making headway with whatever it is you need to do
with that bird in there?"

Miller shook his head.

"Unfortunately, no."

His answer belied his frustration and his growing confusion. He had only succeeded in bringing up more questions than answers thus far. But he was restricted in what he could say to the Marine sergeant, or anyone else here at Camp Lemonnier, for that matter.

Miller was a member of the AFOSI Information Operations team, the cavalry that Henry Purcel and other investigators called in when additional technical expertise was needed. They were the ones to respond to hacks of Air Force systems, wherever they may occur. If some kind of data break-in and theft had taken place, it would be Miller and his teammates who would track it down. While Purcel investigated potential espionage, he had gotten permission from the NSA man Giresi to read into the investigation of two others from IO. Those two were Miller and a colleague, Nate Bolen. Purcel considered them to be the best in the whole of AFOSI in their particular field, and he assigned them to work the other possibility: whether, and where, a possible breach of the Ocelot systems had occurred.

Upon getting the necessary clearances, Miller and Bolen headed out to Creech and got to work. They did a deep dive into the system logs of the SCIF where Lieutenants Moore and Gajewski flew the drones, which revealed no sign of any attacker activity. Using the timestamp on the imagery, they could identify when a hack would have occurred, and they determined that the SCIF's exacting security measures had been solidly maintained throughout that time. The logs showed that the facility's network engineer had done his job and was diligent in monitoring network traffic as well. He had full visibility into network users, devices, and activity. Nothing suspicious or foreign. The network was layered with multiple security solutions, and all of the protocols to keep the SCIF's network isolated from the dangers of the internet were solidly in place, without any deviation. After analysis and re-analysis, using their own version of a fine-toothed comb, the two IO men were confident that no data breach had occurred from the SCIF's network. Even after triple checking the work, at Purcel's insistence, the conclusion was the same.

With that completed, focus shifted to the communication link between the drone and Creech, and that required being physically with the aircraft in Djibouti. Miller was the one to pull the short straw on making the tortuous journey—two layovers and more than twenty-five hours tarmac to tarmac—to the edge of the world. Or, at least, it felt like the edge of the world to him. Witnessing hyenas being fed raw meat by firelight in the desert compounded the sentiment.

Miller and the sergeant watched for a moment longer as the yips and barks continued.

He turned back to Gordon. "I need to get into the SPAF; think it's time to make contact with the mothership."

"Right on, I'll let you get to it."

Miller walked ahead of the sergeant and back into the hangar to fetch his laptop. As he left the restricted area to make the short walk to the Camp SPAF, an unassuming hut made of metal siding with an aluminum roof, he pulled out his internationally enabled phone and typed out a quick text.

Video call in 5?

As he strode up to the SPAF door, his phone buzzed back.

See you in 5.

Miller nodded to the Marine standing guard outside the SPAF and showed him his special visitor's badge, reflecting he had the proper clearances to access the facility. The Marine returned the nod and punched in a code on the keypad next to the door, letting Miller in.

It felt like walking into heaven compared to the blast furnace outside. Despite all the whirring computers, or rather, because of all those machines, the room needed to maintain a consistently cool temperature. Miller just wished they'd extend some of this air conditioning to the drone hangars. He was relieved to see he had the place to himself, as he'd have to ask any occupant to please step out, an awkward request coming from a visitor. He set up his laptop on a small work station in the far corner and opened up his secure video chat capability. He made a couple of clicks on the keyboard, and the application started beeping as a connection was attempted. After a few moments, his screened filled with the grainy image of Henry Purcel.

"Sir, can you hear me alright?"

"Yep, I got you, Miller. So, what have you got so far?"

That was Purcel. Straight to business. Miller imagined him at his desk, fidgeting, knee bouncing up and down, anxiously waiting for Miller to provide an update.

Miller cleared his throat. "Well, sir, I've had two full evenings with the bird now and—"

"Evenings?"

"Yes, sir. I found out pretty quickly that working in that hangar during the day is nigh-on impossible. The powers that be here haven't yet deemed the UAV hangars to be worthy of air conditioning."

"I see."

"Even this time of year, it's pretty brutal outside. Anyway, I'm able to focus better as the sun sets. I've run the rule over that drone, and, sir, I have to say, this one is a mystery. No revelations, everything looks and works as it should."

"Run me through it."

"First off, zero signs of physical tampering. I know the folks at Creech keyed you in on how all that works, but even so, it's clean as a whistle. There's not a trace of malware on this thing. I ran all the necessary diagnostics, and it's clean. As you are aware, these Ocelots have the latest and greatest in NSA encryption algorithms. It's a specialized design such that, even if the encryption were to fail, no data will be released in the clear, as it were."

This was known as a fail-secure design. In recent years, the systems security people at NSA had perfected those things. Miller had yet to see one fail. Purcel being Purcel, though, he knew what was coming next.

"Is it possible that the design failed?"

I owe myself five bucks, Miller thought.

"Well, I gotta say, sir, it would be a freak thing. The NSA designs are as robust as they come, and I've gotten well acquainted with them in recent years. But, even so, I didn't want to leave any stone unturned, so I considered the possibility. I studied the on-board Fault Detection and Diagnostics, or FDD. Are you familiar?"

"Give me the CliffsNotes."

"The FDD tracks the drone's functionality. If any fault were to occur during flight, the FDD records it then automatically applies diagnostics to pinpoint the fault's source so it can facilitate on-the-ground repair. This Ocelot's FDD's records showed no faulty behavior during the mission the leaked photos were taken from. The FDD would not have the ability to accurately and completely track failures that it might experience itself. So, short answer, no, all the encryption algorithms were and are operating just fine."

Purcel said nothing, and Miller watched as he leaned back in his chair and opened and closed his right hand in a flexing motion, the image of a man deep in thought. Miller decided to break the silence.

"So, sir, outside of a really bizarre dual failure, inconceivable really, where BOTH the fail-secure design and the FDD monitoring simultaneously malfunctioned, I don't see anything at all that suggests the comms between that drone and its operators were breached. Of course, I'm going to double check all this tonight, but so far, it's about as clean a murder scene as I've ever encountered."

Now Purcel came back closer to the computer, his face filling Miller's screen.

"Did you investigate this dual failure you just mentioned?"

Oh, fuck. Why did I have to say something?

"Umm, no sir that would be..."

"Then do so, please."

"Sir, I don't think that is necessary. We are talking about something REALLY..."

"Miller."

Miller cleared his throat.

"Yes sir?"

"Do it. You said yourself, no stones unturned on this one. However unlikely they are to reveal something."

Miller was silent for a moment. This was going to prolong his stay, unnecessarily, he felt. He wanted to get back to the comforts of suburban Virginia and his own bed. He had been working diligently and had confidence in his findings; this would be wasted time in the desert. But what could he do?

"I'll need some time on that. May require that I stay another night or two."

"That's fine, it's what you're there for. I know Lemonnier isn't Monte Carlo, but this is paramount. I need you on this, Miller."

"Yes, sir, I understand."

"Alright, get back to it, let's touch base again tomorrow. I'll get with the secretary to revise your travel."

Miller nodded, frustration clouding his thoughts. He didn't know what else to say.

Purcel said, "Talk soon. Good work".

And with that, Purcel ended the call. Miller slammed the laptop shut.

Just couldn't keep my mouth shut.

He gathered his things and exited the SPAF, stepping out into the heat of the Djiboutian night. He stood for a moment, realizing it was now almost perfectly quiet. He no longer heard the laughter of hyenas.

16

November 5, 2025. 16:08 hours local time.
Air Force Office of Special Investigations Headquarters, Quantico, Virginia.

Henry Purcel stared at the black screen of his laptop. He still hadn't moved from the table in the AFOSI SPAF where he had the video call with Miller.

Now what?

It had been nearly three weeks since they caught this case, and he felt no closer to an answer. Not even the ghost of one. They were treading water. It was unlike any case he had worked during his time at AFOSI.

As he had suspected after his first visit to Creech, further background checks, reviews of security footage at the base, and a deep dive into the network activities of the Ocelot team, including Colonel Chavez, proved that none of them were culpable in the data leak. All continued to be cooperative, and they displayed no suspicious behavior, which Purcel found would often creep in once a guilty individual came under intense scrutiny.

And now, this, from his two best IO guys. He trusted their abilities more than anyone else at the agency. When it became apparent that no inside job was the cause of this leak, Purcel had been sure that, between the two of them, they would discover something clever the Chinese had conjured. When they reported no findings from Creech, he figured they would unearth the culprit in East Africa. Sending Miller all the way out there felt like the final arrow in the quiver. The answer *had* to be on that Ocelot. According to Miller, though, it wasn't. Despite insisting Miller follow through on the scenario of a nearly impossible simultaneous dual failure, Purcel knew that it was a reach and not to get his hopes up. Miller was going to be proven right on that, he was sure.

He finally stood up, gathered his laptop, and left the SPAF. As he walked the hall heading back to his office, he thought about what the next move might be. Nothing came to him over the course of his short walk.

What are we missing?

When he stepped into his office, Purcel placed his laptop on the edge of his desk and slumped back into his office chair, exasperation getting the better of him. As he tried to gather his thoughts, he looked at the cork board over his desk. As was the case lately, his eyes automatically settled on the picture of him and Hani Khatib at Petra.

Purcel remembered, for a moment, how inquisitive his Jordanian counterpart had been. Not just about things related to their work, but also about life in America. Khatib had shown great interest in the United States: its history, landmarks, and national parks. He had surprised Purcel with his knowledge of bits of Americana. Purcel had not expected a member of the GID to know about fried butter at state fairs. Khatib had hoped to visit the states one day. Letting that thought once again pass through his mind made Purcel shake his head, knowing it was very unlikely to ever happen given Khatib's current condition.

Purcel recalled how Khatib had expressed this desire to see America, and he had put it in the context of life in the Middle East. Despite what he did for a living, Khatib felt the stress of living in the region, and he feared it was even worse for his wife and son, which added to his anxiety. Their existence was constantly on a knife's edge. The last two years in particular had seen stop-start violence between Israel and Iranian proxies in surrounding countries. The threat of a full-scale war in the region, one that could drag in Jordan and others, continued to loom. Sitting there at his desk, Purcel let his mind wander to the conversation he and the Jordanian had shared one night, sitting outside the villa Purcel had been provided for his stay.

"Besides all of the cities and sights in America, I'd like to experience life there. It must be so different from here. I do not mean the culture or life-style, either, but just...the feeling you must have," Khatib had said.

"What do you mean?"

"I mean....to be able to pass your day and not have to think about what is going on around you, the countries on your border. There must be a peace to it."

Purcel remembered he was about to respond with something about how it was not necessarily true, that while maybe Americans did not think as much about the world around them, they certainly had domestic politics to stress about, but he had decided to let it go. Hani was right. Even if things seemed bad, no one in America was worried about bombs dropping in Canada or Mexico.

Purcel shook his head again, trying to refocus. He sat up in his chair and removed the key card required to log onto his computer from a holder he kept on a lanyard around his neck. He slid it into a card reader next to his desktop and hit a key on the keyboard to bring the machine to life. He was going to look through the file he had thus far built up on the Ocelot case. Maybe something in there would give him another avenue to investigate.

As the computer monitor lit up to show the log-in screen, Purcel went to type in his pin but paused before doing so. Another part of the conversation with Khatib that night came into his mind:

"You know, the whole situation, the...umm... the politics of it, I guess you say, I do not agree with, but I will say, I am glad that Jordan has made peace with Israel, and that, for now at least, we find ourselves on their side," Khatib had told him.

"Why is that?" Purcel asked. He felt like he knew the reasoning but wanted to give Khatib the chance to elaborate.

"Well, it's quite simple really. They almost always seem to come out on top. They are a small country, but their military is strong, and their intelligence, the Mossad and Shin Bet, are the best. No offense to your CIA."

Purcel gave his trademark half smile and said nothing in return.

Khatib continued, "They are just so damn clever, you know? It seems like they are always on the...how is it you say? Sharp edge?"

"The cutting edge?"

"Yes, right, the cutting edge of technology and weapons systems. They have become so good at this that they scared their enemies into going low-tech, and even then, they find a way to...to..."

Purcel, thinking he knew where Khatib was going, interjected, "Exploit?"

"Right, yes, exploit, to exploit that, and deliver a blow."

"You're talking about the pagers?"

A little less than a year before Purcel's stint in Jordan, the Israeli intelligence services had found a way to rig the pagers of several figures in Hezbollah, the Lebanon-based terror organization Israel had been at war with for decades, and detonate them remotely, killing or maiming a number of the group's members.

"Exactly, the Hezbollah pagers. I mean, just incredible. Hezbollah had become so convinced that Israel had any number of ways to monitor or strike them by hacking their cellphones or computers that they starting using pagers. I do not need to tell you, that is like going from a car to a horse cart. Hezbollah thought going to lower technology would make them safe, yet the Israelis still found a way. They took their time and made a fake supply chain so they could rig the hardware of those pagers."

Now, Purcel leaned back in his chair, thinking.

The hardware of those pagers.

That line from Hani Khatib gave him a thought. He sat for a moment, running through his mind exactly how that could possibly play a role in his investigation.

The hardware.

Concern over the reliability and safety of the chips in DOD computer and weapons systems was not a novel concept to AFOSI and its sister organizations, Purcel was aware. He had seen it given space in various defense-related publications and recalled a lengthy article in Bloomberg from a few years ago that called attention to hardware Trojans. If his memory served, these all had to do with the fact that so much mass computer chip production, including chips that would eventually find their way to DOD systems, took place in China.

Purcel thought about that and realized it did not necessarily help him with this particular investigation. He was beginning to wade into a technical area that was outside of his expertise, but he had to figure that even if the Ocelot drones contained chips that had been manufactured in China, the Chinese had targeted that system *specifically*, and the likelihood of a chip with malware in it landing in the exact intended system was akin to winning the lottery. Twice in a row.

But is there some other way?

Could the Chinese have somehow infiltrated the Ocelot drones via a Trojan in the tiny microcircuits that comprised all of the aircraft's inner-workings? He really did not know. As Purcel sat and thought, his first intu-ition was that this was something he would need to run by Miller and Bolen. It was a technical question, and that was what he had them for. However, Purcel also recognized that, while some acknowledged the possi-bility of compromised chips, far more dismissed it. Software security ruled the day. That is what should be on everyone's minds. The thinking was that America's adversaries, especially China, represented unique threats via cyber-attack. He knew Bolen and Miller well enough and knew that they fell into the latter camp. Purcel himself would have to admit he hardly gave the matter any thought. Nothing involving hardware security had ever come across his desk.

Maybe now it had.

His two colleagues would rebuff the idea. Of this, he was sure. Before he broached them, he needed someone else's opinion, someone who could perhaps give him a better understanding of the situation, and maybe even something to propose to his two info ops guys. It didn't take him long to think of a candidate. He sat back up in his chair, this time reaching for the phone on his desk.

Might be time to call an old friend.

17

November 5, 2025. 16:11 hours local time.
Offices of Indiana Integrated Circuits, South Bend, Indiana.

Jason Lizac eased back in his office chair away from his desk, the wood top of which was barely visible beneath an assortment of papers, folders, pens and pencils, and a couple of empty Diet Coke cans. A Notre Dame football player bobblehead smiled at him from its perch at the corner of the desk. Next to the bobblehead and atop a pile of loose papers sat a small box with a white plastic cover, similar to a smaller version of a fishing tackle box. Jason considered the box from a distance for a few seconds then yawned, ran a hand over his face, and scratched the salt-and-pepper stubble he had let form over the last couple of days.

He stood, stretched, and strode over to the large floor-to-ceiling window just to the right of his desk. The company Jason had founded, Indiana Integrated Circuits, or IIC, had some office space and a laboratory on the top floor of a massive brick building that was the centerpiece of Innovation Park. A home for technology startups, Innovation Park was located right across the street from South Bend Indiana's most famous resident, the University of Notre Dame. Jason's office faced north towards the campus. It wasn't the most picturesque of views. Immediately in the foreground was

East Angela Boulevard, the main road in the area. Sadly, most of the campus's handsome Modern Gothic architecture was not visible from where he stood. The view mainly captured athletic facilities. Not the football stadium—that was situated in the center of the school grounds rather than the edge of campus abutting a busy road. But the baseball and track and field stadiums could be seen, as well as their associated parking lots. Jason didn't mind. It was at least *something*. Better than a narrow alleyway with a dumpster. It provided some people-watching opportunities, too, which were nice for the occasional mental break. He also liked being so close to the road, as he enjoyed the metronome of daytime traffic, which was now beginning to pick up as the working day reached its end. There was no activity in the parking lots or around the athletic fields. It was not the time of year for any of the related sports.

He thought about the white-topped box on his desk, the focal point of his work for the last few weeks. Not long after he graduated from Notre Dame, almost fifteen years ago now, Jason and another researcher had taken advantage of the university's business and technology incubation program to spin off and found IIC, the goal being a company to commercialize the technologies and patents they would license. More simply, IIC was all about getting the products in front of customers and into their hands to actually be put to use. Customers, in IIC's case, were most often elements of the Department of Defense. The business had its successes and failures but more of the former than the latter, and Jason had been content with the current state of the company. It had been a good run, Jason thought, especially for a guy from a working-class Polish family in Pittsburgh who, for a time, worked at an elevator repair company to help cover college expenses. But Jason fretted over each new project as if it were his very first. Right now, that meant what was contained in that unassuming box on his desk, a technology Jason and his team had christened with the acronym RECORD. They had all agreed it should share its pronunciation with the noun, not the verb. He saw real utility in what it could do, but thus far it was not getting much traction with potential customers. In his view, fixing this was a matter of changing the mindsets of some of these decision makers and dispelling their preconceived notions.

Jason's reverie was broken by the ringing of his office phone, perched

precariously close to the edge of his cluttered desk. He returned to his desk
and picked up in the middle of the third ring.

"Jason Lizac."

"Jason, it's Henry Purcel. How are you doing?"

He broke into a smile. Jason and Henry Purcel went way back, having
met fresh out of high school at Notre Dame. Jason's religious upbringing
drew him to the Catholic institution, and he was just working his way
through the mundane prerequisites required for an electrical engineering
degree, while Henry, who hailed from the nearby Chicago suburbs, was
enrolled in the school's famous ROTC program. Henry was dating a friend
of Jason's, and that is how the two of them first met, but they hit it off almost
immediately, bonding over mutual interests in world affairs, literature, and
sports. Henry's tall frame equipped him more for basketball, while Jason's
steady diet of the Pittsburgh Steelers growing up gave him an inclination
for football. But each could appreciate the other's preference, so the two
had attended many school football and basketball games. Henry's relationship with Jason's friend ended up being short lived, but the friendship
between the two young men had endured. As was so often the case,
differing career paths, physical locations, and in Jason's case, the raising of a
family, meant he and Henry had grown distant over time, but they still
occasionally stayed in touch. Jason made sure his wife included his bachelor friend on the Christmas card list.

"Henry Purcel, as I live and breathe. Nice to hear from you, man. I'm
doing well, staying busy. How are things on your end? How are you
feeling?"

A few months prior, Jason was visiting Washington, DC, on business
and had tried connecting with his old friend. But Purcel had to turn him
down, as he was not up for venturing out following the surgery for the
bullet wound to his arm. This was how Jason found out what had
happened in Jordan. It was the last time they had spoken.

"I'm well, thanks. Did I catch you at an OK time?"

"Oh, yeah, I'm good to chat for a few. So...you've progressed in your
recovery?"

"Yes, much better. I appreciate you asking."

"I'm glad to hear that, Henry. So, this is a pleasant surprise. What's going on?"

Purcel cleared his throat and said, "Sorry for calling out of the blue on a work day, but I was wondering if I could pick your brain on something."

"Absolutely. Always happy to help."

"Great. First, forgive me if I misuse terminology here, but I want to ask you about what I believe are called hardware Trojans."

Hearing those last two words caused Jason to raise his eyebrows. For a moment, he didn't say anything. That was not what he would have expected to hear in this conversation.

"Sure, go on."

"So, over the last few years I've seen, in passing, questions about trust in microcircuits as a defense-related matter. You know, proliferation of counterfeits, and, more saliently, how much we can trust those produced abroad, namely China. It is kind of on our radar but kind of not. Software security, at least, as far as I can tell, still dominates."

Jason reflexively nodded as he heard this.

Henry does not realize he is preaching to the choir.

Purcel continued, "But I have a situation, a hypothetical one."

"Of course."

He knew Henry did not really deal in hypotheticals. He had a case, for sure, and that more than likely meant something of a sensitive, secret nature. Jason liked the idea he could end up having input on something like that.

"Say an attacker wanted to infiltrate a secure system via a hardware Trojan, but it is a very specific system that is targeted, one of only a handful in existence. Would I be right in saying that the chances of the attacker's Trojan making it in, even assuming the system made use of commercial chips produced overseas in a facility the attacker had access to, are infinitesimally small? I mean, it would require an almost unfathomable stroke of luck, right?"

Jason smiled at Henry's use of the term *stroke of luck*, as Jason felt he may be the one experiencing such in the moment. He looked down at his desk at RECORD. He knew he shouldn't get excited; the conversation was still young, but the prospect that an opportunity might be brewing with his old friend was enticing. He cleared his throat.

"Correct. In the scenario you're describing, if an attacker was attempting to get a compromised chip into a very specific system, then trying to do so via a mass-produced chip would require, as you say, an unimaginable amount of luck."

"Ok. So, would I be safe in ruling out a hardware Trojan in such a scenario? The likelihood of an attacker hitting paydirt would be too far-fetched. Or is there something I'm missing?"

"Well, there is, actually."

There was silence from the other end of the phone. Jason imagined Henry now raising *his* eyebrows. Jason felt the excitement well up inside of him once again. The conversation had veered into his wheelhouse.

When it was evident Purcel wanted him to continue, Jason said, "Well— and perhaps this doesn't fall in line with your hypothetical, but since it appears pretty broad—what if the software used to create the chips used in the system was corrupted? Then it doesn't matter where or who has access to the physical production of the chips. The whole batch is going to have the Trojan buried in there."

Silence again. This time, for more than just a beat.

Jason shifted his feet, waiting for Purcel to say something. After a moment, he said, "Henry, you still there?"

"Yes, Jason, sorry. Listen, I have to go. Thanks so much. I may be back in touch."

"Sure, anyt—"

But Purcel had already hung up.

That's a pretty urgent hypothetical.

Jason thought this as he slowly placed the receiver back in its cradle. He wondered if, perhaps, this conversation was to be continued. Looking once more at the plastic box resting on his desk, he certainly hoped so.

18

November 5, 2025. 16:21 hours local time.
Air Force Office of Special Investigations Headquarters, Quantico, Virginia.

Immediately after hanging up the phone, Henry Purcel pulled out his cell phone and texted:

Can you talk? In the SPAF

He set the cell on his desk and stared at his blank computer screen, considering what he'd just heard from Jason. Purcel was no expert in computer chips, but he had to figure that anything for military hardware like the Ocelots would be domestically produced. What Jason was suggesting pointed them back to an insider threat, but one spread across a wider cast of players. Purcel knew how the DOD operated; such work would invariably have been farmed out to a contractor. How many could have been involved? He supposed he could get that answer from Giresi; he'd have likely had some say in delegating contracts. But depending on what companies were involved and the scope of work for each one...he shook his head thinking about the can of worms this might open.

Finding a needle in a stack of needles.

His cell phone dinging brought him out of his thought. He looked at the text message.

Sure. Give me 10.

He checked the time and figured it was OK to make his next call. He reached over and picked up his desk phone, hitting an inner-office extension.

After one ring, Nate Bolen answered. "Bolen."

"Nate, Purcel. Meet me in 10 in the SPAF? Want to talk with both you and Miller. He'll conference in."

"Sure, see you in there."

————————

Ten minutes later, Purcel sat next to Nate Bolen in a secure conference room, looking at a large display where a grainy image of Kurt Miller sitting in the SPAF at Camp Lemonnier looked back at them.

"Kurt, can you hear us OK?"

"Yes sir, I got you."

"OK. My apologies, I know it's late over there."

"No worries, I was still awake. Body hasn't quite adjusted yet."

Purcel nodded in understanding, then said, "So, I wanted to run something by you two. Have you considered a hardware Trojan?"

The room fell silent. Purcel sensed both men were waiting for the other to speak up.

Bolen cleared his throat and said, "A hardware Trojan, sir?"

"Correct, hardware. Like in an actual physical computer chip somewhere within the system."

Again, both Miller and Bolen were quiet for a moment.

Miller spoke up, "Maybe it's the jet lag, sir, but I'm not entirely sure what you may have in mind here. The idea that the Chinese might have somehow snuck in dirty chips and they happened to land in these drones is...I can't even really express how small a chance of that happening is."

Purcel held up a hand to the screen.

"Right, I get that. But what about if it was put in at the *design* stage? The *software* used to design the chips."

Again, he was met with silence, but this time the two were really considering what he had just said.

Bolen leaned back in his chair and said, more to himself, "Huh. I hadn't thought of that."

Miller nodded as he spoke. "No, neither had I. You...came up with this idea, sir?"

Purcel thought about how to respond. They knew him too well to believe that he would come up with something like this on his own. The "techy stuff," as he sometimes called it, was their realm, not his. He wasn't keen on divulging that he'd sought outside help, however.

"Let's just say I had a muse."

Both men simply nodded, deciding not to press.

Bolen said, "I certainly think it's possible. I'd need to ruminate on it a bit more, but from the jump, I'd say it's possible. Kurt?"

"I agree. Given what we have thus far and what I'm getting from being out here...it's an avenue worth exploring."

Bolen said, "So that would mean...someone inside one of the contractors that worked on this thing? I doubt the design work was done in house."

"Right, I agree," Purcel replied, "That's where we'd be looking, and I know what you're thinking...even a handful of companies could mean a huge pool of engineers we'd have to investigate."

Bolen leaned forward now so his chest abutted the edge of the table. Purcel could practically see the gears in his head turning.

"Well, maybe not. Maybe we can, at least to start, narrow the search window. For one, these Ocelots are partly made of components that are legacy systems. Sure, they've been upgraded a bit, but they have an established chain of trust. I'd begin by looking at new features, particularly those in and around the camera. If you're looking to leak imagery or video, the camera is the place to do it. Back me up on that, Kurt?"

"Right, I agree. I'll take it a step further. The cameras for these birds have a built-in image enhancement function. You know, the aircraft are sometimes up in less-than-ideal conditions...sandstorms, clouds, smoke from ordinance blasts, all that kind of stuff. Shit, I can tell you from being on the ground here in Djibouti there's a fuck-ton of sand and dust floating around. Anyway, the image enhancer, as the name suggests, cleans up the video or images the drone takes to present a cleaner view that gets sent back to the operator. From what I've gathered from pouring over the specs of these Ocelots, that image enhancement piece is very state-of-the-art, and it's precisely where I'd want a Trojan."

Purcel nodded, already thinking of his next move.

After the three of them were silent again for a moment, Purcel said, "Ok. Let me start working this angle. You guys keep up the good work. I'll let you know what I come up with. Kurt, safe travels, look forward to having you back."

"Believe me, sir, I'm looking forward to being home."

———————

Back at his desk, Purcel sat before his computer, awaiting a return phone call. As he did so, he sifted through PDFs of articles he'd compiled in a folder on his desktop labeled *CF051189*, the official designation given to the Ocelot drone case. The articles were from open-source material he had reviewed for background information when he'd first caught the case and were primarily from the online version of magazines dedicated to defense news. The articles revealed very little about contracts that had been awarded on the Ocelot drones when the program had been announced a little over five years before. Lockheed Martin had been the lead contractor in the actual manufacture, but subcontractors were not given any ink in the articles.

His desk phone rang.

"Purcel here."

"Hi Henry, Steve Giresi returning your call."

"Yes, thanks for getting back. Are you in town? Able to meet?"

There was a pause. Purcel figured Giresi was considering the time of day. For Purcel, these were not things that could be scheduled around the regular nine-to-five.

"Umm...sure. What's on your mind?"

"A new thread to pull on. I was thinking maybe you could point me in the right direction. In current traffic, I can be at Fort Meade in about two hours."

"OK, sounds good. I'll get a conference room for us and have a visitor's badge waiting for you."

"See you in a bit."

———————

Two hours later, Purcel and Steve Giresi sat across from each other at a desk in a secure conference room at the NSA headquarters in Maryland. Purcel had explained how they wanted to look into the possibility of a hardware Trojan and how that might involve a person or persons who designed the microchips that ended up in the drones.

"So, you're saying that you want to look into the party that helped implement the Ocelot camera?" Giresi asked when Purcel had finished speaking.

"Correct, my guys thought that would be the most logical place to begin. Was that something that Lockheed Martin headed up?"

"No, much of the work around the camera was done by a smaller firm. BTP Technologies."

"What can you tell me about them?"

Giresi shrugged.

"Not much to tell really. They've been bidding contracts with the DOD for some time now and have won a good number with my outfit. They're not a very big company, probably under fifty total personnel, but their engineers tend to come from solid northeastern universities. RIT, Rutgers, University at Buffalo, may have even snagged one or two from MIT over the years."

Henry thought about what he'd heard. Small was good; it meant fewer personnel that needed checking out. Giresi interrupted his thinking.

"What led you to this particular avenue of investigation?"

"As you know, this investigation has been at an impasse. Zero evidence of human malfeasance from within, and thus far, my info ops guys have come up with nothing. Trying to think outside the box, I was struck by the idea of looking into the drone's hardware security situation."

"Specifically, the software to design the hardware? It's a clever thought. I have to admit it's not something I might have come up with. This is your idea?"

Purcel decided to come clean.

"Well, that part, no, I can't claim it. That came from an old friend, an engineer. Always been a creative thinker. I put the scenario in front of him as a hypothetical, and this is what he suggested. He told me that nowadays, designing hardware is like creating software, so putting a Trojan in a chip can be about as easy as inserting a line of code in a program. My engineers had pretty much the same reaction; it simply hadn't crossed their minds. But they think it needs to be looked into, anything that could be a lead. It was they who suggested starting with the onboard camera, and it sounds like BTP may be the place to begin. What is your experience with the company?"

Giresi smiled. "Well, I know the founder and CEO of the company. He's former intelligence."

That figures, Purcel thought to himself.

Seemingly reading Purcel's mind, Giresi said, "I know, you're probably thinking *that's how all those NSA contracts were happening* and yeah, what can I say? It's the reality of the business. Anyway, they do good work. Insofar as I know, all employees are vetted and given the necessary background checks. Most carry the highest-level clearances, SCI. Certainly for the Ocelot work that was a requirement."

Purcel nodded as Giresi spoke. It was true. He was a cynic about the way so much of the DOD operated on associations and friendships. Individuals left government service for the private sector and leaned on old connections at their former agencies to win contracts and line their pockets. But, as the NSA man said, it was the way of the world.

"Ok. This is going to be my next area of focus. I at least need to run it down and eliminate it as a possible point of intrusion. I want to go to BTP and meet with the necessary individuals."

Giresi nodded.

"That's not a problem. I can put in a call to my former colleague to let him know you're coming and have you two sit down. John Woods is his name. Make your travel arrangements, and I'll handle the initial introduction."

"Great. I appreciate that."

Giresi gave a single nod in acknowledgment.

Purcel made to stand up but paused and asked, "BTP...does that mean anything?"

"I rather like what the acronym stands for, actually. Beyond The Pines."

"Beyond The Pines?"

"Yes, it's from a Native American language, Mohawk, I think. The city in New York where BTP is located means 'The Place Beyond the Pines' in Mohawk."

"What city is that?"

"Shit, it's been a while since I've been there. Near Albany."

Giresi had to think for a moment, pausing for a few seconds while he recollected.

Finally, he said, "Schenectady."

19

November 7, 2025. 13:10 hours local time.
Offices of BTP Technologies, Schenectady, New York.

Eddie Voss picked up the second half of his sandwich, his usual ham and cheese, and continued to stare out of the break room window, his mind blank. He felt exhausted. He couldn't remember the last time he'd had a good night's rest. It seemed like forever ago. His whole life, sleep had never come easily to Eddie, but this was something else: full blown insomnia ever since his meeting in the Utica Denny's with Tony.

After that sit-down with his handler, Eddie had done whatever he could to cover his tracks, to hide the evidence of what he had done, but it did little to bring him any peace of mind. Anxiety over being caught, with a bit of guilt mixed in, now invaded his sleep. Sure, various sleep aids got him to nod off, but he was constantly waking up at odd, dark hours, and his mind would just begin racing, his heart pounding with panic. *What the fuck have I done?*

He tried to reassure himself that he was protected, that the chances of being found out were small, but the thought lived in the back of his mind: *you never know.*

He took a bite of his sandwich and contemplated the campus of Union

College, which was just across the street and clearly visible from his second-floor vantage point. It was another typical cloudy upstate New York day, and it appeared to be threatening rain. He could see some students darting between buildings, trying to get indoors before the clouds opened up. *Such a pretty campus.* Eddie remembered thinking when he had first joined BTP that it almost seemed a crime that his company's three-story glass and steel monstrosity sullied it with its presence on the other side of Nott Street. A college with a history going back to the late 1700s and its picturesque buildings sharing a block with BTP's soulless box just didn't seem right, at least in Eddie's mind. But it afforded a pleasant view during lunch time, though lately, it did little to bring him any comfort.

Eddie set down the rest of his sandwich and went to rub his tired eyes when he heard footfalls on the tile floor come from behind him.

"Hey Eddie."

Voss turned in his chair to see his colleague, another systems engineer, Alex Linden, come into the breakroom carrying a plastic food container and turn towards the bank of microwaves on the counter on the far wall.

Eddie smiled weakly and said, "Hey Alex."

Linden was one of the few, really the only employee at BTP that Voss got along with at all. Eddie was a quiet loner, limiting interaction with others as much as he could, and Linden picked up on that right away and respected it, never really trying to engage in mundane workplace conversation. Just a quick "hey, how are ya?" and, if there was nothing work related to be said, he just moved on. He didn't seem to judge Eddie for his aloofness either, still remaining cordial. Voss appreciated that.

Eddie turned back to looking out the window and heard Linden begin warming up his lunch in the microwave.

After a few seconds of the microwave's whirring being the only sound in the room, Linden said from behind him, "Hey, you don't happen to know what's up with this visitor today, do you?"

Voss looked over to Linden, confusion on his face. "Visitor? No, I don't know anything about that."

Linden shrugged. "Ah, ok, just curious. We don't get many people coming through here."

That was true. It was odd. Normally it was someone from BTP going to "customers," usually DOD agencies, to make pitches or give demonstrations. It was rare that someone would come to the office. Eddie didn't quite know what to make of that.

He went to look back out at the Union campus, but then his colleague added, "Particularly an investigator."

The last word in Linden's statement cut through the space between them, and Eddie felt a sudden rush of dread plume inside his chest. Did he hear that right? He looked back at Linden.

"What do you mean? An investigator?"

"I had to run out to my car a little while ago and when I came back in, I got to chatting with Stacy, and she mentioned this visitor had just come in, and she, of course, had signed him in, and he had put AFOSI as his agency on the sign-in form. Was just wondering what someone like that might be doing here."

"AFOSI?"

"Yeah. Air Force Office of Special Investigations."

───────────

"I've known Steve Giresi for a long time. He's a good man. He's the reason why I agreed to your visit here on such short notice. But, Agent Purcel, I have to say that what you're suggesting troubles me."

John Woods sat in a huge leather desk chair, his hands folded in front of him on top of an enormous oak desk. Henry Purcel faced Woods from a visitor's chair on the opposite side. Upon sitting down, Purcel was put in the mind of a dignitary or general visiting Vladimir Putin, for the Russian president had, in recent times, become known for having sit-downs at cartoonishly large desks or tables. John Woods was apparently no stranger to important personnel, for behind him on the wall, Purcel spotted framed photographs of Woods smiling and shaking hands with a former governor of New York, a general in combat fatigues Purcel seemed to recall seeing on television, and the current secretary of defense. There were also some smaller picture frames on a long bureau behind Woods's desk against the wall, and they appeared to show a young Woods in more exotic locales.

The two men were seated in a cavernous office on the top floor of the

BTP building. Upon first entering, Purcel had noticed the expansive views of Union College through the room's floor-to-ceiling windows, which were now to Purcel's right. It made him think for a moment about his friend Jason Lizac's view of the Notre Dame campus. An interesting connection, he thought, given that Lizac was the reason he was now having this meeting.

The CEO and founder of BTP was not what Purcel had anticipated. Giresi had alluded to a prior career in "intelligence" and had not elaborated, but Purcel had taken that to mean CIA or DIA, where the stereotype of an agent was of someone a bit unassuming, easily lost in a crowd.

Purcel did not expect a wrestler's physique: squat, broad-shouldered, with biceps straining his sport coat. Woods's tie must have seemed like a noose around his thick neck, and he had hands that, when Purcel had shaken them, felt like bear paws. Woods kept his silver hair close-cropped. He appeared to take good care of himself. He put Purcel in the mind of a seasoned homicide detective or maybe even a retired general. Instead, he was the head of a technology company that specialized in microcircuit design. The design happened at BTP, but the fabrication of the chips took place elsewhere. Like other American companies in the chip business, BTP outsourced the work to manufacturers—typically overseas. However, Purcel had already learned that the chips for the Ocelot drones were physically made onshore in a designated DOD-trusted foundry.

Purcel held up his hand in a placating gesture. "Mr. Woods, I understand. I am not here full of suspicions or making accusations. We simply need to consider all possibilities and avenues. As I explained just now, and as Giresi may have told you himself, this investigation has, thus far, yielded nothing of substance, despite all the manhours being dedicated to it. And any scenario, however unlikely, has to be considered."

Woods lifted a hand to rub his freshly shaven chin, not saying anything. Purcel shifted in his seat, causing the visitor's badge he wore on a lanyard to clatter against his shirt buttons.

Finally, Woods spoke. "So, what exactly would you like to do?"

"Two things. The first concerns software. We are going to need the design files for the Ocelot's chip and the code from whatever computer-aided design programs were used in creating those files. I am assuming you have those here on your internal servers."

Woods nodded and motioned with his head to his right, indicating outside the room.

"Our server room is just down the hall here."

"Right, so we can make arrangements to get that securely to my info ops guys to analyze at Quantico. Alternatively, I can fly one of them up here. Second, I'd like to speak with the engineers involved in designing the chip. Ideally, I'd like to make that happen now."

Woods nodded and was once again quiet, his eyes shifting to a spot beyond Purcel. Something about the other man's expression made Purcel feel odd in that moment, but he couldn't quite identify what it was.

Woods looked back to him and said, "That would be Eddie Voss, one of our principal engineers. He led that one up. Good at what he does. Dedicated. Socially awkward." Now, he allowed himself a little smile. "Typical engineer, I guess. When we won the contract, he requested to take the assignment."

Purcel cocked his head slightly. "That so?"

"Yes. Saw it as a challenge, I guess. Again, he's good. Maybe one of the best here."

"I see. Yes, if I can sit down with him now, that would be great."

Woods reached over to his desk phone, hitting and holding down a button. "Heather, would you have Voss come upstairs to the conference room?"

A woman's voice came back. "Yes, sir, I'll call down to him right now."

"Great, thank you."

He turned back to Purcel.

"We have a conference room across the hall here. Why don't you hop over there now. Voss will be with you in just a minute or two."

Purcel sat at a long conference table, the only sound in the room the rustling of his pants as he bounced one knee up and down in impatience.

He checked his watch. More than ten minutes had passed since he'd left Woods's office. *How long does it take to ride an elevator up one floor?*

After another minute, frustration got the better of him, and he stood to leave the room. He turned left towards the elevator bank where Woods's secretary's desk was, but no one was there. As he moved to the door marked *EXIT* next to the elevators to take the stairs down, one of the elevators dinged, signaling its arrival. The door slid open, and a petite woman in a blouse and skirt stepped out. Heather, the secretary. She had a worried look on her face.

"Sir, I am so sorry. Mr. Voss has left."

"Excuse me?"

"I couldn't get a hold of him at his workstation, and I called to the break room as well, with no luck. I went downstairs to look for him, and someone told me they saw him leave."

"Just now?"

"A few minutes ago, yes. It seems like he was in a bit of a hurry."

20

November 7, 2025. 13:44 hours local time.
Chinatown, Manhattan, New York.

The vibrating sound emanating from the desk drawer was nonstop. He had already ignored two rounds of calls, but Bao Jiaotong knew he was going to have to open the drawer and answer the cell phone he'd tucked away there, the one he hoped he'd never need to use. It could only be one person calling that phone, and it could only mean there was a problem. Bao muttered *cao*—"fuck" in Mandarin—under his breath, low enough so that his partner at the travel agency sitting a few feet away couldn't hear. The moment he noticed the vibrations in the drawer, his mind started racing about what could possibly be wrong. They had agreed that a call to that particular phone was to be made only in the case of a true emergency. Over more than five years, it had never rung. Something was going on.

Bao leaned over and opened the drawer, removing the phone. It continued to buzz, so he hit the "Send to Voicemail" icon and then texted the caller.

Give me a moment. I'll call you back.

He stood up, removing his light jacket from behind his chair and slipping it on, and told his office mate that he had to step out for a few. Stuffing his hands into the jacket's side pockets, he headed out the door, hoping the angst wasn't evident on his face.

The New York fall chill meant that activity around the Sun Yat-Sen statue was a little thinner than in previous weeks, but there was still a pick-up basketball game going on in the adjacent courts, and the elderly Chinese chess and mahjong players, now wrapped in warmer clothes, still occupied most of the tables. Bao took up a position on the north side of the statue, away from most of the park's occupants. He pulled out the cell phone from his jacket pocket and opened up the call log, clicking on the number shown in the missed calls. Eddie Voss answered on the first ring.

"Tony, they know, they fucking know!"

He sounded on the verge of tears, his voice choked with terror.

Bao swallowed, and before Voss could continue, he said, "Eddie, what do you mean? What are you saying? Who knows what?"

"The fucking US government, Tony! They know what we've done! They are at my company building right this very moment!"

"Eddie, slow down. Just, calm down for a moment. Who is there? Your company is a US government contractor, Eddie. How could this be out of the ordinary?"

"No, no, you don't get it. Some *investigator* from the US government is there. It was on the sign-in sheet at the front desk. AFOSI. You know what that is, Tony? That's Air Force Office of *Special Investigations*."

Bao didn't say anything. He had knowledge of all US Department of Defense agencies, so he knew full well what AFOSI did. An agent from their office showing up at BTP wasn't completely out of the ordinary, he thought, but he had to admit the coincidence in timing was unsettling. Bao's command of English might not have been as strong as some of his comrades who had spent time in English-speaking countries in their youth, but he knew enough nuance to pick up on the fact that Eddie had said there, not here.

"Eddie, where are you right now?"

"I'm in my car. I left as soon as I found that out. I need to get out of here. I am not going to prison. Do you understand me, Tony? That is *not* happening."

I should have killed this guy when I had the chance.

"You idiot, Eddie. Don't you see how that looks? Even *if* the agent is there to investigate this matter, and we cannot say that for sure, didn't you cover your tracks on site? It would take them time to find your work, no? Time we could have used to develop a plan of action, but now, you might as well have stood on a tabletop and admitted your guilt."

That was met by silence. *It must be dawning on this fool what a mistake he just made,* Bao thought.

Finally, Eddie spoke up, "It doesn't matter. I am not taking any risks. They know something, and if they got to this point already, it is only a matter of time. I have to look out for myself."

"What are you planning to do, Eddie?"

"I need your help. My passport is long expired, not that it matters. They will likely be on the lookout for that soon enough, anyway. I need a way to get out of here. Tony, you gotta help me. You must know someone down there who can make a fake passport or something?"

The pleading in his voice made Bao sick. It was pathetic. Bao would be content to leave him to the wolves, but Voss was proving to be volatile and now unpredictable. If Bao didn't do something, Eddie could just turn himself in and begin talking, and that could create even bigger headaches. He quickly formulated a plan in his head.

"I am not a miracle worker, Eddie. I cannot snap my fingers and magically make something like that appear. It will take a little time, and I will need you to come this way."

"Ok, ok, but you can help me? You can do something?"

"Yes."

"Ok, alright. What do you need from me?"

"If you have it, bring a passport sized photo. If not, it is no big deal. Pack a bag. I will send you a location to meet at shortly. Can you come this way soon?"

"Yes, yes, I can."

"Good. Be on the lookout for the location. By the time you get here, it will be dark, but that is better for us anyway."

Well, really just better for me.

"Ok, Jesus, thank you, Tony, thank you."

"I'll see you soon."

And with that, Bao ended the call. He moved around to the other side of the statue so he could look out at the elderly Chinese men enjoying their board games or smoking cigarettes. He stood for a moment, looking like he was people watching, but he was actually envisioning in his mind's eye how the night would play out. He had no intention of helping Eddie obtain a fake passport or otherwise evade the authorities, who surely were now suspicious of Voss. No, nothing of the sort. He just needed to get Eddie away from the Schenectady area, where it was possible that he would soon be the target of a dragnet. Hopefully, Voss could get on the road and make the three-hour drive before things really heated up. Once he got to the city, well, crime statistics had greatly improved in recent years, but bad things could still happen to an unsuspecting solo tourist.

21

November 7, 2025. 14:01 hours local time.
Schenectady, New York.

Henry Purcel turned on the windshield wipers of his rental vehicle. The intermittent droplets of rain that had been coming down when he left the BTP building had now gathered pace. He peered ahead along State Street and saw, coming up on his left, what he was told to look for: an old stone home with a long-sloped roof. He slowed as he passed, looking towards the home. In front, hung on a black wrought-iron fence, was a large green sign with bold all-capital white lettering:

VALE CEMETERY. ESTABLISHED 1857

He knew the next left after the gate for the cemetery, Moyston Street, would be where he needed to turn.

At first, Woods and his secretary had been reluctant to provide Purcel with Eddie Voss's address, wanting first to consult with legal counsel before giving out private information. After some pressure from Purcel, however, Woods relented, conceding that the optics of the situation were not good. Voss's leaving in such a hurry was curious enough, but a BTP employee who had just seen Voss in the break room told them that, when he'd mentioned Purcel's visit, that seemed to trigger Voss into making a hasty exit. Time was now of the essence; Purcel didn't want to run the risk of Voss disappearing into the ether while BTP waited for their lawyers to chime in.

As he made to head out, Purcel was stopped by the secretary, who wanted to let him know that Voss's Street, Moyston, could be easy to miss if you weren't familiar with the town, even with a GPS app guiding. She instructed Purcel to look for Vale Cemetery, most readily identified by the stone house—the former groundskeeper's quarters that was now falling into disrepair—and that Moyston was the street immediately after the cemetery. Learning that Eddie Voss's home was so close to a cemetery gave Purcel an uneasy sense of foreboding.

Purcel had Google Maps open on his phone, and the GPS voice sounded at the right moment, indicating his turn was just ahead. He hit his turn signal and made the left onto Moyston. The street was lined on both sides by two-story homes outfitted with vinyl siding. Some appeared to be duplexes. Curb appeal and upkeep varied. A few of the houses looked in desperate need of a power wash or had slouching porches, while others showed some pride of ownership, the siding clean and lawns manicured. To Purcel, it gave the impression of a lower-middle income neighborhood, not quite where you'd expect to find a chip designer with a salary easily into six figure territory.

He glanced down at his phone, balanced in the center console cup holder, to see the number he was looking for, 48. It was the very last home on the left. The map indicated Moyston was a dead-end street, and now Purcel could see exactly how that manifested itself: at the end of the street was a large concrete barrier, about thigh height, and beyond that lay rows of headstones. Vale Cemetery.

What about you?

Eddie Voss thought this as he stood looking down at Layla, who looked back at him, one eye ocean blue, the other brown, sadness in both. She had followed him upstairs, as she did every night, despite the fact her hips were beginning to fail. This time, instead of taking it slow like he normally did so she could keep up, Eddie had burst into the house and practically sprinted up to the second floor, taking two steps at a time. He wasted no time pulling a piece of luggage from his closet and stuffing it with a couple days' worth of clothes. He had no idea what Tony had planned for him, or where he might be going, but he couldn't show up with just the clothes on his back.

It was only a matter of time, though, before someone would come looking for him. Tony was right; by rushing out of the offices, Eddie had virtually put a brightly lit "guilty as sin" sign on his back. But what was done was done. He needed to get his things and get out of there. After a few minutes of frenzied packing, he stopped when he realized Layla was in the room, laying near the doorway, watching him. The look in her eyes broke his heart. She knew something was up. Dogs always know.

Voss hadn't thought about what to do with her. He felt ashamed that the consideration hadn't even crossed his mind until just now. It was obvious he couldn't take her with him without knowing what the plan was. Her advanced years didn't help either. No, this was where he and his old dog parted ways. He thought for a moment, still looking at her, with her eyes not leaving his. He blinked away what felt like the onset of tears.

I didn't see it ending this way.

He figured the best he could do now was leave some food and water out for her and then leave a key to the house somewhere outside. He'd call his neighbor while he was on his way downstate, explain that an emergency had come up, and ask them to please take care of Layla. He got along well enough with his neighbors, the Franklins, and Layla knew them. He didn't really have any friends he could call upon. The Franklins would have to do.

Lost in thought, Eddie didn't hear the car door slam outside. Layla did though. She quickly jerked her head to the left, the direction of the bedroom window that overlooked the front. Seeing her reaction, Eddie went over to window, standing off to the side, and moved the curtain slightly so he could a have a look. Rain had begun to streak the glass, but he could still see down below. Parked on the other side of the street across from his house was a blue sedan, and next to it stood a tall man with a buzz cut wearing a suit and tie. An agent of the United States' government if ever Eddie had seen one.

———

The Voss residence was one of the better-kept homes of Moyston Street, Purcel noted as he stepped out of the Hyundai into the rain. He stood for a moment to take in the house. The paint job looked fresh enough, the lawn and landscaping nicely appointed, the front porch outfitted with a rocking chair and side table. The wind chime hanging next to the front door gave off a faint song. A concrete driveway to the left of the home appeared to lead all the way to the back. A waist-high chain link gate ran across the drive from the side of the home, connecting to a fence that ran to the back-yard. A dark colored Tesla sat in the driveway, which Purcel assumed was Eddie Voss's vehicle.

On the drive from the BTP building, he tried to think about how this conversation might go if he found Voss at his home, and it now seemed like he had. Unfortunately, he had not been able to get any intel on Voss's background, his personality, or how he might handle adversity or a contentious conversation. Part of him knew that this wasn't the way to go about this, even from a pure safety perspective. He felt prisoner to the moment, though, forced to act by Voss's actions. Waiting for backup, which in this case would be the local police department, or to gather more information on Voss, would more than likely mean his suspect getting away with a decent head start.

He took a deep breath and made his way to the steps up onto the front porch.

Just gonna roll with it.

Was that a little movement of the curtain on the second floor that he had noticed?

———————

The sight of the federal agent in front of his house turned Eddie's viscera to water. He felt his face and throat flush.

This can't be happening.

He knew someone would show up eventually but had figured he'd be long gone by then. The only way the agent could have come so quickly was if someone at BTP let him know right away where Eddie lived. And Woods would have had to approve such a move. That was what being a good solid worker got Voss: not even the benefit of the doubt. He hoped that BTP suffered whatever fallout came from this. They deserved it.

The urge to vomit crept in. Eddie swallowed and took a deep breath, hoping it would subside. He moved to his bedstand, hurriedly ripping open the lone drawer. He pulled out his gun, a Glock 19. He had never been one for firearms, but the onset of the COVID pandemic a few years prior had changed his feelings on the matter. Worried that rioting and looting could result from a collapsing economy and spurred on by a healthy dose of right-wing talk radio, Eddie decided he needed some form of self-protection. A gun was the only way to be on a level playing field in America. Luckily, he had never needed it, but in the early days of the pandemic, Eddie had taken a firearms course and then continued to hone his skills with regular visits to a local gun range. He impressed himself with how he had grown to handle the weapon. He was no James Bond but felt he could deploy the Glock effectively should the need arise.

He hefted the gun for a second, knowing he kept it loaded, then slipped it into his waist band at the small of his back. There was an additional magazine in the bedstand drawer. He reached in and grabbed it, quickly shoving it into one of his front pockets. Layla was up, sensing the increased tension in the room. She abruptly turned and made her way to the landing to head downstairs. Eddie took that to mean she heard the man approaching the front door. There was no time to think; this was it. Eddie was terrified of jail, of being sequestered in a gray box with hardened criminals who were no better than brute animals. He'd heard stories about how the corrections officers often were little better. It was no place for someone like him. The very thought of it made him sick to his stomach. He wasn't willing to risk prison time when he became entangled with the Chinese, and he wasn't going to now. He had no choice; he had to run. Now.

Purcel knocked. He knocked loudly but in a normal manner, with his knuckles. Pounding with the bottom of one's fist was an attention getter, but it came off as adversarial. He was hoping to avoid any confrontation with

Eddie Voss and still had in his mind how he knew next to nothing about the man.

He waited. Nothing. He knocked again, this time a little louder. He turned his head to lean one ear closer to the door, hoping to hear some movement inside. After a moment, he heard a clicking noise, like the kind produced by a dog's nails on hardwood, from just on the other side of the door. The huffing sound of a dog sniffing at the bottom of the door followed. Was that the creak of a floorboard he heard? Purcel waited another second. The door had a rectangular transom window at the top. Despite his height, it still wasn't enough on tiptoe to get a clear view through, so he grabbed a large empty ceramic flowerpot that sat to the side of the door, flipped it over, and climbed atop. Peering through the transom, he caught the glimpse of a figure running towards the back of the house. Eddie Voss was on the move.

Purcel stepped off the flowerpot and ran to his left, vaulting the porch rail down to the driveway. As his feet hit the ground, he heard what sounded like a back door crash open.

Years of sitting at a computer, poor diet, and neglecting regular exercise had not served Eddie Voss well. He was not built for a foot chase under normal circumstances. He couldn't recall the last time he moved at any pace above walking. Now, though, he was running on pure adrenaline, and that carried him out his back door and through the chain-link gate located in the middle of his back fence, into Vale Cemetery. A gate letting into a cemetery from a private residence would seem odd, but Eddie was aided by history. His father had been a groundskeeper at Vale for decades and could simply walk out his backdoor in the early hours and through the gate to his place of employment. Lucky for Eddie, for he knew that without it, he didn't stand a chance. There was no way he could vault even a waist-high fence and have any hope of keeping ahead of the athletic-looking federal agent.

He was now among the tombstones, a strip of the cemetery that ran behind Moyston and Catherine Streets. A small gym bag he had haphazardly stuffed with clothes was slung over his left shoulder, slapping against his back as he ran. He gripped the Glock in his right hand. Eddie cut to his right, heading towards the main part of the cemetery, aiming his run for the adjacent Vale Park, surrounded by woods. Pines. Eddie had played in these pines as a kid, and he could still navigate them. He could lose the agent in there. He just needed to make it into that tree line.

"Voss! Stop!"

Voss broke his stride to turn around. The agent was about 30 yards behind him, a pistol held downwards in a double grip.

I can't go to jail.

Eddie raised his Glock and fired.

———————

As soon as Henry Purcel saw Voss come up with his weapon, he dove to his left, onto the rain-slicked grass, behind a headstone. It was a normal-sized headstone, nothing close to ideal cover, but it was the nearest thing for protection. Two bullets struck the ground, not far from where Purcel had been. Luckily for Purcel, Voss was firing one-handed and was likely pumped full of adrenaline, not an ideal combination for supreme accuracy. Purcel felt a jolt of pain run from his elbow down his forearm, a reminder of his last encounter with a shooter. His body was splayed out perpendicular to the headstone, the crown of his head nearly touching it. Another shot rang out, this time hitting off to the right of the grave. Henry waited a beat and took a deep breath. No other shots came. He breathed out and rolled to his left, coming up in a crouch, his Glock 19 out in front of him. He could see Voss running between two graves. He looked down the sights of his pistol, centering on Voss's figure.

"Voss, STOP!"

Voss turned once more, again bringing his pistol up and aiming in Purcel's direction.

Fuck.

Purcel fired twice.

Eddie Voss dropped to the ground.

Purcel got up and quickly covered the distance between them, his pistol aimed at Voss.

"Don't move! Do NOT move!"

Voss had turned onto his side and used an elbow to inch himself closer to an obelisk-shaped tombstone immediately to his left, clearly struggling. He rested his shoulder and head against the bottom of the stone. Purcel could see the Glock a couple of feet from the bottom of Voss's shoes. He kicked it to one side and stood over Voss, his gun still at the ready. He looked down at the wounded man.

He was in bad shape. A blossom of blood filled the top portion of his shirt, emanating from a wound just above his heart. Voss was breathing rapidly, the breaths shallow. His eyes were darting back and forth between Purcel standing above him and some spot off to his side. Rain pelted his face.

Purcel holstered his weapon on his hip and took off his sport coat, making to press it against Voss's wound.

"Goddamn it." He crouched down, pressing the crumpled-up jacket down onto Voss's chest. "Voss, hold this there, can you do that?"

Voss didn't respond, his gaze now fully off in the distance.

"Goddamn it."

With his right hand pressing down on the jacket, Purcel used his other hand to fish his phone from his pants pocket. Rain drops hit the screen, inhibiting his ability to swipe up to open his home screen.

"Just hang in, Voss. I'm gonna get an ambulance out here."

Purcel sensed movement behind him. He turned, taking his hand away from Voss's chest and moving it to the pistol on his hip. A few yards behind him, an old-looking dog, a shepherd of some kind, lay completely prone in the wet grass, head on the ground, its eyes focused on the two men. It lay still, emitting a soft whimper.

Perplexed briefly by the scene, Purcel took a moment before looking back to his task and tried to wipe his screen with his sleeve, which itself was already thoroughly soaked. Then he heard something. He looked back to Voss, slumped against the gravestone.

"What was that, Voss? What did you say?"

Voss continued to look away from Purcel, seeing something only he could. "I didn't see it ending this way."

From somewhere behind him, Purcel heard sirens approaching.

22

November 7, 2025. 18:43 hours local time.
Chinatown, Manhattan, New York.

Still no response.

What's going on?

"Cao."

Bao Jiaotong tossed the cellphone he used to communicate with Eddie Voss onto his desk in frustration. It had now been over three hours since he first texted Eddie a location for them to meet at. In the intervening time, Bao had sent three more texts asking for a status update, all unanswered.

He sat down at the desk, running a hand over his face in frustration. In the silence, he could hear shouting and movement from down below, dishes clattering and the heavy *thud* of knives striking cutting boards. Bao lived in a small loft above a restaurant on Mott Street, a short walk away from his travel agency office. It was cramped and sparsely furnished, but he didn't need much. His mattress simply lay on the floor. The kitchen was the size of a phonebooth but all he needed to whip up a quick meal here and there. His desk doubled as a place to do his work and eat. He looked down to the left of the desk where he kept his only other piece of furniture, if it could be called that. It was a steel safe, about two feet high by a foot and a half wide, secured by a fingerprint scanner. In it, Bao kept several fake pass-ports; around one thousand dollars and roughly the same amount in both Canadian and Chinese currencies; a MP-443 pistol and accompanying silencer; and a balisong, better known to many as a butterfly knife. He had intended to bring the balisong with him to the meetup location, Hunt's Point in the Bronx, a part of the city still dealing with high levels of street crime, and use it to dispatch Voss. Eddie would be the unfortunate tourist finding himself in the wrong part of town on the wrong night.

"Cao."

Bao picked up the phone and called Voss. After several rings, the call went to the automated voicemail message. He placed the phone back down, thinking. Something was definitely wrong. Given how panicked Eddie was when they had spoken earlier in the day, it just did not track that he would all of a sudden stop communication. He would have felt a sense of relief that Bao was making an effort to help him. He would have been responsive to that.

Bao opened up the laptop that sat on his desk and pulled up a browser, searching "Edward Voss" in the address bar.

And there it was. Within seconds, his screen was populated with links to articles from various news outlets, with some variation in titles, reporting a shooting in Schenectady, New York. Bao clicked the first link, from a news station in the Albany region.

"Schenectady man killed in shooting involving federal agent."

As he read, Bao could feel his face flush with dread. The room suddenly felt warm, the cold fall evening outside his window no longer evident.

Edward Voss, 43, of Schenectady, was pronounced dead at the scene in Vale Cemetery after being shot by a federal agent around 2:30 p.m. this afternoon. The agent, whose name and agency have not yet been released, was unharmed. Schenectady PD Homicide Detective Richard Conkling, the investigating officer, declined to give further details at this time. Conkling and his colleagues at the department are continuing to investigate the matter, in full cooperation with federal authorities. More details to follow.

Bao leaned back in his chair, his mind now racing. This had devolved into a disaster. He had no way of knowing where the investigation into Voss might lead. The American authorities were now going to do a deep dive into Voss's life and background. What was on Eddie's home computer? Had he kept anything that might tie him to Bao? Bao himself was extremely cautious and always urged the same in his assets, but you can never fully trust what someone is doing without you watching their every move. He figured his connection to Voss being unearthed was unlikely, but that was the same feeling he'd had about Voss's work even being dug up by the Americans. Now, Voss was dead, and not even a month had gone by. No, he couldn't take any chances now. He had no diplomatic protection; his government would not even acknowledge his existence if it came to light he was operating as a spy. It was time to burn this operation and get out.

Wait. Was that phone I just called now sitting in a plastic baggie in an evidence room, waiting for analysis?

Bao looked at the phone on the table. He picked it up and slipped the back cover off, removing the battery and SIM card. He stood up, placed the SIM on the ground, and stomped on it. He did the same to the phone, shattering the screen. He then knelt in front of his safe, unlocking it with his thumb. He rifled through his passport collection, finding the one he wanted.

He paused for a moment, thinking about his other contact in this operation. After he met with Voss in Utica, he had considered also touching base with them but had thought better of it. Contact between him and the other individual was strictly prohibited unless extraordinary circumstances merited it. Now might be sufficient cause, but it was too late. With Voss dead, the wheels were already in motion.

He stood and went over to the studio's tiny closet, taking from the upper shelf a gym bag, already packed and ready to go. As he made his way to the door, the image of an encounter with Zhang Hudao came to him. The idea of having to explain all of this to his superior made him stop in his tracks, and he felt his pulse quicken. He tried to shake the thought. He could not stand there and dwell on what the future might hold.

It was time to run.

23

November 7, 2025. 21:13 hours local time.
Schenectady, New York.

The door to the interrogation room opened, and Henry Purcel looked up from his chair at a metal table to see Detective Richard Conkling of the Schenectady Police Department enter the room. In some ways, Conkling fit the bill of the classic disheveled detective in the movies: chin showing three days' worth of stubble, tan suit coat needing a trip to the dry cleaner. Contrary to the popular portrayals, however, the detective was rail thin, his white hair shaved so closely to the scalp that he appeared nearly bald. Purcel figured Conkling would not have been out of place teaching a philosophy course at a university. During Purcel's interview a couple of hours earlier, Conkling spoke in a manner and with a vocabulary Purcel expected from an academic, not a veteran detective from a mid-size snow-belt city.

As Conkling closed the door behind him, he said, "Apologies for the wait. You know how it can be sometimes."

Purcel nodded without saying anything. Conkling pulled out the chair across the table from Purcel and took a seat. In his other hand, he gripped a gallon-sized Ziploc bag, and Purcel could make out a holstered firearm within it. Conkling placed the bag on table and slid it across towards Purcel.

"Your firearm, Special Agent."

Purcel looked at the detective.

"I'm good to go?"

"You are. No eyewitnesses to the shooting, but forensics at the scene seem to indicate the shooting transpired just the way you say. Your story also checks out with the people at BTP, and having read your file, I would say this is a pretty open-and-shut case of self-defense. I did speak to your Lieutenant Colonel Reed down at Quantico. He backs you to the hilt. I'm sure you will be giving him the full rundown soon enough."

Purcel gave a tired smile but said nothing.

That was followed by an awkward silence.

The police detective broke it. "You OK, Special Agent?"

"You can call me Henry. And yeah, I'll be fine."

Conkling nodded once. After a moment, he said, "Alright then, keys to your rental are in that baggie as well. It's parked out front. You OK to drive?"

"Sure."

"Good. Head back to the hotel, get some rest. Hopefully your next visit to Schenectady won't be so eventful. Try us in the summer, though. Much more agreeable weather."

Detective Conkling slid back in the chair, making his way to get up, when Purcel said, "Did you always want to be a detective?"

The detective didn't say anything at first, instead cocking his head in surprise at the question. Then a smile broke across his face.

"No. I always had an interest in reading and writing. Fancied myself an author, or at the very least, a writing instructor. Started college an hour or so away in Utica but didn't quite settle into academic life. It didn't help that my mom got sick not long after I went to school, so I came back to help out. At the time, the police department was hiring, so, for the lack of a better idea..."

He spread his hands in a *here we are* gesture. After another brief silence, Conkling added, "All of it a lifetime ago."

Purcel just nodded.

Conkling asked, "Why do you ask?"

Purcel shrugged and said, "Just curious. I suppose, if you don't mind my saying, you don't have what I would call the 'typical detective' look about you."

"What would you say is the 'typical detective look'?"

Purcel shrugged again. "You know. Heavy set, squat. Cynical. Looks like they're battling hypertension. That kind of thing."

The detective gave a small laugh.

"Sounds like *L.A. Confidential.*"

"Ha. Yeah. Like that. Great movie. Anyway, that's all."

"Life can be funny like that, the paths we end up taking."

"Yes, it can be."

"How about you? Was this what you had in mind?" He nodded towards the ziplocked Glock 19 on the table in front of Purcel.

"In a roundabout way. I tried being a fighter pilot but wasn't quite cut out for it. The Air Force was always in the cards in some way, though. Runs in the family."

"Ah."

Purcel nodded. The two of them were not good at small talk. He wasn't entirely sure why he decided to engage the detective in this way. Perhaps he needed some human connection after just having shot and killed a man.

Conkling cleared his throat and said, "Actually, this reminds me, I failed to ask earlier. Did the departed say anything to you before he succumbed to his wounds? Was he able to speak at all?"

"Just one thing."

"And what was that?"

"*I didn't see it ending this way.*"

Another pause.

"*I didn't see it ending this way?*"

"Correct."

The detective looked off at a space over Purcel's shoulder, silent yet again, clearly thinking to himself. After a moment, he finally stood up and turned towards the door.

Before he could reach it, Purcel spoke up again, "Detective, one last thing. Voss's dog had followed us out. With all the commotion afterwards, I didn't see where she went or what happened with her. Again, out of curiosity, what will become of her?"

"One of the uniforms at the scene brought the dog over to a neighbor, but he told me they weren't really interested, so I had him bring her over to the Humane Society. Now, it looks like the departed has no next of kin, none that we can find, anyway, so I guess she'll remain there. Tough for older dogs, but maybe she'll find a home."

"I see."

Conkling opened the door and turned back to Purcel. "Take care of yourself, Henry."

––––––––––––

November 8, 2025. 12:22 hours local time.
I-95 outside of East Brunswick, New Jersey

Purcel listened to the rings from the dashboard speaker of his rental vehicle, his cell phone connected to the car's Bluetooth.

On the third ring, there was an answer. "Mark here."

"Mark, Purcel. What do you have for me?"

"Good afternoon to you as well, Henry. Me? I'm doing well, appreciate you asking."

Purcel smiled to himself. Mark Bizon was the office jokester. No conversation with him could be 100 percent serious. He was a good agent, though. Purcel would never let Bizon know it, but after himself, Purcel thought Bizon was the next best investigative mind in the unit. For that, he tolerated Bizon's less-than-serious approach to the job.

"Alright Mark, anything you can tell me?"

Bizon cleared his throat.

"Well, thus far, Special Agent Purcel, your boy Edward Voss is no international man of intrigue. I have turned up nothing of interest. No criminal records, just the odd speeding ticket, nothing on the sex offender registry, which comes as no surprise given his security clearances. Very little on familial relations, not seeing any associations with known bad actors. Umm...shit what else can I tell ya...I'm not sure, pretty boring guy, at first glance. Bachelor's and master's degrees, couple different jobs with DOD contractors before landing at BTP. That's it thus far. Then again, it's only been a few hours working on this. Despite appearances, I'm no miracle worker. And before you say anything, no I didn't see the message you sent at one a.m. until later this morning around, you know, normal people hours."

Purcel muttered *shit* beneath his breath. He then said, "Any thread at all that we can pull? Some avenue we can look down that might lead to a connection to the Chinese?"

Bizon made a raspberry with his lips before saying, "Well, he did do his schooling at the University at Buffalo. Big research institution. Yours truly went there, matter of fact. Anyway, lots of foreign students, a healthy portion of which are Chinese. That could be an intersection point."

"You went to University at Buffalo?"

"Yea, stayed close to home. Would have missed mom's cooking too much otherwise."

"Any connections there still? Someone who might have crossed paths with Voss?"

"Hmm, I'm not sure. I'd have to think on that. Voss is a little younger than I. Also, consider the fact we were in radically different fields of study. Political Science and Computer Engineering didn't exactly share buildings."

"No, I know. But you never do know. Keep at it. Soon as I make it to Quantico, we can put our heads together."

"Roger that. What is your ETA?"

"Looking at around four, 4:30. Will stop for lunch soon then continue on my way."

"Stop for lunch? Planes pull into Chik-fil-A now?"

"Not flying. Got a one-way rental. I'm in Jersey right now."

"You're *driving!*? Christ, I know flying sucks, but you got about three different places you could hit that'll snarl you in traffic between here and there."

"Yea, well, something came up."

Purcel half turned his head to look at the back seat where Layla lay silently. She did not stir, but her eyes looked up at him when she heard his movement.

"Well, whatever it was, good luck with that. You're out of your mind."

"Thanks, Mark. If you come across anything at all, call me immediately."

"You got it."

24

November 9, 2025. 22:54 hours local time.
Chaozhou, China.

Zhang Hudao checked his watch and stole a glance at the proprietor of the noodle shop, a stooped old man, who flicked a tattered straw broom beneath unoccupied tables, his back to Zhang. Zhang sat at the back of the tiny hole-in-the-wall restaurant—there was room for only five small tables —facing the open entryway. Water still dripped off of the roof line into a puddle in front of the entry, a brief rainstorm having just passed over. Humidity filled the cramped space, making Zhang miss the crisp autumn air of Beijing. It never got cool here in China's south. He had only been in Chaozhou a few hours, having taken the overnight bullet train from the capital, and already wanted to head back.

His contact was late. They had arranged to meet at the noodle shop at 10:45 p.m., right before the closing time indicated on its glass window. Despite the hour, the old man said nothing to Zhang, who had already laid cash for his meal on the tabletop. Despite Chinese customs against tipping, the pile of cash included a large gratuity.

Zhang heard footsteps approaching on the wet asphalt outside the restaurant and watched as an athletically built man in his thirties wearing a track jacket stepped up onto the tile floor of the shop. The owner watched first as the visitor made eye contact with Zhang, then he turned towards Zhang and did the same, acknowledgment in his eyes. Zhang nodded, and the owner leaned his broom against a table and walked past the new visitor to step outside, closing the glass door behind him. Zhang watched as the old man pulled a pack of cigarettes out and stuck one in his mouth, staring out into the night.

The visitor, whom Zhang only knew as Tian, pulled out the stool across from Zhang and took a seat.

Zhang cleared his throat and said, "You're late."

"I am sorry, I got held up leaving the base. What is this about? We really shouldn't be meeting like this."

"I want to know how preparations are coming with the operation."

Tian sighed and looked behind him, ensuring the restaurant door was still closed.

"You know I cannot be discussing that with you."

"Then what good are you to me?"

That caused Tian to pause. Tian was a commander in the Special Operations force of the Chinese Navy Marine Corp, known as the Dragon Commando Unit. He was in peak physical fitness and much younger than Zhang but was still intimidated by the veteran agent.

Before Tian could respond, Zhang said, "Need I remind you that you and your friends in the Navy are only in a position of strength due to my efforts."

"Of course, your contribution has been critical, but you know how things are. This is not your area. It is strictly need-to-know."

Zhang shook his head. He shouldn't be surprised. They were all on the same side, but paranoia and jealously guarding information was endemic in the security apparatus of China. He would know. He was guilty of it himself.

"You've passed me information before."

"This is different. Command is keeping all of this very close. Even from our brothers at State Security."

Zhang looked beyond Tian towards the door. The shop owner continued to idly smoke his cigarette.

"I didn't travel all the way to this shithole to leave with nothing, Tian."

Tian once again looked behind him.

After turning back to Zhang, he leaned across the table and whispered, "Preparations are progressing, but we are still not there. Some drills have been run. We have only just come out of monsoon season, so the weather is now more cooperative. We still get a steady stream of video of their coastline and defenses, so that is good."

"That is what I am here about. I have concerns that that information feed may be in jeopardy."

Tian leaned back, eyeing his counterpart. "Why is that?"

"I won't say. There is no need for alarm, but out of caution, I would urge you to step things up."

"What is going on, Zhang?"

"That is for me to worry about. Carry on but quicken the pace."

Tian shook his head. "I am not sure I have that kind of pull, but I will see what I can do."

"Good."

Silence hung between the two men.

After a moment Zhang said, "Should anything happen, contact me immediately."

Tian nodded his acknowledgment. "I had better be heading back."

Zhang gave a single nod and watched as Tian made his way out. The owner did not acknowledge him as he walked past. After Tian had disappeared from view, Zhang stood up and stepped out into the soft glow of the single bulb that hung lit above the shop. From his leather jacket pocket, he extracted his own pack of cigarettes, turning to the old man.

"Light?"

Without saying anything, the old man handed over a box of matches. Zhang appreciated the old school touch.

The two men stood in silence, smoking.

Zhang had reason to be worried. Something was up. It appeared that Bao Jiaotong had abandoned his post. Zhang did not know why, but he had to assume it could have implications for what was happening on the home front.

He knew something was amiss with Bao because he had bugged Bao's vehicle in New York City with a tracker. A connection Zhang had at the Chinese consulate in the city had placed it. Bao was Zhang's pupil in the art of espionage, but there it was, the unshakable suspicion. While he wanted to keep track of Bao's movements, he was disappointed his protege had failed to find the tracker or, at least, suspect it might be there. His behavior indicated he did not.

Zhang knew that not long after their exchange about the San Lang engineers with American forces, Bao had made a trip to a town in central New York, which Zhang knew to be near where Bao's asset lived. He could only assume Bao had gone to tell the asset about what had transpired, which was precisely what Zhang had told him not to do.

More troubling, now, was that Zhang had seen that Bao's car was parked at John F. Kennedy International Airport. Bao had no orders to travel. Taking his personal vehicle was a mistake. He should have used public transit. Bao was not thinking clearly. It was clear to Zhang that his agent was panicking.

Zhang would also be notified if any one of Bao's passports were scanned, but it would have to be at a Chinese port of entry or a border crossing in a country where his agency had a connection. He very much doubted Bao would abscond for the charms of North Korea, Iran, or Syria, however. Guinea in West Africa didn't seem likely either. If Bao made his way to Europe, for example, where Zhang had zero people on the inside at any border control, then Bao really would be in the wind.

He had sent a message to Bao via their system but knew it was for naught. He did not expect any reply. Bao leaving so abruptly and without any warning told him all he needed to know.

The old shop owner finished his cigarette, flicking the butt into the darkness of the street. He nodded to Zhang, turned, and went back into the restaurant. Zhang stood for a moment more, thinking about his next move. For the first time in a very long time, he was unsure of what to do.

He dropped his half-smoked cigarette and mashed it underneath his shoe. He then turned and made his way into the night.

25

November 10, 2025. 09:01 hours local time.
Air Force Office of Special Investigations Headquarters, Quantico, Virginia.

"What can you tell me so far?"

Henry Purcel sat across from his two info ops analysts, Kurt Miller and Nate Bolen, in the AFOSI secure conference room. He had requested that both men come into work over the weekend to get started on analyzing the chip design files and other data that BTP had provided. Immediately following Purcel's encounter with Eddie Voss, the company was quick to cooperate and get the requested files over to AFOSI.

The two analysts shot each other side-eyed glances.

Miller gave a couple of clicks to the pen he was fidgeting with and cleared his throat. "Umm, well, sir, we can't tell you anything, nor will we really be able to."

Purcel showed no reaction. After letting a beat pass, he said, "How do you mean?"

This time Bolen spoke, trying to show that he backed his partner.

"There's nothing to analyze. We sifted through BTP's 'vault,' if you will, of its contracted work for the Ocelot program, and the chip design files simply do not exist."

"How could that be?"

Bolen continued, "Well, someone deleted them. Safe to assume it was Voss, unless he had someone covering his tracks for him—"

Purcel cut him off. "Doubtful. From what I gather, Voss was pretty much a loner. Didn't alienate himself, but he wasn't cozy with anyone."

"Right, so he deleted his work. Each piece of work has a digital signature from its creator, and from BTP's Ocelot files, nothing has Voss's name on it. We know that can't be. He was lead designer for this particular contract. Doesn't make sense that none of his work would be there."

"Is it common practice at all for someone to erase files like this?"

Miller chimed in now, "No, sir, not at all. Maybe for someone operating in their garage with limited storage capacity, but a company like BTP doesn't have that concern. There's something else."

Purcel raised his eyebrows.

Miller continued, "As you can imagine, in instances like this, BTP is contractually required to furnish whatever government agency they are working for, in this case the Air Force, with the chip design files. This is so the government can have them on hand and be able to reproduce the chips if they need to."

Purcel nodded his understanding.

"So, naturally, we ran down that thread. Your contact at the NSA, Giresi, told us when we were read-in that we could contact him if we needed anything, so we reached out and had him put us in touch with the relevant program office at the Air Force. Well, to put it frankly, they fucked up over there."

Purcel shifted in his seat, concern now clouding his face. "How, exactly?"

Miller cleared his throat again. He said, "Well, they didn't properly inspect the deliverable, or so it would appear. Whoever was in charge of certifying BTP's product marked it as such, when in reality, what Voss gave them was a basic 'straw man' design: all bones, no meat. Obviously, BTP itself has no one in the loop verifying this either. Voss must have sent it directly."

"And if the government office had caught it? A risk on Voss's part, no?"

"Not really. He could have simply claimed that he goofed and sent a preliminary file. He could have then provided a real one, only without what we suspect could have been a hardware Trojan."

Purcel nodded along as this was explained to him. Finally, he shook his head. "Jesus Christ. Unbelievable."

"It's a double whammy. Not only can no real forensics be performed, but there is no possibility for chip replacement. They'd have to start from scratch," Bolen added.

"OK. So, he was covering his tracks. Is it possible that Voss's design files could be somewhere else?"

Miller responded, "Sure. He could have slipped them out on a thumb drive. I can't speak to BTP's security protocols, so I can't say how difficult or easy that may have been. But generally speaking, it's possible he has them tucked away somewhere else."

Purcel nodded again and was quiet a moment. He thought about the search warrant that was quickly executed on Eddie Voss's home. Thus far, he hadn't heard anything from Detective Conkling, whom he'd asked to call him if anything of interest came up in the house.

He looked back to Miller and Bolen and asked, "So, we can't say for sure what exactly we have here, can we?"

Both men said in unison, "Right."

They each began to elaborate, with Bolen then nodding to Miller, allowing him to respond.

"That's correct, sir. Without seeing Voss's chip design files, there's no way of knowing definitively what we are dealing with or how to deal with it, for that matter. I mean, given how everything has gone down thus far, it is safe to assume that Voss was up to no good, and as the lead chip designer for this project, that is where he would cause his trouble. But exactly how he was going about creating a Trojan and, if he succeeded, how it works, we can't say for sure."

Bolen added, "I suppose we should add this: despite Voss's deleting the design files, there is still some remnant of them."

Purcel raised his eyebrows in a way that suggested he liked the sound of that.

Bolen, not wanting to instill a false hope in his boss, quickly added on,

"What I mean is that design files give a complete top-down description of the chip. At the top is the software description of what the chip does—sort of like a computer program describing the hardware's function. At the very bottom is all that we have left because Voss deleted everything else. We obtained all that remains from the chip manufacturer that caught the contract, a small DOD-trusted firm in Vermont. The manufacturer is not at fault because they got what they needed from BTP to build the chip. Nothing more was expected. You see, the lowest level of the design Voss created was the only piece he delivered. It was only the machine-readable file that describes how to create the intricate, maze-like circuit patterns of the photomasks."

Purcel held up a hand. "Photomasks?"

"Ah, right, sorry. Photomasks are what the manufacturer uses to create the physical chips. The photomasks are plates of transparent and opaque glass that selectively allow light to etch, as part of a chemical process, the chip's microscopic design onto silicon. Of course, that silicon becomes the physical chip."

Purcel indicated for Bolen to continue.

"Anyway, they have those photomasks, as well as the physical chips themselves, but it is not going to do us any good. It has been common practice for some time now for chip designers to make it such that the chip can't be reverse engineered. Certain preventative techniques are applied. Usually, this is done with counterfeit prevention in mind. Anyway, we could attempt a reverse engineering of our own to try and find that Trojan, but it would take a tremendous amount of effort, and possibly—hell, probably—with no payoff. Either way, you're looking at situations that are going to require time. A lot of it."

The room was once again silent. Miller and Bolen saw their boss was in thinking mode, and they didn't want to interrupt his train of thought. Miller clicked his pen once. Purcel's eyes had settled on the table in front of him, focused on nothing in particular. He was trying to think of what exactly all this meant for his investigation, and he was quickly realizing that he wasn't exactly sure what the next step should be.

Finally, he brought his eyes back up to look at his two analysts and asked them point blank, "So, what do you think we should do now?"

The two men once again stole glances at one another, with Miller clearing his throat, indicating he was going to be the one to answer.

"Well, they definitely need to keep those two Ocelots grounded, and it is going to have to be for some time. Based on the evidence we have, those cameras need to be removed and new ones, containing new motherboards, put in place. We simply can't risk flying them again with those same cameras."

Purcel took a deep breath and, as he exhaled, said, "I'm assuming that's not something with a quick turnaround either."

"No, definitely not. Ironically enough, there are a bunch of spare chips still. I spoke with someone at BTP, and they told me the Air Force just recently purchased a batch. I guess excess funds were available, and someone in the chain figured it would be good to have extra on hand. Of course, as we know, those chips are all dirty. BTP is also now aware of this, and I'm sure they'll be informing the depot where the chips are housed and how they need to be destroyed. Anyway, that's all neither here nor there. Someone will have to design new chips, and I'm sure BTP won't be handed that work. The Air Force is gonna have to find a different outfit."

The three men were quiet for a moment.

Finally, just to break the silence, Bolen added, "Bit odd that the Air Force would order a batch of spare chips like that in this case."

Purcel looked directly at him. "Why do you say that?"

"Well, aren't there only two of these Ocelots in circulation?"

Purcel agreed with that sentiment, but after a moment, he remembered an article from *Defense News* he had saved in his file for this case, and also something that had been mentioned when he spoke with Major Maya Decker at Creech.

"Taiwan and South Korea."

Miller and Bolen took on confused looks at the non-sequitur.

Bolen said, "Sir? What was that?"

Purcel didn't bother to respond. Instead, he stood up quickly and headed for the conference room exit, leaving his info ops team in bewildered silence.

26

November 10, 2025. 13:55 hours local time.
University at Buffalo North Campus, Buffalo, New York.

303, 305…

307. Here we are.

Special Agent Mark Bizon checked the name plate directly below the room number to confirm the office did, indeed, belong to the person he sought, Dr. Paul Richards. He was happy to see the directory on the building's first floor had not misled him.

He was standing in Davis Hall, home to much of the University at Buffalo's computer engineering school and a place where Eddie Voss presumably spent a great deal of time during his graduate studies. Bizon's investigation into how Voss came to be a Chinese asset had brought him here, what he considered the best prospect for identifying a connection. Bizon could not claim to be familiar with the inner workings of education beyond a bachelor's degree but figured that graduate studies were pretty much the same as undergraduate: you went to class, took exams, stressed out, stayed up late, and rarely interacted with your professor. Lucky for him, however, after using some charm with the secretary in the Registrar's office and getting Voss's official transcripts sent down to Quantico, Bizon discovered that Voss had been doing a master's thesis, and that necessitated closer collaboration with a professor or professors. After some more phone calls and deployment of his charisma, Bizon now knew the names of the two professors involved in Voss's project. In the intervening decade since Voss obtained his master's, one of those individuals had retired, but the other was still at the school. That was Dr. Richards.

Bizon gave the office door a light knock.

"Come in."

He opened the door and stepped into a small office with a single window offering a great view of the parking lot outside. Richards, tall and wiry and with a hairline that had been beyond rescue for some time now, was coming around his paper-cluttered desk to greet him. Had they known each other, Bizon would have made a comment about the professor's bow tie.

The academic offered his hand. "Special Agent..."

"Bizon."

"Bizon, right. Pleasure to meet you. Please, have a seat." He motioned to the single straight-backed chair in front of his desk while turning to return to his own seat.

Bizon sat down and crossed his legs, giving the professor a moment to settle in. "I appreciate you taking the time to meet with me, Doctor."

Richards smiled and nodded. Bizon had hoped he might tell him not to worry about the "doctor" title, but no such luck. Bizon would readily admit that he wasn't the best with formality, and that sometimes made dealing with academics difficult. One time, when he neglected to refer to a professor who was visiting Quantico as "Doctor" and was corrected, Bizon asked the professor if he had a ring he could kiss. That joke hadn't gone over very well, and he remembered that the glare from Lieutenant Colonel Reed could have shattered a mirror.

"Not a problem. You have my curiosity piqued, I must say. It's not often I have a federal agent darken my doorway. I guess I should be thankful for that. You mentioned you are located in Virginia. That is quite a trip for what I imagine may be something we could have talked about over the phone."

"Ah, I see it as an opportunity for a nostalgia tour."

The professor cocked his head. "You went to school here?"

"Not only that, born and raised in Buffalo. So, I can come see the old stomping grounds and pop in on my mom. Miss her cooking and all that."

"I see."

"Anyway, I don't want to take up too much of your time. I guess, given your curiosity about my being here, you don't keep up much with the news."

Richards once again cocked his head, looking perplexed.

"Edward Voss. Is that name familiar to you?" Bizon asked.

"Hmm. Vaguely. Student of mine but can't really put a face to the name. I've been at this school for coming on fifteen years now. A lot of faces have come and gone in that time."

"I can imagine. Anyway, the reason I'm here is, yes, Voss was a student of yours, about twelve or so years ago. Just a few days ago, Voss was killed in Schenectady in a shooting involving a colleague of mine. He had been working for a defense contractor there and was the subject of an investigation. Still is."

Dr. Richards leaned back in his chair, a look of genuine shock on his face. "Oh my God. No, I...I hadn't heard anything about this. I read the *Buffalo News* still with my breakfast, but they didn't carry that story. Otherwise, I don't keep up with much. Oh, dear."

They were both silent for a moment, Bizon thinking about how to best broach the subject he came to discuss. He knew he had to tread somewhat lightly. They weren't at Quantico or some other government facility. This was the professor's territory.

Before Bizon could say anything, Richards, apparently sensing an awkward silence might be forming, said, "That is tragic news, certainly not something I expect to hear about a former student of ours. But now I am curious how this matter brings you here."

"It had come to light that Voss was very likely working for a foreign government—"

Richards raised is eyebrows in a show of concern, and he muttered, "Oh, dear."

"—And we are hoping to establish how his connection to this foreign entity came to be, and—"

Richard's expression changed, his eyes narrowing, and he once again interrupted Bizon, "And you believe that Voss's academic background is the place to discover such a connection?"

Bizon picked up on a hint of irritation in the question. It gave him pause. Not only did he not want to make this a combative conversation, but he was also surprised that Richards couldn't discern what was, at least to Bizon, a very obvious point.

"Well, Doctor, I think it goes without saying that your field of study is dominated by..."

"Yes, yes, I'm aware, dominated by international students, a huge proportion of which come from India and China. I'm also aware that the latter is a country with which ours is not on the best of terms. However, Special Agent—"

"Mark is fine."

"—Special Agent Bizon, I'll have you know that across my time in academia I have collaborated with dozens of individuals from those countries and have not once ever considered any of them to be untrustworthy. Also, is it not the case that international students, particularly those arriving from, let's say, *adversarial* countries, are often vetted by colleagues of yours?"

Bizon cleared his throat and thought to himself, *this is going well.*

"Yes, that would be the Department of Homeland Security. You are right, there is a vetting process, but, as I'm sure you can appreciate, it is imperfect. Not only is there only so much information we can obtain, but also, many of these individuals are barely twenty years old when they first come here, so they do not have much personal history to be reviewed."

He waited a beat to let Dr. Richards consider that.

"Having said that, I should make you aware, Doctor, that no one at my office suspects you of anything. Nor are we necessarily saying, definitively, that a colleague or former colleague that may have also worked with Voss is guilty of anything. I, we, are trying to establish Voss's connection to the foreign government in question and possible representatives from that country that may be operating here on our soil. Spies, really. Again, I know it may not be the politically correct thing to say aloud, but given the nature of computer science and engineering, we felt that Voss's educational history represented a likely intersection point with foreign nationals."

Hearing that he himself was not the subject of the investigation seemed to soften Richards some. Bizon could see his body language loosen, and the scowl left his face.

"No, I understand. I can see why you would pursue this particular avenue."

"Right. And that brings me here. Voss was involved in a master's thesis, and my research indicates you were a part of that project. I was hoping you could tell me anything you might remember about him or anyone else he may have worked with in his time here."

Richards sighed, and Bizon started to get the feeling he wasn't going to be of much help.

"Well, I'm afraid I can't be much help in that regard."

Figures.

"I mean, now that you mention the project, I do recall working with this individual, umm, Voss. But at that time, I was pretty new to my professorship and was only tangentially involved in some of those projects. The lead on that would have been Dr. Soto, who had taken me under his wing and had me help his students here and there. But I can't claim to have been too hands on."

"Dr. Wesley Soto, yes, I saw that he was the other professor in on the project. You are the one still at the university, though, so I figured I'd try you first."

"I understand. But really, I don't have much I can offer you. I would encourage you to speak with Dr. Soto."

"I was afraid you might say that..."

"He doesn't live very far," Richards said as he reached over to the desk phone sitting on the corner of his desk. He glanced at the clock as he did so, and to Bizon's complete surprise, said, "It's late enough, the lazy bastard should be up and about."

About a half hour later, Bizon sat in a private residence on Tillinghast Place, a tree-lined street in an upscale part of the city near its famous Delaware Park. It was a far cry from the blue-collar east-side neighborhood filled with the descendants of Polish immigrants where he had come of age. The home of Dr. Wesley Soto, retired from the University at Buffalo Computer Engineering Department for three years, was pretty striking. When he first sat down on the couch in the professor's living room, Bizon made mention of it.

"This is a beautiful place you have, Doctor."

"Thank you, and please, just Wes is fine. I'm not in the classroom anymore."

I think I like this guy.

Soto continued, "Frank Lloyd Wright designed this home."

Bizon wasn't much of an art historian, but he knew who that was. As a student, he had visited the famous architect's Darwin Martin house for an elective class, long now a museum and just around the corner from Tillinghast.

"No shit? Oh, I mean...ah, excuse me...wow."

Soto chuckled. "It's ok. I get that reaction often. No one expects that one could be living in a Wright home. It's like being in a piece of history. All should be on the Register of National Historic Places, but some are still private residences. There's another not far from here. I got lucky. I knew the previous owner, also a professor at UB. When he passed, his estate asked if I was interested. I couldn't pass up the opportunity."

After his brief lesson on local architecture, they were now into the heart of the matter of Bizon's visit. Soto sat across from him in a leather chaise that, to Bizon's eye, seemed expensive, but he wasn't sure it looked all that comfortable. The professor sat with his hands, fingers interlocked, over an ample belly. He put Bizon in the mind of a Santa-like figure. He sported a dark gray goatee and had a darker complexion that suggested an origin somewhere in Latin America. Even late in the afternoon, he had the disheveled look of someone who had just gotten out of bed. Before leaving Richards's office, the professor had noted his old colleague liked to sleep "until the crack of noon" in his retirement.

"Wes, can you tell me then about any other students or individuals that Voss collaborated with, or maybe palled around with, during the time you worked together, something that might help me establish a connection?"

"Given what you said thus far, I fear we may be talking about a connection to China."

Bizon gave him have a smile and a *well, yeah* tilt of his head.

"I certainly know of one possible connection. It is one that I made."

Bizon raised his eyebrows, encouraging Soto to continue.

"Despite being a diligent student and a hard worker, Eddie still struggled with some concepts. Even when working with someone on a master's project, I cannot dedicate too much time to one individual. I have other responsibilities. So, to help Eddie, I arranged for an assistant I had at the time, another graduate student, to work with him. That assistant was from China."

Bizon brought his pen to his notebook on his lap. "And this person's name?"

"Heping Gao."

As he jotted the name down, he asked, "And is Gao still associated with UB?"

"No, he moved on after another two or three years to the University of Michigan. We stayed in touch for a little bit, but I've since lost track."

"Did you ever have any suspicions about Gao? Anything you can recall that now might seem like a red flag to you?"

Soto thought for a moment, eventually slowly shaking his head. "No, not at all. Very affable individual. Well, hmm..."

Again, Bizon gave a raised eyebrow.

"Before I even assigned him to help Eddie, he had come to me, offering to work closely with Eddie. At the time, I guess I didn't think anything of it, but now, with all of this..."

Soto paused again briefly. Then he said, "When Voss was my student, he was working for a company here in Buffalo. A defense contractor. Again, it didn't strike me as noteworthy at the time, but maybe Heping knew this, and it was why he was eager to get close to Eddie." He started to shake his head at the thought.

Bizon took some more notes.

Soto continued, "You know, if all this is true about Eddie Voss, I would say I am not completely surprised, for whatever that is worth."

"Why is that?"

"Eddie very much kept to himself. He was a loner. Very quiet. He spent a lot of time on campus in Davis Hall. I never heard much about a social life or a girlfriend or anything like that. If I could play the role of an amateur psychiatrist for a moment, I can see how someone like Eddie could be easily influenced or manipulated. If he could be made to feel important, I suppose. I'm inclined to think that if Eddie became the target of bad actors, he probably wouldn't have had the psychological armor to hold them off."

"I see. Is there anything else you might be able to tell me about this Gao or anything else that might be helpful?"

The professor sat for a moment, thinking. After a few seconds he shook his head slowly. "No, nothing comes to mind." Another pause, and then he added, "Voss was a good student. Smart. If he put his mind to it or got the proper guidance on something, he would become proficient at whatever it was. It's a shame he may have put that skill to ill use. I came here as an immigrant what seems like a lifetime ago. It's home. It would break my heart if a student of mine came to be involved in harming or attempting to harm this country. And with Heping...we worked closely for some time. That would hurt even more."

Bizon nodded at that. "You can't blame yourself, Wes. Even people who work in intelligence and espionage sometimes miss things like this, right underneath their noses."

They were both quiet, and Bizon made to get up.

"One other thing, though maybe it's nothing."

Bizon, now standing, nodded for Soto to continue.

"Heping often made trips down to New York City. He said he had family there, but it was with some frequency, and that's no short journey. I always thought it was just a sweetheart he was visiting, and he wanted to keep it private. Maybe that's all it was, but I figured I should mention it."

27

November 10, 2025. 15:07 hours local time.
George Bush Center for Intelligence, Langley, Virginia.

"So, Henry, why the five-alarm fire?"

Steve Giresi leaned against the wall, his arms crossed, as he considered Henry Purcel seated a few feet away from him on the opposite side of a long conference table. Purcel looked back up, his hands folded on the table, his posture ramrod straight, as if he were interviewing for a job he very much wanted. It was he, however, who had requested this meeting. Shortly after abruptly leaving his sit-down with Bolen and Miller, he had called Giresi, telling him that they needed to meet as soon as possible. It was decided that Langley would be the best place to do so.

They were in the very same room they had met in when Purcel first came to the CIA headquarters to learn about the Ocelot case. Fitting, he thought, as he felt they may finally be coming full circle, or close to it. Seated across from him were Chris, the CIA agent who handled China matters, and another agency employee who had introduced himself as Mike from the Near East Division a moment ago when the three of them filed through the door. Purcel assumed this was the agent from the Somalia mission where the Ocelot leak had been revealed.

Giresi looked agitated. Purcel's urgent manner on the phone made him think that the AFOSI man was on the verge of some kind of breakthrough. It was why, unlike the two CIA agents, he hadn't yet sat down.

Special Agent Purcel cleared his throat before speaking, "Before I answer, let me ask you something. Was BTP, and therefore Edward Voss, at all involved in the Ocelot II subprogram? Any specific work performed related to this geological identification capability?"

Without hesitation, Giresi responded, "No. Only one non-government contractor was read-into that work, and it wasn't BTP."

Purcel let the silence hang, giving Giresi a moment to fit the puzzle pieces together in his head.

After a few seconds, Giresi said, "Then how—"

"Exactly," Purcel cut him off, "Amidst all of the madness of the last seventy-two hours, I never considered to what level BTP and Voss were immersed in this Ocelot program. Before coming here, I checked the contract statement of work and saw nothing related to the Ocelot II. But I figured, given its level of secrecy, that it may not be reflected there, so I wanted to double check with you."

"Ok, so..."

"So, either the Chinese found, worked, and turned Voss, and in an extreme stroke of luck, his work just so happened to end up in a piece of technology they wanted to exploit, or..." Purcel paused a split second for dramatic effect then continued, "The Ocelot II drone was never the original, intended target."

The three men opposite Purcel all gave him blank stares. He shifted his eyes between each of them before settling on Chris, the China expert.

"It's out there on the World Wide Web, open source, and has been for some time: Ocelot I drones were sold to South Korea and Taiwan."

Giresi moved from his position against the wall and pulled out the rolling chair in front of him to join everyone at the table.

Chris leaned back in his chair, saying out loud to no one in particular, "I'll be doggone."

Giresi, now seated, looked across at Purcel, thinking about what he had just said. Finally, Giresi said, "That has to be it. Anything else would have been the espionage equivalent of the Chinese covering their eyes and throwing darts at the board, just hoping something landed. If there was any thought behind it—and I'm sure Chris will back me up here, the Chinese are always calculating—going through Voss to get access to drones going to Taiwan makes far more sense."

For the first time, Mike spoke up, "Ironically, it appears that they did stumble their way into something possibly even more valuable in the Ocelot II. A massive stroke of luck."

Purcel nodded his agreement. "Precisely," he said, "One of BTP's contracted tasks was related to the chip design of the Ocelot onboard camera, with all its bells and whistles. I assume that this was something that made its way onto the Ocelot II as well."

He looked at Giresi for confirmation. "Correct. The only difference between the two instantiations *is* the geological identification capability. Otherwise, the two are identical. Voss's work would also be found in the Ocelot II."

Purcel continued, "So, gaining access to the Ocelot II was simply gravy to the Chinese, a totally unanticipated side benefit. A big one, at that."

The room fell silent. Giresi, Purcel, and Mike turned their attention to Chris, waiting for his thoughts on the matter. He sat with his elbows on the table, hands in a tepee in front of his face, lost in thought. Eventually, he brought his hands down and bobbed his head up and down a couple of times, as if agreeing with his inner monologue.

Chris said, "It makes sense. I think I may have an idea what the Chinese are after, and we could be discussing something potentially earth shaking here."

The other three men waited for him to expand on the thought.

"The Ocelots are surveillance drones, and I know the Taiwanese purchased their first batch specifically to use along their coastlines and out over coastal waters, part of the local Navy's efforts to boost homeland defense. Seeing what those birds see would be invaluable to the Chinese."

Giresi asked, "How so?"

"Well, wouldn't you want to not only use Taiwan's own systems to recon their coastal defense, but also see what they are seeing in real time and possibly be able to spoof it, particularly if you were planning on invading the island?"

Henry Purcel tapped the steering wheel of his Hyundai Sonata impatiently. Looking out his windshield, a sea of taillights stretched out and filled the darkness in front of him on the George Washington Memorial Parkway. Total gridlock. The meeting at the CIA headquarters had gone on for a couple of hours, meaning that the sun had set, and it was the absolute heart of rush hour when Purcel left to head back to his house in Arlington. For the beltway, that was nightmarish.

Not quite as nightmarish, Purcel thought, as the situation that he and the others in the Ocelot Drone investigation had waded into. Or, he hoped, maybe not.

After his revelation that the target of the Chinese operation may, in fact, have been the Taiwanese Ocelots and Chris's offering that it may mean an invasion of the island country was in the works, Purcel and the three others had crowded around the conference table, going over their options. Mike, the Middle East-centric CIA man, had half joked that it might be the most urgent discussion that room had seen since bin Laden's whereabouts were confirmed.

Purcel, in his eagerness and, he soon realized, his naivete, first suggested that the Taiwanese defense forces be informed and advised that they ground those Ocelot drones for now. Surely, they had other, albeit inferior, surveillance drones in reserve that could at least monitor the coastline while the Ocelot situation was rectified, even if that required an undetermined amount of time.

Giresi shot the notion down so quickly that Purcel was temporarily taken aback. "No way. Strike it from your mind, not an option."

"But they can't just keep those things in operation…"

"Forget it. First off, that is not a call any of us in this room can make. That may very well be a decision for the SecDef. I can't say for sure without some consultation with contacts of mine at the Pentagon, but it is *certainly* much higher up the food chain than us. I'm pretty confident someone from the office of the SecDef would be the one actually making that call to their counterpart in Taiwan."

"Fair enough, but—"

"Second, it's a completely moot point. There's no way we can let the Taiwanese know that those Ocelots may have Trojans in them. *May* being the operative word."

Both Mike and Chris nodded along in agreement.

Purcel still pushed back.

"Well, I think it is well beyond *may*. You have to admit, *very likely* is what we are looking at—"

"Even so—"

"How can we possibly—"

"Purcel," Giresi said with some force to bring the back-and-forth assertions to a halt.

Purcel stopped. He motioned with his head, indicating Giresi had the floor.

"I get it, trust me, I know where you are coming from. But we cannot, at this time, on a hunch, no matter how strong the hunch is, raise alarm bells with the Taiwanese. You have to think of the possible political, and yes, economic, ramifications of that. 'Oh, you sold us dirty drones?' It would set back confidence in the US defense industry for who knows how long—not to mention the damage to our military ties not just with Taiwan, but also South Korea, Japan, the Philippines, hell, even Vietnam. These are going to be important partners going forward. We *cannot* risk our standing with them. Not now."

The room went silent for a few moments. Purcel was considering what he had just heard. Giresi's logic made sense. But what good was it if Taiwan could soon be overrun?

He shook his head. "I understand, but what if—"

"Exactly. What if. I'm sorry to keep interrupting you, but as much as I trust his judgment, I'm sure Chris," Giresi said, motioning to the CIA agent, "will admit that his assertion is still just speculation. We know China has had its eye on the island for ages now, but do we otherwise have any solid evidence something is forthcoming?"

Chris shook his head.

"Nothing concrete, no. We haven't seen any satellite imagery showing a massing of munitions or troops, or any unusually high number of practice flight sorties from coastal airbases."

Chris paused for a moment, thinking, then added, "The Chinese do have a base in the Inner Mongolia region where the design mimics the street layout around the Taiwanese Presidential Palace, and over recent weeks, we have seen a bit more buzz at that facility, but they have a history of doing that, probably to keep us guessing. Having said all of this, it doesn't mean nothing is in the works. It wouldn't take much for China to cross that strait and take over the island."

Giresi continued, "So, it's possible we have some time on this. Again, I get it, I know it sounds absurd, but given what we have, we must consider the bigger picture. Don't get me wrong, this is priority. We just need to find another way."

And another way is what they had discussed, with very little to show for it by the time Purcel left. But not long after he slipped his Sonata onto the Parkway, he had been struck by a thought. Amid all the angst and back-and-forth in the CIA conference room, it hadn't come to him, but the quiet of his car allowed his mind to clear. *Why not revisit the well?*

He inched his Sonata forward, checking the time on his car's dashboard. 5:37 p.m. He was mindful that Layla needed to be let out. He worried about her acclimating to new surroundings, given her advanced age. But he was more curious about the time for an entirely different reason. He reached for his cell phone laying on the arm rest next to him. He could never remember which time zone South Bend fell in, but it was worth a shot.

It might still be working hours in Indiana.

28

November 11, 2025. 07:03 hours local time.
Haidian District, Beijing, China.

He had just sat down and placed his handgun and pack of cigarettes next to each other on his desk when Zhang Hudao heard a knock on his office door. He looked up to see Fei Chengang, one of his subordinates, standing in the doorway. Fei looked like he could still be in high school and had the nervous energy of someone always trying to please. This was particularly pronounced around Zhang. Fei, who spoke fluent English, was one of the Foreign Intelligence Department's analysts, specializing in foreign media and open-source material. He stood there staring at Zhang, holding a piece of paper. Zhang didn't say anything, instead raising his eyebrows as if to say, *well?*

The young analyst cleared his throat.

"Umm, yes sir. Ahem, first, good morning. I was doing some research and—"

"Get to your point."

"Right, right. I thought you should see this."

He stepped into Zhang's tiny, cramped office and approached the desk. He slid his one-page report onto the desk in front of Zhang.

"I have here a summary of something I came across that I thought might be of int—"

"I'll read it. Thank you."

Fei stood there awkwardly for a moment more. Zhang motioned with his eyes towards the door.

"Right, yes, sir. I'll be at my workstation if you need me."

He then turned and left. Zhang picked up Fei's report and scanned it. As he read, he felt his face flush with anger. His grip tightened around the paper until he crumpled it in his hand and whipped the balled-up sheet against the wall across from him.

"Fuck!"

A number of outlets in the American media had run a story a few days before: a man, a government contractor, was killed in a shooting with a member of law enforcement in the upstate New York town of Schenectady. The law enforcement officer involved was a federal agent, and the deceased was one Edward Voss.

Edward Voss. That had to be Bao's man on the inside. Zhang had never been given that information; all he knew was that the asset was based in Central New York. He wasn't a big believer in coincidence. A government contractor in that part of the state being killed by a federal agent right around the time that his own spy disappears without a word? The chances that it was an unrelated event were exceptionally small.

He sat and stared at the blank wall across from the desk. This was a situation he was unaccustomed to. He was used to being fully in control and, even when things did not break his way, knowing how to pivot. This was different. It was a chessboard with many pieces, one that stretched oceans away from his ability to influence. Somalia, New York. It hadn't helped that so much of this operation had been siloed. Bao alone was responsible for handling the assets within the United States, and that likely included this Voss. Now, Voss was dead, and Bao had disappeared. This is what happens when you entrust too much to others.

He pushed away from his desk, standing to leave his office. Years before, he'd been offered a larger space on one of the Ministry's higher floors, something with a window overlooking Beijing's scenic Kunming Lake, but he preferred to stay in his old, cramped space in the basement. It kept him close to the actual work, the real intelligence gathering. Just down the hall from him, behind steel doors only accessible by code, was a huge area filled with computers, so many that the room ran warmer than the space outside of it despite constant air conditioning. The lighting was kept low. Most of the room was lit by glow of computer screens. It was there that intelligence analysts worked around the clock gathering, analyzing, and interpreting data. And that included intel coming out of Taiwan.

But right now, Zhang felt he had no other choice than to take this higher up, literally and figuratively. He turned down the hall in the opposite direction from the intel room and came to a bank of three elevators, taking the first available up to the eighth floor of the building. Many of his colleagues wanted to be on this particular floor. The number eight was considered auspicious by the majority of Chinese people.

Alighting from the elevator, he went straight down a wide hall to the end office. He knocked on the closed door.

"Come in."

Li Yong was the head of the Foreign Intelligence Division and Zhang's boss. Zhang hated the man. They were about the same age, but Li was a lawyer by trade and had never served in the field. Li's grandfather had served alongside Mao during the Long March, and his father and an uncle had been ranking members in the Politburo. The uncle, as Zhang understood, still liked to play kingmaker despite being a retired octogenarian. Besides such a lineage, what else qualified Li to be a decision maker in the Ministry of State Security, Zhang did not know. As a Chinese idiom went, Li stood on the shoulders of giants. The irony never escaped Zhang that his government loved to laud itself for being run by technocrats, which is how large-scale projects—high-speed rail, massive dams, water diversion schemes—could be achieved, but the reality was, it was just as susceptible to nepotism as anywhere else.

Zhang entered to find his boss seated behind his desk, leaning back, reading a multi-page document. He allowed Zhang to stand silently for several seconds before finally looking up from the paperwork. He removed his reading glasses and set them on the desk. Despite being a heavy smoker like Zhang, Li's face was oddly devoid of any wrinkles or age lines. Zhang suspected his boss was a regular user of Botox.

"Yes?"

"May I sit, sir?"

Li motioned for him to take one of the guest chairs on the opposite side of the desk. Zhang sat down and told him all about the San Lang engineers' encounter with US Special Forces in Africa, the losing contact with Bao, the news article about Voss, and the concerns for the operation going forward.

When he was done, Li wore a scowl, at least as much as his stiff face would allow. "And you're only just telling me this now?"

"I didn't see reason to worry you with it initially, sir. It was under control, but I believe Bao disobeyed orders and went to his asset, and it likely caused a chain of events bringing us here."

"It wasn't exactly under control then, was it?"

Zhang didn't respond. He clenched his fist in his lap below the desk, out of Li's view. Li leaned back and ran a hand over his face and looked up at his office ceiling, swiveling gently left and right in his chair.

Keeping his gaze upward, Li said, "Bao had someone else over there, did he not? His linchpin for the entire mission?"

"He did. Deeply embedded. I have no contact. I know communications between the two were severely limited for operational security. Hopefully, enough distance existed between the other asset and this Voss that they are able to remain hidden."

Zhang could see Li was slightly shaking his head.

Eventually, Li said, "So, what are you thinking? How might this play out?"

"Perhaps, if I were given more access to the plann—"

"That's not happening," Li cut him off, making himself upright and now facing Zhang, "You know how this works. Strict need-to-know. Communication with the Navy and Special Operations goes through me. Now, give me your thoughts; this has been your part of the mission."

Zhang had to keep himself from slamming his fist on the desk. Or worse. He paused for a moment then said, "My concerns are twofold. If the Americans are wise to what we've done, will they decide to warn the Taiwanese and Koreans? Or can the Americans have them replace our infiltrated chips without warning them? Maybe something under the guise of necessary maintenance, thus taking the drones out of the air only for a short period. I don't have the technical nuance to answer that question. It is the more significant consideration of the two."

"Why is that? What makes you think the Americans won't tell them to simply take the drones out of service and temporarily use older equipment?"

Zhang nearly grinned at the question. He wasn't surprised at his boss's lack of critical thinking.

"Anything is possible, but think about it. Think about the ramifications for the US military and government if they were to notify the Taiwanese that they sold them an untrustworthy product. This isn't like recalling a tainted food product, where all is simply forgiven. Nor is it something that can be remedied by a software patch. No, this is *hardware*. Not only would trust in the US defense industry take a massive hit—and we know Taiwan is a huge market for that—but also, possibly, even trust in the US military as an able defense partner. There's also a potential cascading effect. You think word would not get out to others in the Pacific coalition the US has built against us? Japan, South Korea, Philippines, Thailand. How would their leadership take the news that hardware in US products is potentially compromised? All of these countries that rely upon US-manufactured defense systems suddenly would want an accounting of their systems."

Li nodded as Zhang finished his point.

Zhang added, "Remember, too, there is no concrete evidence that they know exactly what they are dealing with. Does that merit such drastic action with your ally? I'd think no."

"No, you're right," Li noted as he reached over to his desk phone and punched in a number. After a second, he said, "Send Deng to my office, now," and hung up. He picked up a pen and clicked and unclicked it idly, looking at a point beyond Zhang. After a few moments of silence, Li said, "Go to Dandong. Close up things with the Koreans."

"Why?"

"Head it off. Easier to just break it off with them now on our own terms than to be suddenly cut off and then have to explain ourselves. What you say about the Americans warning everyone is sound but no guarantee. Besides, we aren't getting anything useful in return."

"I can just have Hu communicate this—"

"No. You go. This is your mess. You clean it up."

Zhang glared at him without saying anything. Li looked away at the gray morning outside his window. After they sat in silence for a couple of minutes, they heard a knock at the door. Li said to come in.

Deng Shanlou entered the office. A gaunt man with thinning hair and pronounced liver spots on his face, Deng was one of the Ministry's technical experts with a background in the computer sciences and was intimately involved in the Ocelot Trojan mission. It was he who had passed on instructions to Bao Jiaotong to be given to Eddie Voss on how they specifically wanted the Trojan designed.

Li motioned for him to take a seat besides Zhang and said, "The Trojan in the Ocelot drones...tell us how it works."

Deng shot a nervous side glance at Zhang. He cleared his throat and spoke, "OK. Our Trojan is housed in the drone camera's imagery enhancement capability. Rather simply, the camera picks up imagery and routes it through the enhancement chip. It is then encrypted, and the imagery is shared with the drone's antenna, from where it is transmitted to whomever is operating the drone."

Deng paused to make sure the two others were following him. To his left, Zhang shifted in his chair, his impatience evident.

"The asset in America provided us with the US-government-supplied specifications for the chip. It called for storing the enhanced image and signaling the encryption unit when the data was ready for encryption. Timing is crucial in this process. Normally, the image enhancement chip would only output its data when it received acknowledgment from the encryption unit. There are safeguards to prevent a fault that would cause the inadvertent release of the stored data onto the wires shared by the encryption unit and the antenna. The asset put the safeguards in his chip because they would be tested for. But these safeguards were intended for naturally occurring faults—not ones that are human made. So, without any acknowledgment for the encryption unit, the Trojan leaks the buffers. The antenna picks up the data from the shared wires and transmits the data using a Trojan-supplied frequency that only we, here, are tuned into. The Trojan we instructed him to build runs continuously but so inconspicuously that the drones' operators are never aware of it."

The room fell silent while Zhang and Li digested what they'd just heard. Zhang knew that Li would have barely followed Deng's details. Zhang felt like he understood, but he still needed to know more. He looked at Deng.

"If the Americans knew about the Trojan, could they do something about it?"

Deng looked at Li.

"The Americans know?"

"I said if," Zhang said. He raised his tone slightly. His voice sounded as if it were passing through corroded pipe.

Deng nodded and didn't press any further. He explained, "The Americans are certainly aware of the threat of hardware Trojans and are keen to counteract them. We've been monitoring their developments in this area, and they do have some tools, even a couple commercially available, but they almost exclusively attempt to detect or prevent Trojan insertion. Obviously, given what we've accomplished with the Ocelot drones, we've thought of how they might be doing with their efforts in disabling a hardware Trojan post insertion."

The last line caused both Zhang and Li to raise their heads in heightened interest.

Deng held up a hand in a *be calm* motion and continued, "From what we can tell, and there's no evidence to the contrary, anything they're developing would only be for new microcircuit designs—not ones already in use." He paused before adding, "If the Americans know about our Trojan, then they need to physically replace the chip with a brand new one. That's the only way."

"And how long would that take?"

"A whole new chip would need to be designed. And that is assuming they know exactly which one is infiltrated. And then it would need to be fabricated. We are talking months and months of time."

Zhang glanced over at Li, who returned the look. There was another moment where none of the three said anything, until Li nodded, seemingly to himself.

"Ok, thank you, Shanlou," Li said and signaled the door with his hand. Once Deng had left the office, Li looked back at Zhang. "I'm going to hold off on communicating this to my contacts in the Armed Forces. I trust what Deng says, and let's hope you're right about the Americans coming clean with their counterparts. Get up to Dandong but also make your man in Taiwan aware. Have him keep his eyes and ears poised for developments."

Zhang nodded his acknowledgment and stood to leave.

Just before he crossed the threshold of the door, Li said, "Oh, and Zhang."

Zhang turned to look back at him.

"Your phone was off the other day. Where were you?"

Zhang figured he could only have been referring to Zhang's unauthorized visit down south to fish for information from his contact in Naval Special Forces.

"I had to make an unexpected trip to Sichuan. I have an aunt there who is going to pass. Lung cancer. She's in a small village, very rural. Bad reception."

"Ah. I'm sorry to hear that. Isn't your family all from around here?"

Zhang looked at him. There was a knowing look behind Li's eyes.

"She and my uncle retired there. Wanted a quiet life. Warmer weather, too."

"I see. If you're going to be away like that, I want to know about it. Especially now."

"Yes, sir."

Before turning to leave, Zhang stole a glance out of Li's office window. It looked ready to rain any moment.

29

November 12, 2025. 09:33 hours local time.
Offices of Indiana Integrated Circuits, South Bend, Indiana.

The first thing Jason Lizac noticed when he walked through his office door was the blinking red light of his desk phone.

Oh, boy.

He wondered how many missed calls awaited him. With yesterday, Tuesday, having been Veterans Day, he had decided to take Monday off as well, creating an extra-long weekend. He had been reluctant to do so, such was his workaholic nature, but that was no match for the ultimate boss: his wife. She had insisted that he take a break and get in some extra time with the kids. The forecast of a few sunny, crisp days of Indiana fall had proven correct, and Jason had to admit that the long walks with the dog, games of touch football, and bouts of yard work had felt cathartic. So, Jason was glad he had listened to his better half, despite knowing he would come back to a tsunami of work.

He arrived at his office much later than he would have liked. A scheduled morning meeting at Notre Dame with a couple of professors was the first item on his agenda, and he had begun the day by heading straight to campus. Naturally, the meeting had run over time, and Jason now felt like he was already behind the eight ball after the long weekend.

Jason strode over to his desk, setting his laptop bag down and not even bothering to remove his Notre Dame Fighting Irish quarter zip. He sat down and pushed the play button to hear his messages. After a couple of messages left on Monday by colleagues, a third message from late Monday afternoon played.

Hi Jason. It's Henry Purcel. Please call me back when you have a moment. You can reach me at 703-525-6777. Thanks.

Jason first smiled at Purcel's dictation of his cell number. It was probably muscle memory for Purcel to leave his number on voice mails, even for people he knew, who likely had his contact saved. Jason played the next message, left just about an hour ago.

Hi Jason, Henry again. Really hoping we can talk soon. Again that's 703-525-6777.

Jason leaned back in his office chair, thinking for a moment. It had been just about a week since he'd heard from his old friend to discuss Purcel's "hypothetical," and now he was back with something that seemed pretty urgent. Jason leaned forward to grab the telephone receiver. As he did so, he said aloud to himself, "Henry, you have piqued my curiosity."

November 12, 2025. 10:04 hours local time.
Air Force Office of Special Investigations Headquarters, Quantico, Virginia

"Great, thank you, Jason. I'll be back in touch shortly. I just need to game plan this a bit, but you'll definitely be hearing from me. OK, talk soon."

Henry Purcel hit the "End Call" button on his cell phone laid on top of his desk and removed his Bluetooth earbuds. He opened and closed his right hand, flexing it several times as he thought about the conversation he just had with Jason Lizac. He once again had to couch the situation in hypothetical terms. He knew Jason was too smart to not see right through that, but even so, he had to play it that way. He smiled to himself and shook his head, thinking about the outsized role his old friend was beginning to take in this investigation.

As Purcel had described the situation at hand, he could sense Jason's impatience on the other end of the call, eager to weigh in. When Jason finally started to give his input, he didn't try to hide his excitement. He had advised Purcel to consider playing the lottery, because as luck would have it, Jason felt he might have a piece of technology tailor-made for Purcel's situation. It was something he'd been working on for a while, something known as RECORD.

He had given Purcel a brief overview of how it worked, and Purcel had to admit that a good portion of it went over his head. Jason was insistent, however, that it would be best demonstrated in person, and Purcel agreed. As their conversation came to a close, Purcel was already thinking of who should be in on such a demonstration. Miller and Bolen from the office made sense, but really, it needed to be someone intimately attached to the Ocelot program.

Purcel broke his own reverie, remembering that he had something immediate to address. During his call with Jason, he'd missed a call from Special Agent Bizon. He picked his earbuds up off his desk and put them back in, waiting for the little *bing* noise indicating the Bluetooth had connected to his phone. On his cellphone, he went to missed calls and hit the name *Bizon Cell*, displayed in red in his call log.

After two rings, his colleague was on the line. "Purcel. Had me nervous for a second. That call was over ten minutes ago."

"Apologies, Mark. Was on the horn with someone. Related to this, actually."

"Oh yea? Anything juicy?"

"Possibly. I'll fill you in on that later. What's up on your end?"

"Still here in my old stomping grounds, waiting at my gate for the flight back to DC. Anyway, knowing you, fellow Special Agent, I didn't want to keep you waiting with bated breath."

Purcel smiled and said, "I appreciate that, Mark."

Bizon was a pain in the ass at times, but he was hard not to like.

"So, I dug up what might be a potential lead on how Voss got mixed up with the wrong crowd. During his time as a grad student at UB, one of his professors had him work closely with a PhD candidate, someone working as an assistant of some sort. This individual was from..."

"China."

"Bingo. Anyway, that professor seems to recall this student, one Heping Gao, as being only too happy to help our man Voss. He thinks, now looking at it through a new prism, that this may have been due to the fact that, at the time, Voss was working for a defense contractor, a small firm headquartered out here, and had security clearances."

"Hmm."

"Hmm, indeed. Apparently, this Gao would also take fairly frequent, unexplained trips to New York City."

"What do you make of that?"

"Well, someone that is *not* an experienced, crack investigator might simply write it off as a visit to family or to a love interest, but *I* would urge one to consider the fact that that is a long drive to see someone when you are a student with a full slate and also probably cost conscious. And I would call your attention to the fact that the city is home to a Chinese consulate as well as a bustling Chinatown."

"I see. Anything else?"

"Bit of a cold trail. Gao moved on to Michigan for a post-doctoral position, but from what I gathered there, he left when his work visa was approaching renewal and hasn't come back. Nothing on social media, but that's not surprising. His name is attached to some obscure journal articles. Otherwise, the dude is a ghost."

"From what it sounds like, you may have unearthed the connection there. Keep working it. Maybe there's something out there that will lead us to a network that they have here."

"Aye aye, cap."

"Safe flight."

Purcel ended the call but kept his earbuds in. He leaned back in his chair and thought about what Bizon had just told him. He had to give his fellow special agent credit. From what Bizon had dug up, it appeared that Voss's academic history was, indeed, the correct avenue to run down. That had been a good call. The fact that this Gao character might be out of the country was disconcerting, but at least they had a lead. That was for Bizon to continue investigating, however. Purcel had his own matters to deal with.

He opened up his computer and did a quick search. Finding what he was looking for, he picked up the phone once more and dialed a number. After a few rings, a male voice answered, asking how to direct his call.

"Can you put me through to Major Decker?"

30

November 12, 2025. 10:17 hours local time.
Schenectady Police Department, Schenectady, New York.

The Android phone lit up, indicating sufficient charge that it could be used. The flash of life on the dark screen appeared in his peripheral and caused Detective Richard Conkling to divert his gaze from his computer to the phone.

The phone had belonged to Edward Voss, one of two that were found on his person after Voss's encounter with the AFOSI agent Purcel. The other phone was a simple black flip phone that required no password or pin to access. The night of the shooting, Conkling had examined the phone and saw that it had only ever been used that day to make a number of calls, shortly before Voss's death, to a number saved as *Tony*. The associated number was a Google Voice number, which was effectively a dead end for the detective. Without evidence that this Tony was involved in a crime, it would be difficult to extract the ownership of the number from Google. At the very least, it would take some time.

As for the Android, which Conkling took to be Voss's primary personal device, it was just a few moments ago that a junior detective had brought it over from the evidence locker, along with a compatible charger. It had taken a few days—the weekend and a federal holiday coming after the Friday incident hadn't helped—but a warrant had gotten the cell provider to give the Schenectady Police access. Conkling picked up the device, leaving it plugged in, and punched in the PIN the other detective had jotted on a ripped sheet of paper. The screen unlocked.

It was an older model and showed its wear. Voss, despite working on cutting-edge technology, apparently hadn't let that carry over to his personal life. The phone had not been upgraded in some time. Conkling first opened the call log, which only went back about three weeks. No calls had come from this phone the day of the shooting, and much of the log was populated by incoming spam calls. A couple of calls to a local pizza place showed, spaced about a week apart. Nothing else in Voss's calls over the last month caught his attention. No Tony appeared, and no numbers with area codes outside the New York capital region.

The detective next checked Voss's contacts. There were not that many. BTP Front Office. An Alex Linden, whom Conkling knew was a colleague of Voss's. The next-door neighbor, Bill Franklin. The pizza place. A Chinese restaurant. No Tony in the contacts either.

Christ, this guy really was a loner.

He went to Voss's text messages and scrolled. Conkling himself was not much of a texter, and Voss must have been a kindred spirit, because there was very little in his text messages. Alex Linden was there, mainly asking Voss if he wanted to come out for drinks, which Voss usually turned down. It only took Conkling a couple of scrolls to get to the very last text, and it was there he paused.

The last text in the log, and therefore chronologically the oldest, was to an unsaved number and was sent over six years ago. It was a short message,

Sonya, I am so sorry. I did not know.

Conkling opened up the text thread, but there was none. That was the only message. No response and nothing above it. The text did not show as delivered, which indicated the receiving phone was not an Android and more likely an iPhone.

The detective looked away from the phone at a space somewhere next to his computer, thinking about that text.

There's something there.

He turned back to the phone and clicked on the number, a 212-area code, which he knew was Manhattan. He brought the phone to his ear and listened as it rang.

Finally, a male voice answered, "Yeah?"

"Ahem, hi, I'm looking for Sonya."

"Sorry, wrong number buddy."

The person hung up.

"Shit."

He set the phone down and thought for a moment. He reached over and picked up his desk phone, punching in a number.

After two rings, a voice answered, "Laporte"

"Hey, Bruce, it's Conkling."

"Hey, Dickie, what's happening?"

Bruce Laporte was Conkling's connection at the FBI Office in Albany. They'd known each other for years and were always ready to help each other out. Conkling would be the first to acknowledge, however, that it was usually the FBI man coming through for him.

"Got a number here, was hoping you could run it down for me?"

"Sure, shoot."

Conkling dictated the number to him. When he finished, he added on, "It's in use, but I want to know who had that number about six years ago. Can you get that?"

"Call you back in a few."

"Thanks, Bruce."

––––––––––

About 10 minutes later, Conkling's desk phone rang.

"Conkling."

"Alright Dickie. So, the number is currently being used by a Jerry Difante, and he's had it for about five years now. Before that the number was registered to a Meili Yang."

Meili Yang?

"Any Sonya or something similar in the history there?"

"Hmmm, nope. That Meili didn't have the number very long. Just short of a year, actually. Before that, the previous owner, man, I'm not going to even try to pronounce this one. Looks Romanian or something. This individual had it for a long time."

"I see. Any address associated with Yang?"

"Yea, when they opened the account, the associated address was…60 Elizabeth Street, Apartment 203, New York, New York."

Conkling took that down on a notepad he'd positioned in front of him on his desk.

"Alright, got it. Appreciate it, Bruce, as always."

"Anytime."

Conkling hung up and opened the desk drawer down to his left. He removed a thick stack of business cards bound by a rubber band and slipped out the top one. He picked up the phone receiver and punched in the number shown on the card. He waited as it rang. After two rings, Henry Purcel answered his office phone.

"Purcel."

"Henry. It's Detective Conkling up in Schenectady. Did I catch you at a good time?"

"Hi Detective, yeah, sure, I have a few. What's going on?"

"I came across something that might be of interest to you. I'm not sure how much more time you're dedicating to investigating Voss's background, but I figured I'd pass it on."

"We are very much still investigating that, yes. Another special agent here has taken the lead on Voss in particular, but I'll pass on what you have to him."

"OK, great. Well, I'll take the opportunity to tell you first that Voss had two phones on him. One appeared to be a burner of some sort. He'd only used it that day, and it was shortly before you confronted him. It called a number tied to Google Voice, someone he saved as *Tony* in the phone. The number is now disabled, and we'll have to see if Google will play ball there. I'll keep your office posted on that, but the real reason for my call has to do with his primary cell, which we just got permission to access today. There was one thing in there that stood out to me, a text message he sent just over six years ago. Let me ask you, have you encountered a Sonya during your investigation?"

"Sonya? No, not at all."

"Ok, well, in the message he said 'Sonya, I am so sorry. I did not know.' What's interesting is it's the only text in the thread, and the number is not saved. My initial thought is that he deleted an original, ongoing text thread, but before deleting the contact from his contact list, he sent this one last text. He deleted the contact, which is why it shows as an unsaved number, but forgot to delete that final text."

"I see. Have you been able to get anywhere with the number?"

"Something you might be able to work with. Can you jot an address down?"

31

November 13, 2025. 00:17 hours local time.
Dandong, China.

An icy wind came off of the Yalu River, causing Zhang Hudao to cross his arms over his body. The leather jacket he wore, his usual attire for the autumn months, was quickly proving to be insufficient for the occasion. The night was unseasonably cold in Dandong, even considering its location in China's extreme north, right on the border with North Korea. He let out a deep sigh and shook his head, regretting not having checked the weather forecast before departing Beijing once again. He was also angry with himself, feeling that his usual mental sharpness was slipping. He had done too much traveling the last few days, and over extreme distances. The steamy south one day, then back to Beijing, and now in the deep, dark northern reaches of the country. It wasn't the only cause of his brain fog. He knew that. The situation was weighing heavily on him. This operation could be key to a successful invasion of Taiwan, and now, it was possibly in jeopardy.

So, why was he here? He should be focusing his attention elsewhere. Li sending him to Dandong was a complete waste of time, as Li was surely aware. While Zhang could not stand his boss, he knew the feeling to be mutual. Li had the authority but not the respect that Zhang commanded among so many in the Ministry, and that must drive a bureaucrat like Li mad. It was a power move: send Zhang away when there was a local MSS agent who could have easily done the work. It was self-defeating, of course. Zhang had a more urgent matter to get to, but Li was either too stupid to recognize it or blinded by his own ego. Luckily for both of them, Zhang's asset in Taiwan needed some time before he could meet, so it allowed Zhang to come here first and just do as he'd been ordered.

He was standing in the trash-strewn lot of an old industrial park, much of which was now mothballed, many of the buildings rusting totems to a bygone era when Northern China was an industrial powerhouse. A factory in the park still produced some steel, but that was on the opposite end of the complex, far from the dormant section where he stood. He looked across the river at Sinuiju, the North Korean city on the other side of the river. Despite being home to nearly four hundred thousand souls, the city was almost pitch dark and eerily quiet. Zhang had some connections in the ultra-secretive country, but during his career in espionage and state secu-rity had managed to avoid it by-and-large, much to his relief. He had heard stories from colleagues about just how awful and insane the place really was. Despite the official government line that North Korea was a close and important ally, Zhang knew that most in the Politburo regarded it like a crazy neighbor that was always on the verge of pointing a gun at its own head.

A rustling came from his left. He looked over and saw movement in the ambient light cast off by an adjacent apartment building. It was a bone-thin dog, one of the many feral canines that roamed Dandong's streets, sifting through some trash. As if sensing Zhang's stare, the dog looked up from its task towards him. It considered him for a moment, lifting its snout to sniff the air, then went back to its search.

The sound of a motor cut through the air, and headlights appeared from behind him, beaming across the water. Zhang stepped from the dark-ness into the lights of the dusty Volkswagen that now idled a few feet from his position. He crossed in front of the vehicle to the passenger side and climbed in next to the driver, whom he greeted with a curt nod. The driver was Hu Jinwei, a colleague from the Ministry of State Security stationed in

Dandong. He was younger than Zhang, mid-forties, with thick black hair slicked back. He also wore a leather jacket but still had the car's heater turned on full blast.

After Zhang had closed the passenger door, Hu said, "What's going on? Why the short notice?"

Zhang stared straight ahead through the windshield. "I need you to bring me to your contact. Now."

"What? Why?"

Zhang cleared his throat, his impatience growing. He wanted to get this over with. "I'm to inform him that our information exchange is coming to an end. There will be no more video intel from us going forward."

They were silent for a moment. Hu was not aware of all the details of the operation, just his part in it. He and Zhang were not close, but Zhang at least appreciated that he knew enough not to pry for details.

Hu eventually said, "That required a trip out here? Why not just have me pass the message?"

"I'm sure this is Li's idea of punishment. Whatever's going on, he lays at my feet."

Hu nodded and, without a word, dropped the car into drive.

———————

They drove through the night to Dandong's red-light district, Hu filling the time by giving Zhang some details on his asset. Eventually, they parked illegally in front of a nightclub that lit up the sidewalk with the ugly neon glow from its sign. Hu's license plate bore the marker of a government official, meaning the vehicle would be left alone. They both alighted and walked towards the entrance.

Hu had explained his asset was someone he only knew as Chu and that he was the owner of this club. Owning the club was simply a front for Chu's actual status as a member of the *Bowibu*, North Korea's infamous secret police. He was there to spy and report on any North Koreans trying to flee the country, as well as the locals in the underground railroads that aided them. He somehow flitted over the border between Dandong and Sinuiju and, Hu was sure, also used the club to engage in smuggling drugs and trafficking North Korean women into local sex work—lucrative enterprises in this city of thieves and shadows.

Chu was well connected on the other side of the border, and that included high-ranking military officials. Since Zhang's operation began to bear fruit, Hu had used Chu to pass on video files they stole from the South Korean drones in exchange for information regarding North Korean palace intrigue. The information coming from the South was otherwise not of immediate use to Zhang's agency, but Li and others at the MSS agreed they could offer it to the North Koreans and parlay it into intel of which, when it came to the Hermit Kingdom, one could never have enough. The irony was that the data from the South Koreans was likely of very little use to the North. The South was using their Ocelot drones to perform surveillance over the Sea of Japan, and thus far, this revealed nothing of value, at least in Zhang's opinion. Such was the cutthroat nature in the halls of power in the North, however, that someone would eagerly accept the information anyway, likely in the hopes of boosting their stock or one-upping a rival.

Upon entering the club, the two men were greeted by pulsating dance music, and Zhang hated it immediately. The place was simple in its layout. Round tables surrounded by cushioned benches dotted the bare concrete floor. At the end opposite the entrance was an area meant for dancing. Strobe lights of varying colors lit the space. The patrons were primarily men, some with female companions. A handful of couples danced, the women wearing fake smiles.

Zhang followed Hu to a U-shaped bar to the right of the door where several women, all in short dresses and with too much make-up on, sat forlornly. Zhang figured them to be North Koreans employed by the club. He watched as Hu said something to the bartender; he could not hear him over the din. After a moment of conferring with the bartender, Hu motioned to Zhang to follow him towards the back.

Walking past the dance floor, they passed through a black door with a *Restricted Access* sign in both Chinese and Korean and entered a long hallway dimly lit by a single bulb that hung low halfway down the hall. Hu led Zhang to another door at the end of the passage. Instead of knocking, Hu pressed a buzzer to the right of the door.

The two waited in silence for a few seconds until a voice crackled from a small intercom over the door, "*Oda.*"

Korean for *come in.*

They stepped into a small, cramped office space filled with boxes, folding chairs, and, Zhang noticed immediately, an AK-105 assault rifle leaning against the far wall. The room reeked of cigarette smoke and, like the hallway outside, was dimly lit. A wooden desk occupied much of the space, and behind it sat a man Zhang figured was Chu. His face was pock-marked and had the drawn look of a smoker. His hooded eyes contained a guile Zhang had seen countless times. Someone he knew he could never trust. To Chu's right was another man, Korean by his look, squat and burly and with a tight military-style haircut, sitting in a folding chair.

Hu spoke in Korean to Chu. Chu didn't say anything in return, only nodded.

Hu turned to Zhang. "I told him you're my associate and that you carry a message."

"Tell him this is notice that our information exchange is hereby terminated. We appreciate his help in the matter."

Hu translated.

Chu still said nothing. He let his gaze rest on Zhang, appearing to size him up. Most were intimidated by Zhang's appearance, but the Korean seemed unbothered. Zhang shifted in his stance slightly, eager to get this over with. Chu reached for a pack of cigarettes that lay on the desk, removing one and putting it in his mouth. Without lighting it, he said something.

Hu turned to Zhang. "He wants to know why."

"Tell him that is not his concern. Things have changed from our end. What is important is that he knows not to expect any more from this particular pipeline."

Hu hesitated a moment but then translated.

The cigarette remained unlit. After listening to Hu, Chu leaned forward, resting his arms on the desk. He looked directly at Zhang as he spoke.

Before translating, Hu said something to Chu, and Zhang noted irritation in his voice. Whatever it was, it caused the Korean to slam a palm on the desk and shout at Hu. Hu stared him down for a moment and then turned back to Zhang, giving him a knowing look as he spoke.

"He says that this isn't good enough. This is going to bring him grief. He will need to explain to his source back in Korea, and that source is not an easy individual to deal with."

"I'm sure he'll find a way," Zhang said and made to leave. From behind him Chu said something, more calmly this time. Zhang did not understand Korean, but the threat in Chu's words were unmistakable.

He turned back to face him as Hu translated, "Chu says he wants compensation for his role in this, for protecting the information we have gathered. It would be a shame if it were to fall into the wrong hands."

Zhang stared Chu down. The Korean gave him a wide grin and an insolent shrug. The still-unlit cigarette dangled from his mouth, and now, one hand fiddled with a cheap BIC lighter on the desk.

He held the Korean's gaze. The impatience he felt earlier had now dissipated, replaced by a burning rage. One wouldn't be able to tell, however. Zhang's expression was blank.

Chu broke the silence, "*Guelsse?*" *Well?*

Zhang listened. It was quiet in the room. No pulsating music or other noise seemed to be seeping in from the club outside. Then he thought of the buzzer and intercom to enter. It took him only a moment to realize why that might be. It made sense. Chu conducted business here, maybe even brought one of his girls from time to time. He'd want it quiet.

He had soundproofed it.

He glanced at Chu's sidekick. His thick arms were crossed across his chest. Not a great starting position to reach for a weapon, which Zhang assumed he had on his person. He looked back at Chu and, once again, held his gaze for a moment, looking as if he were considering what the man had said. Instead, without a word, he swiftly reached into his jacket with his right hand, pulling his CF98 handgun from his shoulder holster and bringing it forward in the same motion, firing a round directly into Chu's forehead. Chu's head whipped backwards, and his blood and brains painted the wall behind him. His motion carried his lifeless body backwards, causing him to tip over in his chair. Immediately, Zhang set his sights on the other man who had turned in horror to look at Chu. Zhang's motion was so quick, the man had no time to even look back at him, and his next round punched through the man's cheek. He fired two more rounds, double-tapping into the sidekick's chest. The Korean slumped to the side and joined his boss on the floor.

Zhang held his pistol in the ready position for a moment then calmly slid it back into its holster. He shook his head to clear the ringing in his ears. The last of the bullet casings made the only sound in the room as it completed its bounces on the tile floor. He looked over to Hu, who had turned pale and was staring at the desk that was, up until a second before, occupied by his asset.

"Let's go," Zhang said and turned to leave.

"Hudao! What the fuck?! How the fuck are we going to explain this to Li?!"

Zhang had stepped out into the hallway. He turned his head to look back through the door at his stunned colleague.

"Chu was in a dangerous line of work. These things happen. Now, let's go."

32

November 14, 2025. 09:00 hours local time.
Offices of Indiana Integrated Circuits, South Bend, Indiana.

Jason Lizac glanced down at the corner of his computer screen to see the time when he heard the knock at his office door.

Nine o'clock exactly. That's Henry Purcel.

He stood and turned to face the entryway, a smile spreading across his face as he saw his friend from college step through the open door. Purcel wasn't exactly beaming, but he had a half grin.

"Henry, good to see you."

Both men covered the space between them. Jason thought about going for a full hug but figured Henry would prefer a more standard firm handshake, particularly given that Purcel had company trailing behind him, and the reason for their visit was all business. The two men shook hands.

"You as well, Jason. Again, I appreciate you taking the time."

Purcel half-turned to a man and woman who had followed him in and now stood behind him. The woman wore green-grayish camouflage fatigues and held a cap of the same color scheme in her hand, while the man was in a suit and tie.

Indicating the woman first, Purcel introduced them, "As I mentioned over the phone, this is Major Maya Decker of the US Air Force and Steve Giresi of the NSA. I think they'd very much like to hear about this technology of yours."

Jason shook hands with both individuals, saying, "Jason Lizac," each time he did so. He addressed all three.

"Welcome to IIC. I'm grateful for the opportunity to show you what we have here," He said and nodded towards Purcel, "Thanks so much for thinking of me."

His three guests nodded.

When it was apparent all of them expected him to take the lead, Jason clasped his hands together and said, "Well, shall we?"

He motioned for the group to follow, and he led them out of his office and down the hall to IIC's lab. It was a long room with several granite-topped workstations—or workbenches, as Jason called them—that resembled kitchen islands evenly spaced throughout. It put Purcel in the mind of a high school chemistry classroom. Jason came to a stop at the workbench nearest the entryway.

On top of the counter was a white, clear-plastic-lidded box, similar in size, Major Decker thought to herself, to the box of cigars her ex-Marine father used to always have on his desk. There were two stools on the side of the workbench nearest them. Purcel indicated to Major Decker to take one.

"Steve and I are here primarily as observers. I think the major should be in the passenger seat."

As he said this, both Purcel and Giresi walked around to the other side of the work bench. Despite stools also being on that side, both men remained standing. Jason and the major each slid out a stool and sat down.

Jason considered the box for a second, looked up at Purcel, and then turned to Major Decker. He said, "You two might like to know that what I am about to show you is actually an Air Force invention, out of a research laboratory in Rome, New York. IIC licensed the patents and invested in creating this demo. Nothing else was happening with the patents. I mean, it was almost as if the Air Force were content with just having the invention patented. Seems crazy to say, but if we hadn't done something, I'm confident this technology would still be collecting dust on a shelf, so to speak."

Major Decker nodded, raised her eyebrows in a knowing way, and said, "Declare it a success and move on. All too common, unfortunately."

"You've got that right. Anyway, the laboratory guys' papers and patents all stress that their invention is for dealing with microcircuits that are outsourced to foreign fabrication facilities which are usually untrusted. So, IIC saw this as a business opportunity."

Jason continued, "Anyway, we picked up the patents because they utilize a technology that is the foundation for IIC. It's called Quilt Packaging, QP for short. Microcircuits are fabricated in die form—that is, tiny slabs of silicon, hence their name, *chips*. Usually, a single chip is then encapsulated in a microcircuit package. Microcircuit packages are those ceramic or plastic rectangles with metal leads on their exterior."

Jason formed a rectangular shape with the thumb and index finger of each of his hands to demonstrate.

"Before they are packaged, IIC can take chips and apply QP to them. What QP does is join those chips not only electrically but also edge-to-edge. If you can picture a handmade quilt with conjoined squares, you get the idea of QP. It lets you put multiple chips into a single package."

"Is joining the chips a defense against Trojans from ex-filtrating data?" Major Decker asked.

Jason answered, "No, because Trojans in the chips' circuitry will continue to do that. They have many possible ways. Oftentimes, they create what is called a side channel, which are electromagnetic emissions. I have even heard of Trojans that build a tiny antenna into the chip for data transmission. Or they can find a sneak path to reach a regular communications channel in the system that ends up connecting the Trojan to the outside world and then to the infiltrating party. These types of adversarial activities are done with great subtlety so that the Trojan goes unnoticed."

This time, Henry queried Jason, "Isn't it possible to test the chips for Trojans in the first place?"

"It's a good thought, but for one, hardware Trojans are designed to escape detection during testing. Some may be detectable by triggering them before the chips are put to use. However, I've learned Trojans that leak data are different from Trojans that aim to cause a chip to fail. The last thing the former wants to do is affect the chip's functionality because, rather obviously, you won't get any data from a chip that has been rendered inoperable. These Trojans are designed to go unnoticed indefinitely, even after they have been triggered. So, not only are they small enough to be undetectable but they also do not disturb the chip's normal operation."

Major Decker spoke up, "Right, so, before we really dive into it, there's something I wanted to bring up. As I believe Henry laid out for you, say we have a scenario where there is a hardware Trojan in a chip or chips that has gone undetected, and the systems with the infected chips are already out there, operating in the field, potentially leaking data. A *fait accompli.*"

In her periphery, she could see Giresi cast his eyes at her in a look that said, *careful now.*

She spoke neutrally, as if she were describing her preferred coffee order, and in a manner that conveyed the impression that this was a matter of curiosity or a newly found area of concern for the Air Force. When Purcel had called Jason once again, rather urgently, Jason noted at the time, he again had been using terms like *hypothetical* and *scenario.* But the 800-pound gorilla in the room, as Jason saw it, was why his old friend, an Air Force investigator, was involved here. The major and the NSA agent, sure, but Jason was pretty familiar with Henry's job description, and this didn't seem to fit. He also detected the tense look that Giresi had just shot Major Decker as she spoke. Something was going on. He was sure of it, but he knew not to ask. The idea excited him, however, and he felt a slight jolt of adrenaline.

I have to do this right, he thought.

The major continued, "From reading the material you sent prior to this meeting—thank you for that, by the way—if my understanding of the description is correct, it sounds as if it is meant to be implemented in *new* designs, before a microcircuit is even fabricated. I see no mention of viability in chips that are already out in the field. That's a big deal. I'd hate to think we came out here for nothing."

Jason smiled. "Very good question, Major. I got the sense from my chat with Henry over the phone that this is what you had in mind, so I knew our meeting here would be worthwhile. I suppose it's an opportunity to give kudos to our work here at IIC. You're absolutely right; the inventors make no mention of the technology's potential using chips that have already been designed and fabricated. Sounds odd, but it was just a simple oversight, really. Which, I suppose, is understandable to a degree, because inventors are always trying to look ahead, by nature. It was our engineering here that determined it could also have utility in existing chips. We would prefer opportunities to use QP, since it belongs to IIC, but QP requires that the chips be processed in a special way. When using chips already made in a conventional way, then they are connected in simpler ways—such as wire bonding them together—but doing so takes up more space than QP."

This time Major Decker quickly shifted her eyes towards Giresi, whose expression did not change.

She looked back at Jason and said, "Excellent."

His last line had also encouraged her. If her engineers back at Creech did not have to rely upon Quilt-Packaging, and thus be tethered to IIC, they could move forward unencumbered and still use what Jason was about to demonstrate.

Jason cleared his throat and nodded. He motioned toward the box in front of them on the lab table's granite surface and said, "Let me show you what it does."

His guests joined him in studying the box. With Purcel and Giresi both leaning over the counter to get a closer look, they all peered in and surveyed the contents: a printed circuit board with a small video screen and a larger microcircuit package with some smaller ones, all connected by a maze of silver traces on the board. No one showed any reaction.

"Yeah," Jason broke the silence, "it may not look like much, but there is a lot going on inside."

He cleared his throat and flicked the box's power switch on. The small black screen illuminated to become a gray rectangle.

"So," said Jason, "to begin, Major, I know you're a bit read-up on the basics, but again, this technology is called RECORD, and that is an acronym for *Randomized Encoding of Combinational logic for Resistance to Data leakage.* RECORD has two main components: split manufacturing and randomization."

Jason paused for a moment, making sure to not go too fast and potentially leave any of his three listeners struggling to keep up.

He continued, "The split manufacturing refers to combining, on the one hand, a chip that is manufactured by untrusted sources—such as from an overseas factory, which I'm sure you are all aware is a real concern with microcircuits currently—or one that has a suspected Trojan with, on the other hand, a chip that is trusted. RECORD represents the trusted chip."

Again, he paused and then said, "The trusted chip is a relatively simple one—low tech compared to the untrusted one. It is trusted because it is made in a secure facility—an onshore DOD-verified foundry, for instance."

That didn't stop Eddie Voss and his Chinese handlers, Purcel thought as he was listening to this. He decided to interject, "Jason, sorry, just if I may...it was you that turned me onto the idea of a hardware Trojan being slipped in via the chip's design."

In his peripheral, Purcel felt Giresi shoot him the glance that suggested caution was needed.

He continued, "Say that were the case. A DOD trusted foundry producing the chip is moot, as the Trojan is there *before* fabrication. How can one be certain that RECORD's trusted chip is truly clean?"

"That's a very good point, I'm glad you remembered our conversation. Well, for one, as I said, the RECORD chip is quite simple. If one could write the code to implement what is in the patent to design the chip, presto. Say the major here were interested in using this technology, she could design the chip. I can't think of a more trustworthy source in such a case."

Purcel and Major Decker nodded. The NSA agent, still having not spoken, showed no reaction. Purcel asked, "You said for one. Is there something else?"

"I could give you the design files. We had them done right here at IIC. Be a matter of getting them on a thumb drive." He winked at his old friend. "I'd like to think I'm a trusted source."

Purcel gave his half smile. "I'd think so."

After a second of silence, Jason said, "I'll continue?"

Everyone nodded.

"The trusted chip introduced by RECORD actually doesn't contribute to the untrusted chip's functionality. It's oblivious to what the untrusted one is doing. Just to reiterate, the untrusted chip is the 'original' chip, so to speak. It is that which does the intended function of the designer—that is, the useful work. It's more complex, and its creation is almost always contracted out to a high-tech firm."

Like BTP, Purcel thought again.

Almost as if reading his friend's mind, Jason said, "As we just alluded to, that is the potential access point for a Trojan, and again, Trojan testing isn't necessarily a guarantee to find anything."

He noticed Steve Giresi shift his stance, perhaps showing some discomfort with the topic.

Jason continued on, "This is going to sound counterintuitive, but there are actually *three* chips at play, because for RECORD to function, it requires *two* of the original untrusted chips from the same batch. The two being identical."

Major Decker raised her eyebrows. "Interesting," she said, "that *is* counterintuitive."

"I know, but...that's the way RECORD works. Let me explain. As I said at the start, there is a way to join these three chips together. Assume that it has been done, so now we get into the second part of RECORD, randomization."

He paused momentarily for a little dramatic effect then added, "And that is what neutralizes the Trojans." He looked up at his three listeners, eyeing each of them for split second. "Ready?"

Three nods.

"Alright, here it is. In order to function, the untrusted chips need inputs from the system. In RECORD, just the trusted chip in the quilt receives the system's input and supplies the output for the system. The trusted chip is connected with the inputs and outputs of the two untrusted ones. The trusted chip effectively interposes itself before the untrusted chips get inputs from the system and before those untrusted chips supply their outputs to the system. In this way, the trusted chip intercepts the signals from the system and then sends them to the two untrusted chips. But before it does, it randomly chooses to invert the bits of the inputs. That is, it switches a one to a zero and a zero to a one. What does this mean? It means that one of the untrusted chips receives the correct input while the other receives incorrect data. Those untrusted chips do what they were designed to do: the chip receiving the wrong, inverted input will produce the incorrect result, and this is what its Trojan leaks. The other chip, receiving the *right* input, produces a correct result. This, too, is leaked by its Trojan. Now, remember, we are talking bits here. A zero produced by the first chip and a one from the second, or vice versa, makes for total guesswork, and the Trojans contribute nothing to guessing the correct bit. What I've described is just a single instance of a bit, but now, imagine a repetition of this process thousands and thousands of times. The mixture of right and wrong output across a multitude of instances ends up creating, in total, if you will, randomized data the Trojan ends up delivering to an attacker."

The room was silent while Major Decker, Purcel, and Giresi digested what they'd just heard, each forming their own mental picture.

Jason felt like he wanted to tie it all up nicely, so he added on something he'd often used when describing RECORD to interested parties. "Data is bits, and information is data with relevance. With RECORD involved, attackers get all the bits, both right and wrong, but not the relevance, as they cannot discern what is relevant within the data."

Major Decker nodded in a way that indicated understanding, and Jason nearly breathed a sigh of relief.

She then asked the question he figured would be coming. "Ok, so we've jumbled up whatever is being leaked to the bad guys. How do the proper operators of the system, the good guys, still get the correct output?"

"Excellent question, Major. RECORD's chip, the trusted one, remembers which output corresponds to the correct system input and sends that result forward while ignoring the other. To an outside observer or, I guess, someone unaware of what exactly is going on inside, it would appear as if the untrusted chips were acting as one and producing results as intended. In a sense, it would almost be as if RECORD were not there. From the system's perspective, RECORD is operating inconspicuously. To sum it all up: by introducing RECORD, the Trojan is, in effect, being bypassed."

Jason directed everyone's attention to the box. He reached in and pressed a tiny button next to the screen. It showed two lines of text:

!%408*(AhK)@69!?<56HaL57/Flf16B17P51=}k4Fonda!n450ab357!`plıks3;?
</J12Q

&96-$~>82SlU|\X1562;:.Kak!OBn3SU852Ior/\|,,432YoNyM`,+=0zsLe1M-sl@&570k

"These are the alphanumeric representations of the bits used by the chips. The first line is an encrypted message. The second line is the key to unlock the message. Now, see the large chip package here?" Jason pointed to it. "In it are the three quilted chips that I described before. One trusted chip does RECORD's randomization and de-randomization. The two so-called untrusted chips are designed to take in the encrypted message and the key to produce, in decrypted form, the contents of the message. I say *so-called untrusted chips*, but we designed them ourselves and deliberately inserted all-powerful, full-access data-leakage Trojans. In this demonstra-tion, RECORD has to keep these Trojans from leaking both the input key and also the decrypted message that is produced."

He motioned to Major Decker. "Major, if you would, press this button right here by the screen."

The moment she did so, the screen displayed four lines:

804*$%(HvK(!!-?←—→Rrqyzpl17UBew35[JoM673dxzk5%67mi!`pyh45fcvb-dwj*(o^$5k/?

77XcVbo+=(LaK-.rAdC&24_8k1AUkn796FbCxnku45";uHVwqasszmpy j14578(Jt{71!

&*a^%$Fkiu(8boPp%{?48vxmv10000%^abjib33ilvb1qbnjh{wk87m-newq81.#^Xzhobo82

88*@T):hQ1oZSuuB1!`MraPs[APeKkWhD34&8VcI13+--_aurmv2ep-PvIq~`p{/8xCbna123

Jason explained, "These four lines of text are what the Trojans leak. The first two are the inputs from the system that have been randomized. The first is the key to decrypt the message, and the second is the encrypted message—again, both converted to random data. The encrypted message, you might even say, is encrypted again. The last two lines are the *decrypted* message leaked by the Trojans in each of the two untrusted chips. As you can see, total nonsense."

It was Steve Giresi, finally, who spoke. "And the actual message?"

Jason gave a slight tilt of head indicating *coming right up* and said, "Major, please press this third button here."

Major Decker reached in and pressed where Jason indicated. He smiled to himself, as his cleverness—at least, so he thought—was about to become apparent. It had been a while since he'd read Sun Tzu's *The Art of War*, but he thought one of the maxims from there tied nicely into RECORD's using potentially corrupt chips to achieve results. The screen filled with a single English sentence:

The opportunity of defeating the enemy is provided by the enemy himself.

33

November 14, 2025. 10:51 hours local time.
Chinatown, Manhattan, New York.

To be in the large apartment building on 60 Elizabeth Street in Manhattan's Chinatown was akin to entering another country without ever having stepped foot on a plane or shown your passport. A babel of Chinese dialects crept into the dimly lit hallways, shouted over televisions blaring soap operas in the same language. The air still held the aroma of breakfasts sauteed in woks or cooked in bamboo steamers. Some doors were decorated with red stickers of Chinese characters, the hall ceilings dotted with water stains and browned by years of cigarette smoke. If someone told Special Agent Mark Bizon that he was on the set of one of his favorite 1980s Hong Kong action movies starring Chow-Yun Fat as Inspector Tequila, he'd have believed them.

Bizon had arrived that morning at Penn Station, having taken the early Amtrak Acela train direct from Washington, DC. He was greeted there by Detective Sergeant Sammy Ren of the NYPD. Knowing that he might run up against potential language issues on this assignment, Bizon had called the day before to the Chinatown subdivision to see if he could get an officer proficient in Chinese on loan for the day. Sergeant Ren was available.

While walking out of the station to Ren's department Chevy Tahoe and making the necessary small talk, Ren had told Bizon, "My parents immigrated from southern China. I grew up speaking Cantonese, but I know enough Mandarin to get by."

"Which is most common in Chinatown here?"

"Well, all kinds of different dialects are spoken, but I guess Canto is what you'd hear most. Newer arrivals are primarily Mandarin speakers, though. Any idea what the person we are looking for speaks?"

"No clue."

"Great."

Now, the two men ascended the stairs in 60 Elizabeth to the second floor, the elevator shown to be out of service. They came to apartment 203 and, before knocking, Bizon listened for activity beyond the door. He knew someone was there, as he heard dishes clattering. He knocked, loudly, and after a moment, the door opened.

Bizon and Ren had to look down to see the apartment's occupant, an old, stooped woman who Bizon figured would barely be five feet tall if she stood ramrod straight. Bizon, with his long black overcoat over his sport coat and white shirt and tie, looked every bit the government agent he was, and that appeared to register in the woman's eyes. She then noticed Ren in his NYPD jacket and cap, and her eyes narrowed in concern. She said something Bizon did not understand.

"She's asking what we need," Ren told him.

"Tell her who we are first and that we're looking for a Meili Yang."

Ren spoke to the old woman. Bizon saw recognition in her eyes. The woman shook her head and then replied.

"She says this Meili used to live here but has been gone a couple of years or so now. She wants to know if she's in some kind of trouble."

"Tell her no, we simply want to ask her some questions. She may have information important to a case. She is in no legal trouble, at all."

Ren translated. When he finished speaking, the woman was silent for a moment, pondering whether she should trust these two agents of the state. She spoke to Ren.

"She thinks Meili still works at a hair salon on Canal, just around the corner from here. Possible she's moved on, but the last this lady knew, that's where to find her."

"Can she describe her?"

The woman showed confusion to Ren's question. Bizon couldn't blame her. Two guys asking after someone and they don't even know what they are looking for. As she spoke, she put her hand in the air a few inches above her head, indicating height.

"Pretty, long black hair, about yay high, as she showed. Figures she's about 20 or so. I asked for any distinguishing features, but she didn't have any."

"Yea, that doesn't necessarily narrow the field. But we'll see what we find at this salon. Can you ask her what Yang was doing here?"

The woman shrugged to the question.

When she finished speaking, Ren told Bizon, "An acquaintance, that's the word she used. A guy from the same town as she was back in the old country brought Meili around a few years ago and asked the woman to put her up for a bit. She ended up staying a couple years. For taking the girl in, the old lady got a little help on rent from this guy. She says Meili was no trouble, shy, very quiet. They never did talk about her situation; the lady here didn't like to be intrusive."

Bizon was about to nod his thanks and say, *let's get moving*, but he had a thought. He reached into the leather-bound binder he carried and pulled out at photo. It was a little dated, but it was all he could get from the University at Buffalo: a blow-up of Heping Gao's passport photo they'd had on file. He showed the woman the picture and told Ren to ask if she recognized the man.

She nodded her head and spoke before Ren could translate. Bizon did not know a single word of Chinese, but he knew from her reaction that Gao was the person who'd brought Meili Yang to come live with her.

"So, what dialect were you two conversing in?"

"That was Mandarin. She had a pretty heavy accent from one of the southern provinces, but I got the gist."

Bizon nodded and looked across Canal Street at the crossing signal. On the other side of the street, he could see the salon where the woman had told them to look for Meili Yang. Before leaving, he'd asked if she knew where they might find Heping Gao. She shook her head right away, saying it had been years since she'd heard from him. Gao had only spent a year in Ann Arbor at the university there, and then his trail went cold, so that did track, but it was possible she wouldn't share the information if she did know. Someone whose picture is being carried around by authorities isn't likely sought so they can be told they've won the lottery. Bizon wasn't going to press the issue, though; the priority was finding whomever Eddie Voss had texted.

The little green man appeared, and Bizon and Ren crossed the street. They came to the salon and entered. It was a tight space widthwise but ran longer. On each side were five chairs and associated workstations. Six of the ten places were occupied by clients and a worker attending to each of them. All of the employees were young women in their twenties, pretty, petite, and with long hair. When the bell above the door rang, everyone looked up at the two men who'd entered, clearly not prospective clients. After a moment of awkward silence, everyone went back to their business, hoping to avoid any impending drama an NYPD officer and his acquaintance might bring with them. Bizon nodded to Ren, who spoke to the room.

Ren asked if Meili Yang worked here or was available, while Bizon studied the occupants. No one responded, not even a shake of the head, which Bizon took to mean she was probably still associated with the place. Bizon worked about as far from immigration as one could while still being an employee of the federal government, but even so, he knew it was a given that immigrants were wary of authority, regardless of their status. It was especially true of a place like Chinatown, where the legality of many residents was often murky. Add in the fact that these were all young women now being questioned by two men, and he couldn't blame them for their hesitancy. A couple of the workers went back to their business with scissors and hair products. otherwise, the salon was quiet. Bizon surveyed the scene a moment more, thinking about the next move. An idea came to him.

Take a chance.

He said aloud, "Sonya?"

At the farthest chair on his left-hand side, the young lady looked up right at him, clearly surprised to have heard the name. Bizon turned to Ren and indicated with his head to follow him, Ren looking slightly perplexed. They walked the length of the room to her chair. The older Asian woman she was tending to continued to face forward towards a mirror but gave them a side glance, showing annoyance.

Bizon spoke to the worker, "Do you speak English?"

She hesitated, but then she nodded her head, almost as if she were embarrassed to admit it.

"Are you Meili Yang?"

Once again, she didn't respond right away, instead eyeing the two men nervously and glancing behind them to see if any of her coworkers were listening in. Before she could respond, Bizon spoke to her almost like a father would to a child, switching to a different mode, as he often did, depending on who he was dealing with. It was one of the reasons why he was recognized as being good at his job.

"Sweetheart, you're not in any trouble. My name is Mark. I work with the government. I just need to ask you some questions about Edward Voss. You knew him, didn't you?"

She hadn't been looking directly at him, but at the mention of Voss's name, her eyes darted up to meet his.

After a moment, she said, almost in a whisper, "Yes."

"OK, listen, finish up here. We'll wait outside. We'll find a place to sit and have a cup of coffee. I just need a few minutes of your time and then you can come back, OK?"

Meili looked down at her client and then back and him, nodding.

Bizon checked his watch and turned to Sergeant Ren. "Know a place we can sit down around here?"

"Sure, pastry place a few doors down."

"Cool." He turned back to Meili and said, "We'll be right out here."

———————

About twenty minutes later, the three of them sat down at a small table in a tiny bakery that was more set up for pick-up orders—their table was one of only two—and Bizon felt like they were meeting in a phone booth. Both Bizon and Ren had steaming cups of coffee in front of them; Meili asked for a green tea. The girl sat with her hands folded in her lap, fidgeting at times, and looked down at the table, only occasionally glancing up at her interlocutors. There was a fragility to her that broke Bizon's heart. Before she started telling her story, he already had the sense she was a victim in all of this.

She opted to speak through Ren, using Mandarin. Bizon had first told him to ask her how she knew Eddie Voss, and she said she'd been introduced to him a few years ago and that it was all part of a role she was told to play. Bizon showed her the photo of Gao, asking if that was who introduced her, and she nodded. She then got into the sequence of events.

"She says that she was approached back home in her city in Zhejiang province. That's in the south, possibly the same area of the old lady at the apartment. The accents are similar. Anyway, she would be smuggled here to the states and was told that if she did so, her father who was sick with liver cancer would be taken care of. Her family didn't have the money for his operation, so she accepted. She figured it would be to work in a restaurant or something here, but instead, it turned into something else."

Ren then asked her something, and she nodded. He then tilted his head towards Bizon, indicating the photo of Gao now tucked back in the binder, and she once again nodded.

"Yea, she says the old lady and your boy in the pic all hail from the same area."

Meili remained silent, in what seemed to Bizon an attempt to steel herself for the painful memories she was about to wade into. Ren shifted in his seat as if he were about to say something, but Bizon held up a hand to say, *give her time.*

Finally, she continued, pausing at times so Ren could translate.

Things had at first started off as she assumed. Gao brought her to the apartment on Elizabeth Street, and she was given a job washing dishes in a nearby restaurant. This only lasted a couple of months, during which she was told to work on her English with a book Gao had provided. When he'd come to check in on her, he'd make her practice with him. She had learned enough of the basics in school in China, but they wanted her to expand her skills as much as she could in a short time. Eventually, Gao came and told her she had a new job, an important one, and that they'd be going to a different part of the state to meet someone. Gao was to introduce her to this person as if he were setting up two mutual friends. She would be known as Sonya, and she would have to show interest in his friend Edward Voss. It started off primarily with video chats and texting, as she was still in the city, and Voss was first in Buffalo and then a different city—she could not remember the name. On a few occasions, Gao drove her up to visit Voss, and Voss also came to visit. When this happened, they made the woman at the apartment disappear for the evening or weekend, whatever it was. Once, a different man had driven her to upstate New York for another rendezvous.

Bizon stopped them there. "Who was that individual?"

Ren didn't have to translate the question, but she responded in Mandarin.

"She says shortly before she met Voss, Gao brought her to see an acquaintance here in the city. It was late, but they met at an office not far from here, a travel agency. She never got the man's name, but he said what they were asking her to do was extremely important and was for her country, and that if she wanted her father to get the help he needed, she'd do as she was told."

"Could she show us later where this travel agency is?"

Meili nodded. She then went on to explain that, after some time, she was to collect evidence of a sexual relationship with Voss. This included explicit material sent over text, and at one point, hiding a camera in the bedroom at Voss's house. Afterwards, one day, she was told to cut off all contact with Eddie. She had been given the option to stay, and if she did, she would be provided a job in the city. Or she could return to China. She opted to stay to earn more money to send back home. Her mother needed the help. Gao also told her she was never to speak about what had transpired if she cared at all about the safety of her family back home.

When Ren finished translating, they were once again silent for a moment. Meili turned her head to the side, trying to hide the tears welling up in her eyes. She swallowed in an attempt to clear the lump in her throat.

Jesus Christ, this poor girl.

Bizon pushed his napkin across the table towards her, a feeble gesture, but he didn't have any tissues on him. She ignored it. He looked down at his coffee, which he had barely touched. His mind filled with follow-up questions as he pieced the puzzle together in his head.

"Meili, how old are you?"

She looked back at him. A tear had begun to roll down her cheek.

"Twenty-two."

He did the quick math and immediately recognized what the Chinese had been playing at with Eddie Voss. He glanced at Ren, whose face showed no reaction. Before Bizon could continue, she said something in Chinese.

Ren told Bizon. "She says that Voss was a very kind man, gentle, sweet. It was obvious to her he was awkward and shy. He was grateful when Gao introduced them. Despite being much older, he was deferential. She says he didn't deserve whatever it was Gao and this other man had planned."

"He never asked how old she was?"

Meili shook her head then said something.

"No. She assumes Gao told him before they actually met."

"Was it Gao who recruited her back in China?"

Ren asked and she spoke in response. At one point, she ran her finger from her left eyebrow down across her eye. "No, someone else. A scary looking man. Very bulky, with a close-shaved head and a scar over his eye, like she just indicated."

Bizon took this info down in his notebook. He felt he had all he needed from her at this time; she'd given enough to make the Chinese scheme with Eddie Voss evident. There was no point in pressing for more detail from the young woman. She'd been through enough. He'd have her show them this travel agency she spoke of and then send her on her way, back to what he hoped was now a normal life.

Before getting up, Bizon asked one last thing, "They threatened your family over this, yet you are talking to us. Do you no longer fear them?"

After Ren translated into Mandarin, she shook her head and spoke.

Before translating, Ren also shook his head forlornly. "No, there is no reason to. For one, she's had no contact with Gao or the other man for some time now. But her father never got the help with his sickness. He died not too long after the Voss business wrapped up. A couple of years ago, her mother joined him. She says it was because of a broken heart."

34

November 14, 2025. 11:03 hours local time.
South Bend, Indiana.

"Colonel Chavez, please. Let him know it's Major Decker. Thank you."

Major Maya Decker checked her watch as she held her cell phone to her ear. She would have to get moving soon for her 1:05 p.m. flight from the South Bend Airport to make her way back to Nevada. Originally, she had a flight booked for the following day, in case more time was needed to go over what Special Agent Purcel's contact had to say. But she'd heard all she needed to during their meeting, which had lasted little more than an hour. She was convinced, and she wanted to get moving with things. That meant getting back to Creech.

"Major, how's it going?"

"Very well, sir. I think Purcel brought us a good connection. We may have something here, and I want to get it implemented ASAP. I've actually switched my flight. I'm coming back tonight. Should be landing in Vegas around 1800 hours."

"Ok, great news. You can give me more details when you're here. This is something Giresi is on board with?"

"Yes, sir. He had some difficulty with the out-of-bounds manner in which this is happening, given Purcel's contact's lack of the necessary clearances, but I think we navigated it well. He's just as convinced as I am."

As she spoke, she looked down at the desk where she'd placed the silver USB device Jason Lizac had given her. It contained the design files for the RECORD chip.

She continued, "He is actually going to need to work in tandem with us. I'll explain more later, but for this to work, additional chips used on the system will be required, and he has the connections to the company where the problem occurred. He's going to have to ensure whatever stocks were kept in reserve do not end up getting destroyed. Not yet, at least."

Colonel Chavez didn't speak for a moment while he thought about what he'd just heard. Much like when Jason explained it, it seemed counterintuitive. He would just have to wait for her return to the air base to get a complete handle on it.

Finally, he said, "OK. Is this something we can make happen quickly?"

"It won't be overnight, sir, but I think so. Possibly a month. I'll ride my contacts at FMS as well."

FMS was the Foreign Military Sales office at the Department of Defense. Anything involving the sale or transfer of US military hardware to a foreign country had to go through them. Major Decker had more than one performance report that applauded her resourcefulness and problem-solving attributes. She would be putting that to the test when dealing with the FMS.

"Speaking of...have you given some thought about how we are going to handle this with our ally over there?"

"Yes sir...I think I have an idea."

———————

An hour later, Henry Purcel stood with his windbreaker zipped fully up against the midwestern November chill, looking up at the University of Notre Dame's Word of Life Mural, the famous Touchdown Jesus. It had been decades since he'd been back to where he spent the first part of his college career, and he had to admit that the hit of nostalgia was stronger than he anticipated. Probably a sign of advancing age, he figured. There had been some good experiences, some exciting Notre Dame NCAA tournament basketball games attended, some good friends made. A few, it would appear, turned out to be very good friends.

He looked at his watch. He and Jason had agreed to meet here and then go off to lunch after Jason wrapped up some conference calls that followed their meeting with Major Decker and Giresi. Jason was a little late, but that was fine with Purcel. He realized that—to use an analogy befitting the mural in front of him—the football was now well and truly handed off to the major and the rest of those more intimately entwined with the Ocelot program. He'd made the connection between the Ocelot folks and Jason. It was a good one. Major Decker had let him know that when she shook his hand before they all departed the meeting. It was also likely the end of his involvement. He did not have the need-to-know regarding nullifying the Trojans in the Ocelots that were still deployed. Maybe someday he'd find out, but for now, his work on the Ocelot case was rapidly coming to a close.

He felt his cellphone buzz in his pants pocket. He pulled it out to see Special Agent Bizon's name across his screen.

"Mark."

"You got a minute?"

Purcel looked around to see if Jason was in sight at all. Not yet. "Yes, what do you have?"

"They honey-trapped him. Voss."

"How do you mean?"

"The name you got from the detective upstate, Meili Yang, she and the 'Sonya' Voss sent that text to are one and the same. The guy I learned about in Buffalo, Gao, was right there in the middle. Facilitated bringing the girl over from China, basically to act as fucking bait on a hook. He introduced her to Voss, someone who, let's face it, wasn't going to find romance on his own, and directed her to engage in explicit messaging and to record her encounters with Voss. Now, here comes the fucked-up twist. She was just sixteen at the time."

It wasn't hard to make the connection.

"Statutory rape."

"Bingo. They must have gotten what they needed and then put that in front of him. Work for us or say goodbye to security clearances and hello to a prison cell."

"Jesus Christ."

For a moment, Purcel had forgotten where he was. He again looked around to make sure no one was nearby to hear him curse.

"You got that right. Incredibly fucked up method, but it worked. I hope we aren't as ruthless when it comes to working assets."

Purcel didn't respond to that. The image of Eddie Voss laying before him in the wet grass of a cemetery briefly flashed before his eyes.

I didn't see it ending this way.

"The last text must have been him apologizing for inadvertently taking advantage of the girl."

"That's the way I read it. Easy to see it that way if you meet the girl. She's pretty delicate. I'd prefer a combative interrogation with a terror suspect over that interview any day."

"So, she's still in the states, in Manhattan?"

"Yea, long story there. I'll tell you more later. Wanted to give you the bottom line."

"Sure. I do wonder...why register the number in her name and address? Left us a nice trail of breadcrumbs."

"Well, for one, I think they got cocky. With Voss, they had the perfect mark, and that felt like a victory unto itself. Second, I figure to lend credence to the story if they ever wanted to pull the trigger and really run Voss over the coals. If an investigation showed he was talking to a phone registered to someone else, it hurts your blackmail material. They had leverage over the girl, too, threats to family back home, typical stuff. I figure if Voss refused to play ball, they'd twist her arm to bring charges, and any of the main guys involved could remain in the shadows."

"Guys? There was more than just this Gao?"

"Yea, the girl says Gao took her to meet this guy who worked out of a travel agency here in Chinatown. He was the one calling the shots, it seems. He also drove her up to see Voss on one occasion. She walked over with us to the agency to see if the dude was still there, but no dice. Someone was though, a partner in the agency, but he told us the other guy up and disappeared a week ago. Hasn't heard a word from him, nothing."

"That's when I shot Voss. That's not a coincidence. Whoever that was must have seen the news and took off."

"For sure."

"Got a name?"

"The guy said it was Tian Xi, went by Tony. I doubt it's a real name. I'll follow up, but don't expect much from it."

"OK. Good work. Any luck with this Gao? Or also in the wind?"

"The latter. I'll look into it a bit more, but this one may be a dead end."

"OK. I'll see you back at Quantico."

"10-4."

Purcel hung up and put his phone back in his pocket. He checked his watch again to see that Jason was twelve minutes late. He sighed and thought about what he'd just heard. Now, the other end of this investigation was fast approaching a conclusion. While Jason's RECORD had the potential to be a victory, this felt like anything but.

A minute later, Jason appeared in his peripheral. Purcel turned to face his friend, offering his half smile. Jason approached him in a light jog that he slowed to a walk as he got closer.

"Henry, I'm so sorry, I—"

Purcel held up his hand and said, "Jason, it's no problem. I know you got work to do. Don't worry, I was enjoying some quiet time here."

"The campus is good for that."

Purcel indicated to their right with his head. "I'm parked in the lot over there. Any recommendations?"

"There's a Thai place I like just off campus."

"I rarely pass up a good Pad Thai."

"Let's do it."

Both men turned to head towards Purcel's rental car, walking shoulder to shoulder. Jason zipped up his own windbreaker featuring the iconic Notre Dame Irishman in fighting pose. As he did so, he said to Purcel, "So, can you tell me what's going on?"

Jason turned to see Purcel still looking ahead, grinning.

"Not a chance."

35

November 15, 2025. 21:05 hours local time.
Old Lumpinee Boxing Stadium, Bangkok, Thailand.

The two fighters continued to circle one another, their fists raised in the classic boxing position to protect their heads. One lashed out a kick, attempting a blow to the kidney, but the opponent anticipated the move and executed a successful block. It was now the fourth round of the match, and exhaustion was clearly beginning to show in the Muay Thai boxers. Both were bleeding from cuts on their faces, and their movements were becoming labored. It was turning into a battle of stamina and wit rather than the raw brute force both boxers exhibited when the first-round bell had rung. They put Zhang Hudao in the mind of a cobra and mongoose engaged in combat.

He was seated in the cheap seats of what had once been Bangkok's premier Muay Thai area, Lumpinee Boxing Stadium. Despite its title, it was a ramshackle building—dark, dingy, and damp. The seats in Zhang's section weren't seats at all but rather rows of wooden benches that had become loose from years of spectators standing up in haste, cheering their favored boxer on, or simply baying for more blood. The expensive seats were just cheap folding chairs at ringside. Apart from the dampness, Zhang liked it. A new, much more modern complex, New Lumpinee, had opened nearly a decade ago in a different location, but Zhang preferred the bouts occasionally offered at the original.

The bell rang, signaling the end of a tense round. The shouting and cajoling from the scrum of middle-aged men around him in sweat-stained shirts, some waving their betting tickets in the air or carelessly swinging bottles of beer, abated somewhat. As the fighters made their way to their respective corners for a brief respite, Zhang sensed movement towards him in his periphery, and a moment later, the empty space on the bench next to him was filled.

The man said to him in Mandarin, "Again, with the boxing."

"It's the one thing to do in this city that I find interesting."

"I know. Shall we?"

Zhang nodded, and both men stood up and made their way to the exit, stepping outside into the humid night air. Zhang thought of the contrast with the weather in Dandong just one night ago. He wondered if these wild swings in climate over the course of so little time were doing harm to his immune system.

Rama IV Road, the busy thoroughfare that ran in front of the stadium, pulsated with life. Around them, in the open space leading to the stadium gates, mobile cooked-food stalls hummed with activity, anticipating customers in between matches. Several men paced around, talking into cell phones and smoking cigarettes—bookies at work. Despite the activity, it was almost sedate compared to the mayhem inside the arena.

Zhang took a pack of cigarettes from his linen shirt and offered one to his interlocutor, who shook his head.

As Zhang lit himself a cigarette, the other man looked out at Ram IV and said, "City of Angels," a reference to the meaning of Bangkok's Thai name, *Krung Thep*.

Wang Kai was of medium build, seemingly in good shape, with a youthful face. The only thing that betrayed advancing years was the occurrence of silver at each temple of his close-cropped, military-style haircut. He was naturally amiable, his smile the type to put others at ease. He got along readily with almost anyone he encountered. He also, for years, had been Zhang's spy within the Taiwanese military. It was he who, all that time ago, had informed Zhang of the Taiwanese Civil Defense Forces' intent to purchase a new line of state-of-the-art surveillance drones from the United States to be used to monitor Taiwan's shores that faced mainland China. Initial discussions regarding finally invading Taiwan had already been taking place at the highest level in the Politburo, and Zhang and his superiors at the Ministry of State Security immediately saw an opportunity.

Wang turned back to Zhang, who blew smoke sideways out of his mouth in deference to his more health-conscious colleague. "It's not easy for me to leave like this on such short notice. This isn't something that we could have communicated via our system?"

Zhang looked away at the busy road, contemplating it for a moment. Yes, they had various means of communicating electronically, including the same method he used with Bao, sharing an email and using drafts to send messages. Face-to-face meetups like this may have been overkill, but he was old-school and, more importantly, paranoid. He felt more in control having the person right in front of him, in the flesh. Was beckoning Wang here to Thailand, the nearest country to both China and Taiwan that Chinese and Taiwanese passports could visit promptly without visas, disruptive and also somewhat risky? Yes, but to Zhang, it was necessary.

He turned back to Wang. "I know, my apologies. But this is too important."

"What is it?"

"I need to know, has there been any talk of the Ocelot drones possibly being taken out of operations?"

Wang was clearly taken by surprise by the question. "No. None at all. It has been normal operations. No talk of any deviations. Why, what is going on?"

Zhang once again turned his head and blew smoke from his nostrils. He'd already lost interest in the cigarette, so he flicked it away. Despite the fact that Wang, who was actually a couple of years Zhang's senior, was really the one answering to him, he felt like the subordinate in this instance. Some part of him felt partially to blame for all that was happening around the Ocelot operation.

Looking back at Wang, he said, "We believe that the Americans are aware of our access. It's not established fact, but all signs indicate it. From what I gather from my contact at Naval Special Operations, things are not yet ready to move forward. It's all I have to go on. Li has made himself the point of contact with the military and refuses to share details. It is possible this whole aspect of the operation is in jeopardy."

Wang's reaction wasn't what Zhang had expected. There was hardly any reaction at all. He motioned with his head for Zhang to follow him, and he led the way out the gate and turned west up Rama IV. After just a few steps, they entered Lumpinee Park, one of the largest green spaces in the city. Despite the late hour, there was still some activity in the park, couples strolling or the odd jogger along the floodlit pathways, but it was much quieter than it would be during the day.

Finally, Wang said to Zhang walking alongside him, "Tell me."

As they walked around the park, Zhang told him what had transpired to bring them to this point. The San Lang engineers' brush with US Special Operations in Somalia; Bao and Voss, who he was sure must be Bao's asset; Voss's demise. Wang listened silently, only nodding occasionally.

Zhang ended with, "We got greedy. The rare-earths identification capability on the other version of the Ocelot was pure luck, but unfortunately, exploiting it was the first domino to fall, bringing us to our current situation."

"Equally bad luck for those engineers to cross paths with American commandos."

Zhang shrugged. "It's a war zone. We should have been more aware of the risks."

"I'm curious, *how* did you come to recognize this ability? That it was, in fact, minerals that the drone could pick up signals from?"

"That's the beauty of the Trojan. It's been there since the beginning. That means that when the US Air Force was doing test flights domestically —in parts of the western US, from my understanding—we could see what it was picking up. We had some of our analysts look at the data and, over-laying it against what we knew about deposits of certain minerals in that part of the country, they were able to say with confidence that that was what the drone was identifying."

Wang gave a *not bad* expression with his face and nodded.

They walked a few steps in silence.

Finally, Wang said, "So, you say your technical lead is confident that the Americans are a long way from being able to replace the chips that have your Trojan?"

"Correct. But there is still the question of whether the Americans will warn your side of what is going on."

He explained to Wang how he felt that wasn't a forgone conclusion, using the same reasoning he'd given Li back in Beijing.

Wang nodded as Zhang concluded his point.

"I agree," said Wang, "I don't think the Americans would take such action, especially since, as you say, there's no guarantee they know for sure what is going on. The potential for nearly irreparable damage to their reputation with their allies is too great."

"I still felt I should warn you. The mission is now wading into murky waters."

The two men walked alongside each other for a few paces in silence. A young couple passed them, giggling.

Seeing the two made Zhang ask, "Your family is well, I trust?"

Wang nodded. "Yes, all good. My son is getting big, enjoying his basketball. Starts on a new team this summer."

"Perhaps he'll be playing for our Olympic team within a couple of Summer Olympics."

He saw Wang grin in his peripheral. "Yes, perhaps."

They were silent again. Wang didn't need to reciprocate the question. He knew Zhang had no family or any life beyond his work. As they strolled, Zhang pulled his cigarettes out again and went to light another.

"Smoking will kill you."

Zhang didn't say anything back at first. As he blew out smoke, he thought about what transpired in Dandong. Two more bodies added to his ledger. How many did that make now? He wasn't sure. Suddenly, he felt tired, a wave of fatigue washing over him.

"Yes. Maybe. If I live long enough."

Wang stopped and faced Zhang. "I'll be on the lookout for any warning signs. Should something more come up on your end, let me know. I can't be pulled away like this. Use our system for anything urgent."

Zhang turned his head to blow out more smoke. He looked back at Wang and nodded agreement.

Wang looked at his watch. "I have an early flight back tomorrow. I'll be going. Safe travels to you."

Before Zhang could respond, Wang turned back towards Rama IV. He watched as Wang stood by the busy roadside, waiting to flag one of the city's ubiquitous green taxis.

A commotion coming from the old boxing arena next to the park caused him to turn his head in that direction. The crowd was roaring, stomping their feet, and whistling.

A fighter had just gone down.

36

November 19, 2025. 08:25 hours local time.
Air Force Office of Special Investigations Headquarters, Quantico, Virginia.

Henry Purcel faced his boss, Lieutenant Colonel Al Reed, across a small conference table in the corner of the AFOSI SPAF. Reed leaned back in a swivel chair, his body slightly turned away from Purcel, hands interlocked behind his head. Now that AFOSI's involvement was no longer necessary, Reed had asked Purcel to sit down with him and give a final debrief, along-side the lengthy report of the Ocelot investigation Purcel had delivered to him the day before. Purcel had gone through each step, including Jason Lizac nudging him to look in the direction that took him straight to Eddie Voss and having a technology designed to combat the types of Trojans that a Voss might introduce into a system.

"That's the way it is sometimes, Henry. We ride our luck. You would have gotten there eventually. Sounds like your connection just offered a shortcut," Reed told him.

Purcel's chair was pushed a bit back from the table, allowing him to lean his long frame forward, his hands clasped in front of him. He didn't look at the ground, but he did not look directly at Reed either.

"Henry, for Christ's sake, don't look so dejected. I got Giresi calling, practically telling me to hand you a Medal of Honor, that I clearly gave him my best agent, *et cetera*. You should be proud of the work you did here."

"I suppose, sir. Just feel like I won't be able to see it through to the end. That's not my style."

"I know it isn't, but you know more than anyone that this is the way of our world. Let the spooks and our brothers and sisters in the Air Force take it over the finish line. It was their mess anyway."

Purcel offered a single nod in response. After a moment he said, "There is still something bothering me about this, sir, something that we haven't fully addressed. I—"

Reed held up a hand to cut him off. "Henry, if this is about the two suspected Chinese agents—what is it, Xi and Gao? I know they're loose ends, but you gotta let it go. Sometimes, the bad guys do get away. Perfect endings are for the movies."

"No, no, sir, I understand, but it's not that. Trust me, I wish we could bring them in. But there's something else. You know, in the midst of all the...commotion, I guess, for lack of a better term, there's something we haven't considered. Or if we did, we've lost sight of it. How *exactly* did the Chinese ensure that the contract to design the chips for the onboard camera's image enhancement ended up in Voss's hands at BTP? I only really thought of it after I got back from Indiana, and it is bothering me."

Reed adjusted himself so he now fully faced towards Purcel, his hands on top of the table. "From what I read in your report, Bolen and Miller agreed that the tech in that camera was pretty specialized. Is that a BTP thing exclusively?"

"No, it isn't. And even if it were...the Chinese have been working Voss for some time now, over a decade. Given his DOD bona fides when he went for his master's, he represented an opportunity, a potential asset for the future, that I get. But...the fact that their asset just so happened to land at the company that would eventually win this contract, that just seems far-fetched to me."

Reed spread his hands in a *what can you do?* gesture. "They brought him into their camp, he gets hired by a tech firm, and they just see if the chips fall in their favor. Could be as simple as that."

"That's quite an alignment of the stars, sir."

"Our stars aligned with your connection in Indiana, no? It can happen for the adversary, too."

"Sure, but..." Purcel let his voice trail off. Reed clearly wasn't up for the argument at this time.

"Voss took any secret to the grave with him, and I don't think we'll get the chance to ask Xi and Gao. The important thing is that you found the mole, and Giresi and Major Decker will work out the rest. Take the win, Henry,"

"Yes, sir," Purcel replied, his lack of enthusiasm evident in his voice.

Before either man could say anything else, a knock on the metal door jamb came from behind Purcel. He turned to see his colleague Mark Bizon standing in the doorway holding a sheaf of papers.

"Sorry to interrupt, sir, but I was told I could find Purcel here."

Reed motioned for him to take a seat next to Purcel. "We were just wrapping up. Whatcha got?"

Bizon pulled out a chair and sat down. He placed the papers he had on the tabletop and turned to Purcel. "So, I thought you might find this interesting. Not sure it will really lead anywhere, but to satisfy our curiosity at the very least."

He slid the top sheet over so it was in front of Purcel. "This is a blow-up of the image off of a business card for Tian, aka Tony, Xi, the supposed travel agent that helped honey-trap Eddie Voss. I sent that over to Customs and Border Patrol at JFK and asked if they could look through security footage for the day Eddie Voss bought the farm and the following couple of days.

It's amazing what you can accomplish by offering a set of tickets for a Rangers game. Anyway, they actually got a hit."

He slid the next sheet over to Purcel, who looked down at it. It was a blown-up CCTV image of a man presenting his documentation to go through security. Despite the somewhat grainy nature of the image, it was clearly the same man as in the business card photo.

Bizon continued, "Our boy here traveled on a Vietnamese passport as Nhat Tuan. He was on the 11:50 p.m. Korean Air flight to Seoul and was checked all the way through to final destination Hanoi, Vietnam. This was the night of November 7."

"The day I killed Voss."

"Correct."

"Vietnam, though? Why Vietnam?"

Bizon held up a finger and gave a little smile. "This is where the narrative gets a little interesting. Of course, Vietnam is a non-extradition country with the US, but that is beside the point. This individual is clearly Chinese. The whole thing with Voss and the girl and Gao shows that. I think it's safe to say it's a fake passport, which makes sense if this guy is a spook. But it does beg the question, why not just go back to your home country? China is not about to extradite anyone, let alone one of their own."

Bizon gave both Purcel and Reed a moment to consider the situation.

After a few seconds, Purcel said, "Maybe he caught wind of Voss's death and got scared. Scared not only of our authorities but also retribution from home base. So, he cuts and runs."

Bizon smiled as his colleague reached the same conclusion he had. "Bingo. I think that's it. Otherwise, just go back home. You're certainly more protected there."

"Bit close for comfort though, wouldn't you think?"

"I thought the same, but now I get to the *really* interesting part, which might explain why our Tony absconded for Vietnam. After all this probing, and again, not entirely sure to what end, I figured I'd also give his business card pic to the NSA and CIA, see if they have any database hits. I mean, they got facial recognition technology over there that's pretty scary. Jason Bourne movies come to life." He cast a glance at Reed, who shrugged. AFOSI was a small fish compared to those two behemoths of the US intelligence services.

Bizon continued, "The CIA hit me back with something. They don't have anything on this particular individual, but they got a very close match."

He slid the final piece of paper he had with him next to the other sheets in front of Purcel.

"Wenbu Bao. Known to be a high-level Chinese intelligence agent in Vietnam during the late '80s through the '90s. Apparently, based on the file the Agency has on him, he was like a veritable Colonel Kurtz there. You remember Marlon Brando in *Apocalypse Now*?"

Both Purcel and Reed nodded at the reference.

"He was like the King of the Vietnamese highlands, along the Vietnam-China border."

Purcel considered the picture and then passed both the blow-up of the business card and the image from the CIA to Reed. It didn't take long to see the connection. "This Bao is our guy's father."

"You got it," Bizon said.

Purcel leaned back in his chair.

"I guess it explains why this Xi would make for Vietnam. Maybe there are still old connections."

"Correct. And I think it's safe to say his real last name is Bao."

Purcel nodded at that and thought for a moment. He looked at Bizon. "It's really good work, Mark. It somewhat ties off a loose end. At least we know what became of him."

That should have been the end of it. But there was something about the Vietnam connection that bothered Purcel. It touched something deep in the recesses of his memory. He just wasn't sure what exactly it was.

37

December 18, 2025. 08:07 hours local time.
Hsinchu Air Force Base, Hsinchu, Taiwan.

Major Maya Decker stepped from the small military transport plane onto the tarmac and into the bright morning sun. She moved her sunglasses down over her eyes and looked up at the cockpit of the plane, giving a thumbs-up to the young Air Force pilot who had just taken her on the hour-and-a-half journey from Kadena Air Force Base in Okinawa to this Taiwanese air base on the island's northwestern coast. A helmet and sun visor obscured much of the top part of the pilot's face, but she could see his smile as he returned the gesture.

She turned back to the base laid out in front of her. It was a beehive of activity. Men in uniform marched in lockstep, transport vehicles lumbered about, and one fighter jet was slowly taxiing. Among this, she saw a military jeep approaching her. When the vehicle pulled up a few feet away, two men in uniform stepped out. The driver, a young officer, Captain Liu, approached her, stopping to salute.

When she saluted back, he smiled and extended his hand. "Major Decker, so good to see you again."

They shook hands. The other officer she recognized from a previous visit a couple years before. He bore the two stars of a Major General on his lapels. He also smiled, and this time, she saluted first. She noticed him glance down at the titanium briefcase she carried in her left hand.

Liu said, "Major, you might remember Major General Guo."

She shook hands with Guo. "I do, yes. Thank you for receiving me. It's good to be back."

Liu translated for Guo while stepping away and opening up the back door to the jeep. He indicated for Major Decker to step in. "Major, please."

Once all three were back in the jeep, Liu turned the vehicle around and headed towards a large, nondescript, white-washed block building.

He spoke over his shoulder, "Major, how are you feeling? I know it's a long journey."

Yes, yes it is.

Decker was exhausted, her sense of time completely warped. A long journey, as the young Taiwanese captain had put it, was an understatement. Flying commercial from the States to East Asia, particularly Taiwan, could test the limits of even seasoned travelers, but given that Major Decker carried chips destined for advanced military technology in the briefcase with her, commercial wasn't an option. Instead, it required an odyssey via military transport, one that began with a specially arranged flight from Creech to McChord Air Force Base outside of Tacoma, Washington, arriving just in time to run for a regularly scheduled C-17 headed to Okinawa. She then had less than twenty-four hours on the ground in Japan and, despite being drained from the flights, had awoken for her 06:30 flight at one in the morning, wide awake. She had been able to doze a little on the flight from Kadena, but the fatigue of jet lag still weighed behind her eyes like an anvil.

She responded, "Captain, I'm hoping you have some good coffee available here. I could use it."

Liu gave a laugh. "Major, I cannot promise it will be good, but we do have coffee for you."

He pulled them up in front of the building, and the trio hopped out, Liu leading the way. He used a badge to swipe them in. After passing through a small lobby where a young enlisted airman sat behind a counter that resembled a hotel front desk, the opposite wall adorned with framed photos of dour-looking officers in dress blues, Liu once again swiped his badge so they could pass through a set of double doors. They entered a hallway that put Major Decker in the mind of a hospital ward: old 12x12 plain white ceramic tile flooring and harsh fluorescent lights overhead. It smelled vaguely of chemical cleaners. They turned down another hall, eventually coming to another set of double doors that required Liu to first swipe his badge and then punch in a code. Major Decker remembered this as one of the facility's secure rooms. The major and her two Taiwanese companions walked by three rows of computers, many occupied by airmen in uniform, and came to a small glass-enclosed office. Before they entered, Liu turned and said something in Mandarin to one of the airmen seated nearest to them. He then smiled at Major Decker and indicated for her to take a seat at the office's long conference table.

They all arranged themselves around the table, Major Decker placing the briefcase in front of her.

Liu, sitting across from her, motioned with his head toward the briefcase. "So, Major, that is what we need to fix this anticipated issue with the Ocelot drones?"

The issue that Captain Liu referred to was what, a couple of weeks before, the major and Colonel Chavez had described in a secure teleconference as an *anticipated reliability problem* that further testing on the drones at Creech had revealed may be forthcoming. They had told Liu, their main point of contact at Hsinchu and a key player on the Taiwanese side that oversaw the transition of the Ocelots to his country, that this had to do with the Ocelots' onboard cameras and was nothing to be alarmed about. It simply required the addition of a new chip onto the cameras' circuit boards, and this would patch the problem.

This had been the major's way of tiptoeing around the revelation of a suspected Trojan within the Ocelots' circuitry. As Colonel Chavez had indicated to her when she had called from South Bend, as she knew he would, telling the Taiwanese they believed there was a ghost in the system would cause a veritable shitstorm that could do irreparable harm to the two nations' defense partnership. *Reliability issues*, however, were not unheard of with cutting edge military systems, and the major thought that, by couching it in such terms, they could insert RECORD onto the drones and avoid setting off alarm bells with their counterparts. Both Colonel Chavez and Giresi, who still lorded over the program like Godfathers, agreed that this was the proper approach. Technically, as the major had told them, they were not lying to the Taiwanese. There *was*, in a way, a reliability problem. Was it a sin of omission? Perhaps. When she had presented this idea to the colonel, she remembered a visit as a teenager to the lobby of the CIA headquarters, when her father, who spent time in the clandestine service after leaving the Marines, received a service award. One wall in that lobby famously displayed the words *the truth will set you free*, and while she conceded that was often the case, she also had once heard someone use the phrase *the inadequacy of reality*, and that, she would argue, certainly applied here. Luckily for Major Decker and her team, such was the level of trust and reliance on the part of the Taiwanese that, when given this news, they had not pressed for details and had welcomed any updates that would ensure the continued proper operation of their drones.

Now, sapped not just by the hellacious trip out but also by the entire affair, she just needed to clear this final hurdle. It had been a whirlwind undertaking. The major had set a target of thirty days turnaround time, and they had about hit the mark. From her meeting with Jason Lizac in Indiana to now, just over a month had elapsed.

Under normal circumstances, it should have been a long, drawn-out process of planning, designing, and implementing a microcircuit, but by sharing the RECORD design files, Jason Lizac had given them a head start. The relative simplicity of the RECORD chip's functionality helped as well, and when necessity called for it, the major and her squad of engineers would get dialed in, working long days and nights fueled by coffee, energy drinks, and vending machine snacks. No one wanted to be responsible for missing her deadline.

"We can't cut corners here, Major. I know you're the beating heart of this whole program, and I want this resolved just as much as you, but anything that even brushes up against a security violation in the interest of saving time, I won't have it," Colonel Chavez had admonished when she met him upon her return from South Bend.

"I fully understand, Colonel. We'll do this right. We've already put IIC's RECORD chip design files onto an air-gapped computer. We can just take their high-level description of the chip to derive our own and get that onto a FPGA."

The FPGA she referenced was a standard microcircuit in which the hardware was programmable—a one-time programmable Field Programmable Gate Array. Since it was her Air Force personnel programming that chip, it would represent the trusted piece of hardware for the RECORD design.

The colonel had leaned back in his office chair, tapping a pencil against his chin. Decker was seated across from him at his desk, having just run him through how she anticipated implementing RECORD.

"You said over the phone that you could push this through FMS? A month is tight, Major. I know how they can be over there."

"Yes, sir. I've already begun laying the groundwork. Like I said over the phone, I have the inside track with some folks there. It will be all by the book, but it's just a matter of speeding up some of the bureaucracy."

The Colonel nodded. He thought for a moment then said, "As you know Major, your technical acumen runs much deeper than mine, so I'm entrusting you to lead this and see it through to its conclusion. However, I'm not totally rusty. Not yet, at least. Perhaps you can tell me what I'm missing here, Major, but if RECORD is going to require not only a trusted RECORD-ized chip, but also two of the originals, how in the hell is there going to be space on a circuit board for all that? If we are talking about having to outfit these birds with whole new boards to accommodate this thing..."

Decker remembered smiling at his question. She'd learned a lot from the colonel over the years, but his technical acumen *was* getting rusty.

"Do you remember Moore's Law, Colonel?"

"Shit happens?"

"Ha. True, but different law. Moore's Law—though, I'm not sure if *law* is really accurate, as it's more of a trend—but anyway, it posits that about every year and a half, the density of chips doubles. BTP produced those chips not long ago but still used Voss's infected design files from over three years ago. So, given the time that has elapsed, they can be accommodated."

"A bit of luck, then."

"I'd rather be lucky than good."

"You'll need to be both with this thing. Let's hope Giresi comes through with getting those excess chips."

And he had. Giresi had done his part and obtained the Ocelot chips they needed from a depot in Alabama, and the major and her team of three Air Force engineers had done the rest, producing a RECORD-ized chip and bringing her to where she now sat in coastal Taiwan, on the precipice of neutralizing Eddie Voss's hardware Trojan.

"Major?"

Captain Liu's voice broke Major Decker from her reverie. She shook her head to show she was clearing a clouded mind. She tried to hide her embarrassment at having lost her focus, her mind drifting to all the work over the last month.

"Yes, sorry, my apologies. I don't handle jet lag like I used to, I guess. Yes, Captain. I have here seven new chips, one for each of the Ocelots that you currently operate."

The door behind her opened up, and the airman that Liu had spoken to before came in and set a mug displaying the crest of the Taiwanese Air Force down in front of her. The aroma of coffee wafted out.

The young airman asked, hesitantly, in English, "Sugar or milk?"

She smiled and shook her head. "No, thank you."

The airman stepped back, saluted all three gathered at the table, and left, closing the door behind him.

The major took a sip. It was strong and pretty bad.

"You were right, I was being hopeful looking for *good*."

Captain Liu laughed. "Starbucks has been slow to make it here."

She smiled and waved it off. "All good. Thanks for having that brought in. Anyway—"

She popped open the briefcase and first removed a large folder with the US Air Force insignia on it from the top portion. She set the folder aside and moved the briefcase so the captain and major general could see seven chips, all a little smaller than a memory card one might find in a Canon or Nikon camera, spaced evenly within little square slots cut into a piece of foam that filled out one side of the briefcase. Those chips all had RECORD inside.

"These are all that you need. As Colonel Chavez and I indicated in our call, these are for the Ocelot's main camera."

She opened the folder and pulled out a folded document, spreading it on the table between herself and Liu and Guo. As she did so, Liu spoke in Mandarin to Guo, translating what she'd just said. She unfolded the document, revealing a schematic of the Ocelot drone.

"I know you have copies of this, but I figured I would show you so you can demonstrate to your engineers."

She stood up, pushing the schematic closer to the two men, and leaned over the table. She pointed to an image in the top corner of the unfurled document, showing a more detailed visual description of the front end of the aircraft. "The bird's main camera is housed here."

She moved her finger down a trace amount. "I'd suggest they use this access panel. The motherboard for the camera is designated with the heading DCS012398. They'll simply need to remove that and solder in these new chips. That should head off the suspected reliability issue. Of course, make sure to run the necessary tests on the camera before you put the UAV back in the air."

Once she finished, Liu spoke again to Guo, giving him a condensed version of the major's instructions. Guo said something back to him.

Liu then said, "Excellent, sounds easy enough, Major. I think our engineers can take care of this rather quickly. Major General Guo did just ask me, though, this is a long way to come for a major like yourself for some routine patching, is it not?"

She had anticipated that someone would bring this up. The major general wasn't wrong. This was a lot to go through for someone of her rank. The matter of a suspected Trojan embedded in the drone hardware was of the highest sensitivity, however, and the fewer individuals on their side made aware of it, the better. Only a select few, including herself, Colonel Chavez, and three of her engineers at Creech who'd been part of the Ocelot program from its inception, knew of the situation. It was possible she could have sent one of the engineers, but part of her also felt that, as one of the senior leads of the program, it was she who needed to make the journey here. She had dedicated a great deal to this endeavor, and she needed to see this through.

"Yes, Captain, it is, but as one of the senior officers who has been with the Ocelot drones from the very beginning, I thought it appropriate I be here, primarily to show that, no matter what, we take any potential issue with our aircraft very seriously."

She hoped that would suffice as an answer. Liu nodded and, as he spoke to Guo, the major general also nodded, apparently satisfied with what he had heard.

About twenty minutes later, down the hall from the secure facility where she'd met with Captain Liu and Major General Guo, Major Decker looked at herself in the ladies' room mirror, having just splashed cold water on her face. Adrenaline had carried her through that meeting, but the strong cup of coffee, if it could even be called that, had not been of much help. The jet lag once again had taken hold, and it showed on her face. She sighed and stared at the reflection, dark bags under her eyes.

Almost there.

She reached over and pushed the lever on the paper towel dispenser to reveal a lengthy sheet. She folded it up and ran the harsh paper over her face, drying it off. Looking back in the mirror, she ran a hand over her hair, held back in a tight bun, and straightened the jacket of her camouflage uniform. Captain Liu had offered to give a tour of the SCIF where they analyzed data in real time from the Ocelot drones, and then they could have an early lunch in the base canteen, where he promised the food was quite good. She accepted the former but declined on the latter, eager to retire to her hotel in the town of Hsinchu. It was asking too much to get another military transport to bring her back to Okinawa the same day, so she would spend the night in Taiwan and then return to the base early in the morning for the long journey home.

She pushed the bathroom door open and exited into the hallway. As she turned left to head toward the entrance where Captain Liu awaited her, she nearly collided with a man who had been walking and reading a document. They both stopped just short of one another.

"Excuse me," she said, and he said the same, only in Mandarin.

Upon closer inspection of who he'd almost bumped into, the man switched to English. "Sorry, excuse me."

He gave her a pleasant smile and moved slightly to his right so she could continue straight on. She returned the smile. Despite that briefest of interactions, she couldn't help but notice how handsome he was and would have figured him to a be a young recruit if it weren't for the salt-and-pepper at his temples.

38

December 18, 2025. 22:12 hours local time.
Dongcheng District, Beijing, China.

Freshly fallen snow crunched underneath Zhang Hudao's feet as he stepped into the *hutong* from his home. He set down on the ground a small plate topped with reheated rice and some chicken he had mixed in.

He said aloud, "It is too cold out here for you, my friend."

Zhang waited for Xiaogui, the stray cat he fed nearly every night, to make an appearance. He stood for a few moments, the freezing temperature cutting through his heavy fisherman's sweater, listening for movement. Nothing. Perhaps his erstwhile feline companion had already found shelter away from the bitter cold of night and would not be venturing out.

The phone in his pants pocket dinged. He removed it and looked at the screen to see a notification from WeChat, a message from a "friend."

Hey, sorry for the late hour. Busy day. It has been a while since we spoke. How is everything? Did you see that Arsenal might sign that young midfielder from Leverkusen?

The reference to Arsenal, the London-based soccer club, was a signal for him to check the email account he reserved for messages from Wang Kai. He stepped back into the house and went to the laptop on his dining table. He sat and opened it, pulling up the email account. He checked the Drafts folder.

An American was here today. A woman wearing Air Force camouflage. It was only for a moment that I saw her, just passing in a hallway. As I'm sure you can imagine, it is not uncommon for Americans to be here, but I believe she was here with a captain who works with the Ocelot drones. He was waiting nearby while she was in the restroom. I made some inquiries, but no one knew the reason for her visit. I was careful not to show an elevated level of interest. It could be nothing, but I thought you should be aware. I have otherwise heard of nothing happening with those aircraft.

Zhang leaned back in his chair and ruminated on the note. As Wang had said, Americans in uniform walking around Hsinchu should be no surprise. The fact that she may have been seeing personnel tied to the Ocelots did raise questions. If the Americans had discovered the presence of the Trojan, which Zhang had to remind himself was still not a sure thing, they certainly would not sit on their hands. He knew that much. But Deng had been certain in his assessment that the Americans were a long way from counteracting the Trojan *and* keeping the drones in operation. While Zhang felt a level of contempt for Deng, primarily for the way in which he curried favor with Li, he did have a grudging respect for Deng's technical acumen. The man knew his field and knew it well. It had also now been more than a month since Bao went off the radar and Voss was killed. If those two events were, indeed, signs that the Americans had discovered the infiltration, then it served as proof that Zhang had been right in his assumption that the Americans would not simply tell the Koreans and Taiwanese and have them pull the drones out of service.

So, were the Americans likely working towards a solution? Yes, Zhang was sure of that, but it was also possible that *they* thought time was on their side. China was not going about the Taiwan matter the way that fool Putin had Ukraine. No massive troop movements or deployment of thousands of men and machinery along borders for all satellites to see, or bellicose saber rattling for the news cameras. No, Zhang knew his compatriots in the armed forces would be doing this in a surgical way that would rely mainly on special forces landing by sea. Putin may not have cared about razing Ukrainian cities to the ground and turning the country into a World War I battlefield, but such tactics would be self-defeating to the People's Republic in Taiwan. They *wanted* to keep the infrastructure intact and in use. Why would you destroy land and buildings that were potentially useful and, after all, rightfully yours?

And that was why this Trojan in the Ocelot drones was so critical to the mission. Not only could the People's Liberation Army see what the Taiwanese were seeing, but more important was their intent, right before sending troops over the strait, to spoof the Ocelots. This was where Zhang had to give credit to Deng again. While the idea to spoof the drones had not been his, it was Deng who laid the groundwork for it. As he'd explained it to Zhang, he'd had the asset (Voss, Zhang assumed) design a tiny radio receiver within the Trojans. As they crossed the strait, elements of the Dragon Commando Unit would broadcast via antenna a specially coded message, one only recognized by the Trojans, and this would begin the spoofing. The Taiwanese, on their end, would continue to see loops of innocuous, empty water in the feeds from the drones, when in reality, troop carriers filled with Naval Special Forces would be bearing down on them.

And the witching hour was now close at hand. His boss, Li, still revealed nothing of what he knew about preparations, but Zhang's source in the Navy in Chaozhou had finally given Zhang something after another visit. A target date had been set: February 17, the beginning of the Chinese Lunar New Year, now just a couple of months away. No one would suspect a Chinese invasion of Taiwan during such a period of cultural importance, and Taiwanese guard was likely to be down during celebrations. It would be a repeat of the famous North Vietnamese Tet Offensive against the Americans all those years ago.

He looked back at the draft email. It was less than ideal news, but given the context, he wasn't unsettled by it. Not yet. He deleted what Wang had written and typed a message back.

Ok. Keep an eye on the situation. Report back with anything new.

Picking his phone up off the dining table, he opened the WeChat dialogue and responded:

No worries. Things have been good here, no real news to report. Arsenal needs someone in that position, hope they get him.

He tossed the phone back on the table and ran a hand over his face.

Two more months he thought. It was all they needed.

He stood and walked over to the small sofa in the adjoining living room, the only piece of furniture in the space apart from an old TV sitting atop a wooden cabinet. He was ready to sit down with his book, an account of America's chaotic withdrawal from Afghanistan, when he remembered something. He turned and went back to his front door, stepping back out into the cold.

He looked down at the plate he'd left on the ground. It was wiped clean of food.

39

December 19, 2025. 06:40 hours local time.
Arlington, Virginia.

As Henry Purcel sat down at his little breakfast table that afforded him a view through his bay window looking out onto Kenmore Street, Layla slowly got up from where she normally slept at the meeting point of Purcel's kitchen and living room and came over to his side. She sniffed the air with interest, seeing if there was any deviation from Purcel's normal weekday breakfast of shredded wheat with strawberries and blueberries.

He looked down at her. "Sorry girl, nothing for you"

The old dog turned away and went back to her bed, where she'd wait for him to finish eating and then feed her. She lay her head down with a sigh. Purcel smiled at the somewhat dramatic display of disappointment that had now become routine.

As Purcel ate his cereal, he looked at the tablet he kept propped up on the table. His habit was to first scroll the headlines on the *New York Times*, *BBC*, and *Reuters*. If he still had some time to spare, he'd check out ESPN. Basketball, his sport, was in full swing, though he preferred college to the NBA. He also liked to keep an eye on the NHL, with the Washington Capitals being playoff contenders for a number of years now.

On the side panel of the *BBC* webpage was a story about the opening of a new American embassy in Hanoi, the capital of Vietnam.

Vietnam, there it is again.

It had been a month since Purcel and AFOSI officially closed the book on the Ocelot. Even though Lieutenant Colonel Reed had given Purcel new work, the case still bothered him. In the subsequent days, his mind would often wander back to it.

The loose end, as he saw it, was how the Chinese had ensured that their man Eddie Voss was handed the work of designing chips destined for the Ocelot. It was a question that still lingered at the edge of his thoughts.

Though he was done with the case, certain details would occasionally float in front of his vision, unclear and disjointed. He was sure he was missing something. It was the details, after all, that the devil lay within.

He opened the article about the new embassy in Hanoi. After ground-breaking more than two years prior in the summer of 2023, the new, massive, modern glass and steel complex was ready for business. The top of the article showed an image of a beaming US Secretary of State standing in front of the building, shaking hands with the mayor of Hanoi. The picture gave Purcel pause. It called to mind something, but he couldn't quite place what it was. He looked away from his tablet and stared out the window.

He thought about where he had seen something similar. Why did an embassy in Vietnam trigger something in the recesses of his memory? He thought for a moment, flipping through his mental photo book.

US Embassy.

Vietnam.

Men standing in front.

The home was so quiet, he could hear Layla's light breathing a few feet away, but he didn't really notice it. He felt on the cusp of pulling up a memory. Suddenly, he had it.

"Holy shit," he said aloud.

He remembered what it was.

———————

"Giresi."

"Steve, hi, it's Henry Purcel, how are you?"

"Hi, Henry, I'm doing well. Yourself?"

"I'm doing OK. Listen, do you have a minute?"

Purcel sat with his elbows perched on his office desk, one hand holding his desk phone receiver to his ear. Though delaying a call like this was not his style, Purcel decided to wait until he was in the office. He did not want to irritate his NSA counterpart with a call outside of normal working hours. Particularly since this one was very likely to touch a nerve.

"Um, sure, what's on your mind?"

"John Woods at BTP...how well do you know him?"

There was a pause. Purcel knew it was a question straight out of the blue, and he could envision Giresi on the other end thinking about where this could possibly be going.

"I know John quite well. Before going into the private sector, he spent some time here at the NSA. I was a few years into my career, and we collaborated on some efforts. As I mentioned before, we've maintained a working relationship. Why do you ask, Special Agent?"

The switch from *Henry* to *Special Agent* was not lost on Purcel.

"Just some final details on that whole case I'm trying to square off. Been thinking about Voss's time at BTP. He had not been there very long when the contract in question fell in his lap. A fact that still puzzles me a bit. Anyway, so Woods wasn't a career NSA man?"

"I see. Umm, no he wasn't. He was actually CIA for much of his career in intelligence."

"Was he in the field?"

Again, another pause. This time when he responded, Giresi didn't attempt to hide his irritation. "Where is this heading, Special Agent? Your involvement with that case has ended, I'll remind you."

"No, I know. Just, please, I would appreciate some indulgence here. I understand you have a history with Woods, but as I say, some things about this case...I just can't reconcile. Again, he spent time in the field?"

Giresi breathed audibly through his nose, another sign of displeasure. "Yes, John Woods spent the greater part of his career with the Agency abroad."

"And this would have been during the early '90s?"

Giresi didn't say anything for a moment as he thought about the answer, likely confused by what the dates of John Woods's time working as a CIA agent had to do with anything. Finally, he said, "Correct, that would have been the time frame."

"Do you know where he was stationed?"

As he asked, Purcel tightened his grip on the phone receiver. His mind went to a couple of framed photos he'd seen on the bureau behind John Woods's desk in his cavernous office.

A younger version of the man standing, smiling. One was in front of a building, the other in a pastoral scene of rolling hills and rice paddies.

"His background at Yale was East Asian studies, if I recall. He had a hardship posting in Timor-Leste to begin, then I think a couple years in Cambodia. He climbed the ranks, though. After that, he got a Chief of Station position."

Purcel shifted in his seat, bouncing his right knee in anticipation, waiting for Giresi to continue.

"That was in Vietnam."

40

December 19, 2025. 12:55 hours local time.
Schenectady, New York.

Detective Richard Conkling watched through the huge storefront window of Jay Street Subs as a young woman wearing a puffy jacket, her head turtled in against the cold, walked by with her small dog, heading towards State Street. He noticed the dog looked more miserable than the owner. It reminded him of one of the reasons why, despite loving dogs, he didn't have one himself. It saved him from having to walk in the *bullshit cold*, as he liked to call it, of this upstate New York city.

The detective looked at his watch. He figured he should probably get going back to his desk. Another shooting awaited him, this time an incident that appeared to be related to a drug deal gone south. Still, he couldn't believe that within the span of a month, he had two dead bodies as the result of gunshot wounds. That wasn't supposed to happen in his small city. With a sigh, he crumpled up the wrapping paper that had held his Philly Cheesesteak. He was about to stand up from his spot at the bar top that ran along the window when he felt his cellphone vibrate in his pants pocket. It was an unrecognized Virginia number.

"Detective Conkling."

"Detective, hi, it's Henry Purcel, AFOSI."

"Hey Henry. How are you holding up?"

"I'm doing well, thanks. Yourself?"

Conkling glanced out the window at the steel gray sky and snow and slush on the ground. "Hanging in. Hope you're warmer down there than up here."

"Ha, sure. Chilly, but I'm not doing any shoveling."

"Keep it that way."

"For sure. Anyway, catch you at a good time?"

"Yea, what's up?"

"The Edward Voss case...there's still some things I'm looking into there. You did a little background on him afterwards, I imagine, such as his employment at BTP, that kinda stuff?"

"Sure, yea, interviewed a couple of his colleagues and his boss. Ran down a cousin that hadn't seen him in ages. Pretty much it."

"Right. The boss, by that you mean John Woods?"

"That's right"

"Can you tell me what he had to say, if you recall at all?"

"Not much to recall, really. He claimed not to know Voss very well. Voss was just one of the worker bees."

"I see. I know I'm stretching here, but you didn't get any sense of the hiring process over there, did you? Who makes the final call, that kind of thing?"

"No, didn't take it very far, as you can imagine, and to be honest with you, Henry, can't see why we would have needed that kind of info. What's on your mind with this?"

There was a pregnant pause on the other end. Conkling got the feeling that in itself was a signal from Purcel that they were maybe wading into a gray area.

Purcel eventually said, "Some things about this case still bother me. I can't quite get into it right now, but I'm trying to look into something."

"I see."

"So, now, I have to ask you for a favor."

About three hours later, Detective Conkling was sitting in a small cubicle on the first floor of the BTP offices on Nott Street. He felt a slight tinge of guilt being there; the captain was eager to see the new homicide case closed as soon as possible, and at the moment, they didn't even have a potential suspect. But Conkling, for reasons he couldn't articulate, liked Henry Purcel and wanted to help. It wasn't only that, he told himself. Given what he understood about BTP's work and Purcel's involvement as an AFOSI agent, this appeared to be a matter of national security, and that certainly intrigued him.

After hanging up with Purcel, he'd gone back to the police department and made the calls to arrange the meeting he now sat in, pushing it out until 4:00 p.m. so he could dedicate at least some time to the shooting and come here with slightly clearer conscience.

"Ms. Cohen, thanks for meeting with me again. This shouldn't take too long."

Elaine Cohen, the bespectacled woman in her mid-forties whose cubicle they occupied, was the head of BTP's Human Resources and who the detective knew controlled much of the hiring process at the company.

She gave a small smile and said, "Not a problem, Detective. How can I help you?"

"As I mentioned over the phone, we are still looking into the incident with Edward Voss. Still some I's and T's that need dotting and crossing. I understand that Voss had been at the company for six, seven years, something like that, and you handled his hiring, correct?"

"Correct."

"Is it you who handles the final decision? Whether a candidate is a yay or a nay?"

"Good lord, no. A small panel of our engineers interviews candidates, and they make a recommendation to Mr. Woods."

"Was this the process for Edward Voss?"

"Not quite. There actually wasn't an open position he applied for. I mean, we are always on the lookout for good people, so occasionally an employee will recommend someone, and we will consider them."

"I see. And someone recommended Voss?"

"It was actually Mr. Woods. He asked that we take Edward under consideration. If I recall, he said a former colleague passed along Edward's resume, and he took it as a courtesy."

"I see." The detective jotted this down in the small notepad he always carried with him. "And do you know how the reviewing panel of engineers considered Voss, his application?"

"Hmm…I really can't say. They make the recommendation; Mr. Woods has the final say. He usually goes based off their input, so the fact that Edward was brought on makes me think he measured up quite well."

"Do you think I could talk to someone who was part of that process?"

Alex Linden had been getting ready to leave for the day when Elaine Cohen knocked on the frame of his cube, the detective standing next to her. He had spoken with Detective Conkling previously in the immediate aftermath of Eddie Voss's passing. It was not something he was eager to do again. Much of the office was still reeling from the whole episode, and Linden, as one of the only BTP employees who had any kind of friendly relationship with Voss, had been impacted the most. He wouldn't say he considered Voss a friend, but Voss had reciprocated his kindness, and Linden respected the work he did. Voss's violent end was bad enough, but the murmurings in the office that he may have been compromised and was doing the bidding of a foreign entity had really struck a nerve. Linden and his colleagues just wanted to move on. He made no attempt to show his irritation when Elaine left the two men standing in Linden's cube and the detective had made a *may I?* motion towards Linden's guest chair.

"As I'm sure you can appreciate, Detective, the program Eddie was working on was highly classified, and I do not believe you have the proper clearances. I am not sure how much I can speak to you about his time on that particular contract."

The detective held up a placating hand. "I understand. I'll keep it in general terms."

Linden nodded, indicating he could go on with his questions.

"To start, you serve on the hiring panel, correct?"

"That's right."

"Based on Voss's resume and interviewing, were you guys able to recommend him to Mr. Woods?"

"Two of us did, the other thought he wouldn't be a good fit. I felt his technical acumen justified him joining. It was clear he knew his stuff."

"And the dissenter? Do you recall why they objected?"

"Eddie was awkward. A bit nervous at times. That's what I remember my colleague saying after the interviews. I don't put much stock in that stuff. What counts is what's up here." He pointed to his head. Before Conkling could ask his next question, Linden added, "And let's face it. Apparently, Mr. Woods said an old connection asked as a favor that we consider Eddie. I think he's good about taking our advice, but unless we were strongly negative on Eddie, Mr. Woods was likely to hire him."

"What makes you say that?"

Linden shrugged. "Just a sense I got when we first spoke about it. He seemed pretty interested in seeing Eddie succeed."

"I see." Conkling once again wrote something in his notepad. Once he was finished, he said, "Mr. Woods has a pretty deep technical background?"

"Hmm, not that I'm aware. He's obviously highly educated, undergrad at Yale then an MBA from Brown. I'm sure his time at the NSA is what informed his technical knowledge and spurred him to start the company. But no, his expertise is obviously more in the business side of things, saw an opportunity in the market, that kind of thing. I think he can speak at a high level about the work we do but, at the end of the day, relies on us for the technical side."

The detective paused as if he were considering what Linden had just told him. Then he said, "Now, as you say, I am not very familiar with the work in question, but from what little I've been told, and just using some Detective's intuition, I think it's safe to say that the contract the AFOSI agent was most interested in was an important project, no?"

"It certainly was. Not just in dollar terms. It was related to something the DOD was clearly excited about pursuing."

"Right. What I'm wondering is...Voss had not been at BTP for very long, just around a couple of years, when the contract was awarded. How did he come to lead up that particular program?"

Linden hesitated for a second before answering, "It was Mr. Woods who suggested Eddie be the lead on that contract."

"Given Voss's time at the company and maybe his background compared to others here, did it strike you as strange that Woods wanted him as lead engineer?"

"It was a little odd, I have to admit. But Mr. Woods thought it would be good for Eddie. I am not sure how much he knew of him from this connection of his, but I guess he thought highly enough of Eddie that Mr. Woods decided he should be the lead on it. Again, when he first brought Eddie's resume to us, I got the impression he had hopes for Eddie to come aboard. Also, it's not like the rest of the engineers didn't have other work; putting Eddie on that program wasn't hurting anyone around here."

As Conkling jotted something down in his notepad, Linden continued, "Don't get me wrong, Eddie had the bona fides for it. It's definitely not a case of a square peg/round hole he was trying to force. But did we have senior guys more suitable for such a sensitive project? I would say, yes. I have to admit, at the time, there were some whispers about that whole thing, but we all like John and trust his judgment, and these concerns eventually faded away, particularly when it was apparent Eddie was good at his work. He was fresh off his master's, and UB is a great school and all, but we got guys here from more...highly regarded institutions, let's say, in our field. But at the end of the day, it's what you can do that counts. Eddie showed he had it, so Woods looked to be correct in his decision. At least, that's how it seemed before all this happened."

He shook his head at the thought and continued, "I suppose I'll never get the full story, but it just seems like Eddie got mixed up in something bad. I liked him. He kept to himself, and he was clearly very smart. I think he had a sensitive side to him, too, and I have a younger brother like that, so I empathized. The whole thing is just...just really sad, detective."

The detective nodded, unsure of what to say to that.

Linden added on, "Now, I just hope the company and Mr. Woods aren't severely impacted by all this."

41

December 20, 2025. 10:08 hours local time.
Air Force Office of Special Investigations Headquarters, Quantico, Virginia.

"You're out of your mind."

"Steve, I know—"

"John Woods is an American patriot. He's dedicated his life to serving this country. To insinuate he's a traitor, an insider for the PRC? I'm sorry, I simply won't have it."

Henry Purcel, Steven Giresi, and Lieutenant Colonel Al Reed were gathered in the secure conference room at the AFOSI headquarters in Quantico. Upon speaking with Conkling after the detective's return visit to the BTP headquarters, Purcel had asked Giresi to come in on a Saturday for a face-to-face to discuss something *urgent*. He feared revealing the topic of discussion over the phone would lead to Giresi refusing to show. After the three men had sat down, Purcel laid out his theory that owner and CEO of BTP Technologies John Woods was, in fact, a deeply placed insider for the Chinese.

Giresi's reaction had been as expected. The indignation in his voice was such that Purcel feared the NSA man might storm out of the room. Purcel looked over to Lieutenant Colonel Reed, seated on the other side of the conference table. He had barely moved during Purcel's verbal breakdown of the evidence, and his face now showed, to Purcel at least, something more than curiosity.

With the room silent after Giresi's angry protestations, the lieutenant colonel turned to Giresi. "Steve, for my part, having heard all of this, there's just too much coincidence. I believe there is something here, and something we need to address."

Steve Giresi simply shook his head, not saying anything. Reed glanced over to Purcel, indicating he should retake the floor.

Purcel cleared his throat. "Steve, you know as much as anyone, high-level assets are not without precedent. Klaus Fuchs on the Manhattan Project, Kim Philby at MI6. Woods was a career intel officer. It was in his training to hide who he really was."

Giresi interjected, "Philby had a history of communist sympathies. So did Fuchs. Do you have anything to show similar suspicion for John? Other than his time in Vietnam happening to coincide with this other character, what's-his-name, Bao?"

"Who can really say what people's motivations are? But Woods's time as Chief of Station in Vietnam overlapping with that of the father of a prime suspect in this case is simply too much to brush aside, particularly with the other details of this case."

Giresi again shook his head.

"Think about it," said Purcel, "The level of cosmic luck the Chinese would have required for their asset to be in place at the company that won this Ocelot contract is extraordinary."

"OK, tell me, how do you explain the fact that the Chinese even knew these drones were going to be developed? Doesn't your theory posit the idea they knew this was coming, and they moved to place their asset in a pole position? They got Voss in place *before* the Ocelot was even announced."

"I have thought of that, yes. I believe the Chinese have an insider somewhere in our allies, the countries that were first on the list to buy this drone. Either Taiwan or South Korea."

"They just have spies in all the right places, don't they?"

Purcel didn't say anything right away, hoping to calm the mood some.

He proceeded, "Whatever theory one might have to explain that particular question, it is immaterial to the matter of John Woods. Again, we have a connection in Vietnam with a longtime Chinese intelligence officer—"

"An *assumed* connection."

Purcel nodded to concede the point. "A longtime Chinese intel agent, Wenbu Bao, who is very likely the father of our suspect in Manhattan, known to us as Tian Xi but actual surname likely Bao. Again, you can see for yourself."

Purcel pointed to images he had laid out on the table between himself and Giresi. They showed printouts of the head shot of Bao Jiaotong, or Tian Xi, as he was known to the men in the room, and of Bao Wenbu, which had been provided by the CIA from their database of known foreign adversaries.

"The similarities are uncanny. As a side note, I'm told sons are more likely to resemble mothers. Father-son similarity does happen but is not nearly as common. The striking resemblance between the two, I think, further solidifies that they are, indeed, father and son. Anyway, there is nothing on Bao that we can find, meaning he likely came in under a different alias. We have no idea how long he was here. What we do know is that he made for Vietnam, something that makes much more sense if we tie him to Wenbu Bao. The latter likely still had contacts the son could rely upon in a pinch."

He paused once again, letting Giresi take in the information on the second go around.

"Parallel to this is the activity at BTP. Voss is introduced to the company *by* John Woods, after having been turned by the Chinese, by this tag team of Heping Gao and Bao, not long before the Ocelot contract is to be awarded. Then, Voss is given the *lead* on the chip design for the Ocelot camera image enhancement capability at the suggestion of Woods. It is also evident that Woods lied to me, suggesting Voss pushed to be placed on the program. The Schenectady detective found that to not be the case. In my time speaking with Woods, he also gave no indication of having known Voss or much about him, obfuscating the fact that it was he who had brought Voss to the attention of the hiring team."

Giresi sat stone-faced, eventually turning away from Purcel to look at the blank wall of the room to his right, as if seeing something only he could. Purcel looked at Reed, who now leaned back in his swivel chair, expressionless. Purcel hoped the silence from Giresi was an indication he was digesting all that he'd just heard.

Without turning back to the other two, Giresi said, "You believe that this Wenbu Bao turned Woods during their time serving in Vietnam?"

"Yes, I do," Purcel replied.

"And that he's been a sleeper cell ever since, lying in wait?"

"I do. What activity he's possibly been up to in the interim, ever since his return stateside, I cannot speak to that. But, for this matter, BTP and the Ocelot drone, whatever investment the Chinese made is now paying big dividends."

Again, the room fell silent. Giresi continued to stare off into space, trying to think of another explanation that did not implicate his old friend. If he set aside his emotions, he knew what Purcel had laid out was compelling. As hard as it was for him to believe someone like John Woods could be playing for the other side, the number of coincidences that had gathered in this case were legion. One would have to stretch credulity to its breaking point to explain them away. Steve Giresi was himself a spy, and one of the first things one learned in intelligence was that to write something off as a fluke or happy accident was done at one's peril. Coincidences did happen in life, but some were too great to ignore. As he sat there with Purcel and Reed, the realization crept up on him that he could not conjure anything that would be a convincing defense for John Woods. The reality was setting in that Purcel was on to something.

He turned back to Purcel. "This detective up there in New York, he can verify his information?"

"He can, yes."

"And the Chinese girl, the one used to entrap Voss. You have her on board if need be?"

"Yes, my colleague Special Agent Bizon is in contact with her, and she can implicate the younger Bao and his role in all of this."

Giresi paused, then he looked to Lieutenant Colonel Reed. "Well...what do you suggest?"

42

December 21, 2025. 05:43 hours local time.
Chaoyang District, Beijing, China.

The obnoxious sound of a cell phone vibrating against a solid surface jolted Li Yong awake. After taking a second to gain his faculties, he realized what was going on and immediately reached for his phone connected to its charger on the bedstand. He panicked momentarily, not wanting to disturb the young woman next to him, but also because he realized it might be his wife calling, wondering where he was. He kept this penthouse apartment in the city's Central Business District for his occasional trysts with high-end escorts. Owning it through a small holding company, set up by a banker who owed him a favor, meant he could also keep it secret from his wife. Usually, when he decided to spend nights here, he would tell Xiaoping that he would be sleeping on a cot in his office, that there was just so much work to do. Had he forgotten to say something to her?

As he pulled the phone from its charging cord, he stole a glance at the screen and saw it was a number associated with the ministry. He thought that it was far too early in the morning to be fielding work calls. He stood up out of bed, phone in hand. The buzzing stopped but immediately started up again. The woman did not stir. He tiptoed out of the bedroom, answering the phone in a low voice as he closed the door behind him.

"Li here. For fuck's sake, what is it?"

"My apologies, sir, for such an early hour. This is Wen Houdei in the Intel Room. I—"

"Just get to it, what's going on?"

"Ahem, sorry sir, umm, there is something going on here we think you should see."

—————

December 21, 2025. 06:55 hours local time.
Haidian District, Beijing, China.

An hour later, Li stood next to Wen, one of his senior analysts, in the basement of the Ministry of State Security. They were in the back corner of the expansive Intel Room, and before them was a bank of computer monitors. Their attention was focused on two in particular, the two that comprised the workstation of a young, visibly nervous intelligence analyst. Both screens showed visual noise, the snow seen on a television screen when there is no signal.

"What the fuck am I looking at?" Li nearly shouted at his subordinates.

"Sir, at this particular position, we monitor the live video feeds of two of the Ocelot drones. As you can see, something is blocking the signal, interrupting our feed," Wen replied.

"So, fix it you fucking idiot. What are you calling me for? It's Deng who knows this computer shit. Get him in here."

"Sir, it's not so simple. We think the Taiwanese implemented something to make this happen." Wen nodded to the young analyst. "Lu here can explain a bit more."

The analyst sat facing the monitors, his back to the other two men.

He turned around and looked at Wen, not Li, as he spoke. "Last night, these two drones were taken out of the air. It fit with their refueling schedule, so we thought nothing of it.

"However, since the start of my shift this morning, this is all we've been seeing. More than enough time has elapsed for the refueling. They should be back operational by now."

"Is this normally what you see when they are grounded?" Li asked.

The analyst, Lu Entao, looked to Li but avoided his eyes. "No, sir, it just goes blank, as it did when we monitored them being grounded for refueling. This is something completely new. I suspect they are back in the air... but something is interfering with or blocking our access."

Li sighed deeply and ran a hand over his face. "And the others?"

Lu looked back to Wen, who nodded for him to respond. Lu pointed to his left at another analyst who sat a few feet away, his head turned from the three of them in an attempt to avoid being roped into the discussion.

"Two more drones have been grounded; Zhou's monitors have gone blank. But what is curious about that is we believe they still had sufficient fuel for another couple of hours. The Taiwanese have seven of these aircraft monitoring the strait and always have at least four in the air, which is something else that makes me believe the two drones here are back flying. If they were still on the ground, it would only leave three operational."

Li said nothing in response. Lu looked back at his static-filled monitors, unsure of what to do. Wen, standing next to Li, shifted nervously.

Li eventually looked at Wen and said, "Get Deng. Tell him I want him in my office as soon as he gets here. Zhang as well. Make sure that pig knows we have a fucking problem."

———————

A little more than an hour later, Li sat at his desk fidgeting with a pen, staring at Deng Shanlou, who cut a worried figure sitting in one of his boss's guest chairs. A month earlier, Deng had made assurances that he knew of no way the Americans could possibly interrupt the leaks from their Trojans in a short amount of time, and Li had just informed him that this assessment appeared to be wrong. He now sat there beneath Li's glare, nervously attempting to formulate an explanation. It was not discomfort born out of his boss's clear indignation, either. Deng felt he could navigate around Li, a shallow bureaucrat concerned only with his own trajectory in the state machinery. No, Deng had broken out in a cold sweat due to the knowledge that at any moment, Zhang Hudao would walk through that office door and join them.

"Sir, I'll need time to look into this. As I've said before, we know the Americans have had their eye on hardware security, as do their allies in the European Union, but we are not aware of any capability that nullifies an already in situ Trojan. I—"

It was then that Zhang burst into the office, not bothering to knock. He stepped in and remained standing, first looking at Deng and then at Li. He was breathing heavily.

"What is going on? Wen said it was urgent, regarding the Ocelots."

Li glared at him as he responded. "Two of the feeds from the drones appear to be interrupted. Visual static on the screens. Nothing we've ever encountered before, apparently. It was after the aircraft had been grounded for fueling."

Zhang cast a glance downwards at Deng to his right. Deng sat staring straight ahead at the wall beyond Li, still as a statue.

Li continued, "Two other drones are currently grounded, and apparently, it doesn't fit with their refueling schedule. Something is going on."

Zhang turned and spoke to Deng. Deng continued to look forward and did not meet his gaze as Zhang asked, "Is it possible some sort of jamming equipment is currently in use in the vicinity, interfering with our signal?"

Deng finally turned his head slightly in Zhang's direction. "No. For one, if it were interfering with us in such a manner, so it would the Taiwanese themselves. Besides, we can still see three of the drones. It wouldn't make sense they would be uninterrupted while these others are. They are not that far from one another."

Zhang's nostril's flared, and he stepped closer to Deng. If both had been standing, Deng would have looked diminutive next to Zhang's stout figure. Sitting down and with Zhang now looming over him, Deng nearly recoiled in his seat as Zhang moved to berate him.

"You said—"

He was cut off by the ringing of Li's desk phone. All three men simultaneously moved their heads to the source of the noise.

Li picked up the receiver. "Li."

He listened for a moment and then, without a word, slammed the receiver down. He looked back at the other two, but his eyes focused on Zhang. His voice started to shake with anger as he said, "That was Wen. The two monitors that were blank have now just been filled with the same as the other two. Static noise."

The room fell silent. Deng turned his head to look out the window, swallowing audibly.

Li continued, "He also said that two more drones have been pulled from the sky. They are heading back to base. Once again, it doesn't fit with the refueling schedule."

After another second or two of silence passed, Zhang suddenly gripped the guest chair next to Deng and whipped it sideways, sending it crashing into the far wall.

He immediately stood over a now terrified Deng, spittle flying from his mouth as he raged, "You said there was time! You said this couldn't happen! Tell me, huh? How the fuck are the Americans doing this!?"

Li had stood up when Zhang threw the chair, and now Deng quickly found his feet, backing a few steps towards the window, creating distance between himself and his seething colleague.

His voice shook as he spoke. "Hudao, I, I...It is possible there is some capability we have not yet uncovered. There's always that chance, but I—"

"How are you so sure it was the Americans?" Li interrupted him, his voice calm. As he spoke, he was staring straight at Zhang.

Zhang turned his head towards his boss. "Say again?"

"How. Are you. So sure. It was. The Americans?" Li asked again, deliberately.

"Who else would it be?" Zhang turned his head back to face Deng.

"Or perhaps," Li said, raising his voice significantly. Both Zhang and Deng looked at him. "Perhaps it is because a member of the American Air Force was just at Hsinchu. Perhaps it is *that* fact which makes you think this is the Americans' doing? She was seen in the company of a Taiwanese captain who is known to work with the Ocelots, no? I must say, a visit from an American and only days later, this situation? Quite a coincidence, isn't it, Zhang?"

Zhang gave him a blank stare. He blinked once or twice. It was rare he was caught so off guard.

Li continued, "Oh, what is it? You think you're the only one with eyes and ears in Taiwan? That's your fucking problem, Zhang. You think you know better than everyone else, and therefore, only you should have control. When were you going to share that bit of information? I'm sure your asset made you aware. Or were you just going to see how it played out? Just like the entire fucking matter, ever since American soldiers shook down those San Lang engineers in Somalia. You kept that to yourself for long enough. Well, this is how it played out!"

He pointed with his whole hand towards the door, indicating the situation unfolding outside the walls of the office. "Fucking disaster!" he yelled.

No one said anything for a moment. Li and Zhang glared at one another, almost forgetting Deng off to the side.

Eventually Zhang, in a calmer tone of voice, said, "It's early yet. We cannot be sure exactly—"

"Oh, fuck off, man. It's perfectly clear what is going on. That American woman brought them something, and they are implementing it two at a time. The dominoes are falling. It's blindingly obvious. It's over, Zhang. It's over." Li sat down and steepled his hands in front of him, thinking. "I'll need to inform Naval Special Forces. Then the planning committee at the Politburo. This very likely means a derailment of the entire operation. We need to reassess. I'll be sure to let them know your role in this, Zhang."

"We cannot account for what happened on the American side of this operation. We—"

"This was your mission. You were lead man on this, Zhang. Bao was your subordinate. It is you who must shoulder the blame."

"He had full control of the assets over there. I was completely in the dark—"

"And *you* apparently had no control over him. That's unlike you, Zhang. I expect better. Maybe you think too highly of yourself. No, I'll find something more fitting for you. When the dust settles on this, you'll be cleaning latrines in Lhasa," said Li, referring to the remote capital city of Tibet.

Zhang moved to come around Li's desk towards him, violence in his eyes, balled fists down by his sides.

To Zhang's surprise, Li did not lose composure but rather spoke to him firmly, enough to stop him in his tracks. "You wouldn't dare, Zhang. You wouldn't fucking dare. You might have friends but not like I do. If you so much as touch me, yours won't be able to protect you from a bullet to the back of your head in the dungeons of Qincheng." This was Beijing's notorious prison for *special* convicts.

Zhang stared him down, his chest rising and falling noticeably with the fury that coursed through him. "This isn't my doing."

"You can tell that to the investigative commission that will inevitably form over this. Now, get the fuck out of my office."

Zhang turned, glancing briefly at Deng, who had barely moved during the last few minutes.

As Zhang got to the door to leave, he turned back to Li and said, "The Americans can't stop us from taking Taiwan. It will happen eventually. This is only a small setback."

Li waited a moment before responding. With disgust in his voice he replied, "Well, they've ensured it won't happen on our terms now, haven't they?"

43

January 6, 2026. 09:05 hours local time.
Federal Bureau of Investigation Field Office, Albany, New York.

If he is engaged in espionage, then John Woods is very good at it.

That was what Bruce Laporte, Senior Special Agent of the Albany FBI Office, thought as he sat at his desk and sifted again through print outs of communication records and other material. It had been just about a week since a federal judge issued a warrant allowing for Laporte's office to perform surveillance on the founder and CEO of BTP Technologies. Apparently, circumstantial evidence provided by the Air Force Office of Special Investigations and Laporte's old friend at the Schenectady Police Department, Richard Conkling, had been enough to convince the judge that Woods deserved a closer look.

When the investigation was handed to Albany, Laporte flexed his seniority to take the case. Decades at the Bureau consisted primarily of investigating dirty state senators or organized crime with ties to New York City. Laporte liked to joke that Albany made Louisiana look like Denmark. If only people knew some of the corruption that took place in upstate New York. Laporte grew up an hour away in Utica, which held the moniker of

Sin City of the East during the '50s and '60s, when it functioned as a veritable fief of the mob.

An espionage case, though? *That* was different. He wanted in on that. Matters with potential geopolitical ramifications rarely found their way north of the Mario Cuomo Bridge. Why should the agents in the city or in DC get all the interesting ones?

After surveilling Woods for a few days and analyzing records, Laporte's initial takeaway was that John Woods had been careful. His phone records, which they had going back years, showed nothing suspicious. Every call came from or went somewhere innocuous. No calls to a travel agency in the city, which he'd been told to look out for, or to any suspicious or defunct numbers. Text message logs were just as uninteresting. Nothing out of the ordinary for a guy in his early sixties. Woods's bank records also appeared clean. Laporte had been hoping for a large deposit or withdrawal that required explaining but thus far had drawn a blank. In-person surveillance of the target, which Laporte shared with a couple younger agents, had also turned up nothing. Woods went to the BTP offices, to the gym, once out to dinner with his wife. That was it.

The ongoing wiretap had thus far yielded no incriminating evidence, which, given the other intel they had, didn't surprise Laporte. If Woods had gone this long being diligent in covering his tracks, he wasn't going to start acting reckless now. Woods was an ex-spook. He would know, more than anyone, that his employee—ex-employee, rather—having not only been tied to likely foreign intel agents, but also gunned down by a federal agent, would draw scrutiny on Woods and his company.

There were a couple of interesting calls that Laporte had noted, however. The first was made just a day after the wiretap was authorized. It was Woods calling his adult son, Jacob, telling him that he needed to come to the house as they *had something important to discuss.* When Jacob asked what was going on, Woods wouldn't say. Laporte had watched the next evening when the younger Woods came to the big house on Harvest Drive and stayed for over an hour. The second call was one that Laporte was only now seeing the transcript of. It happened early that same morning around 6:00 a.m. from Woods's cell.

The call was to an international number. The transcript noted that the person who answered had an English accent and identified himself as David Strange.

David Strange.

Hi. This is John Woods. I am just calling to see if you received my email from last week. I have not heard anything back.

Ah, yes, Mr. Woods. My apologies for not following up right away. I'll get back to you shortly on your request.

No worries. I'll be on the lookout for your email.

Indeed. Will be in touch.

Thanks. Bye.

Unfortunately, their wiretap didn't give them authorization to see Woods's email communications. Not yet, at least. They were working on it, but that was always a difficult hurdle to clear, so Laporte was in the dark about the email Woods was referring to.

Laporte turned his attention to his computer, pulling up a web browser. Given the note about David Strange's accent, he figured the number would be for the British Isles, but a 971-country code did not seem right. He typed that into a search engine.

United Arab Emirates?

Just then, a knock came on his office door jamb. He looked up to see Special Agent Nick Leary darkening the doorway. Leary was one of the agents assigned to assist with the surveillance of Woods, and he had been the one tailing him that morning.

"Nick, what's up? Aren't you on detail right now?"

"Yes, sir, followed the subject to the BTP offices a short while ago. Abdou relieved me for now; I have a ten o'clock I didn't want to push. Wanted to come see you first, though, couple things I thought you should know." The young agent walked over and stood next to the seated Laporte.

Laporte said, "Hit me."

"First off, I watched as a lady, a real estate agent, I assume, popped a *For Sale* sign in the Woods' yard."

"No shit?"

Leary shook his head. "Nope. Just before Woods left for BTP. She came, stepped it in, and was on her way."

Laporte pointed to the papers on the desk in front of him. "I see nothing in his call logs to a realtor here. Not even going back before the wire-tap warrant."

"I assume they communicated through Woods's wife. Only explanation I can think of."

Laporte nodded, conceding the possibility. "And we never picked up a prior visit?"

"Possible she came over to meet with them before we started surveilling, or they went to her office in that time. I will have to check the logs, but it's also possible we picked up a visit but figured she was a family friend or something. Her vehicle didn't have any advertising or bullshit."

Laporte didn't say anything.

Leary continued, "There's something else. Bigger." He pointed at Laporte's computer screen. "Pull up the Schenectady Daily Gazette."

Laporte went to the online version of the Schenectady local paper. Leary leaned over so he was closer to the screen. He looked at it for a moment and then told Laporte to scroll down some.

After a couple of scrolls he pointed to a headline on the right side of the screen. "There."

The headline read:

Area business owner retiring. Son to take over company.

Laporte clicked it to open the article and began to scan.

John Woods, founder and CEO of local technology firm BTP Technologies, has issued a press release stating that, effective immediately, he is resigning his position and giving full control to his son Jacob. Woods only cited personal reasons for the sudden change...

Laporte leaned back in his chair and ran a hand through his thinning hair. "Holy shit."

"Yep."

After pondering for a moment, Laporte sat forward towards his computer and said, "Hang on a sec."

He went back to a search engine and searched the terms: *David Strange United Arab Emirates.*

The top hit indicated a profile on a web page for a company called Falcon Real Estate Management Solutions. The page contained a full body photo of Strange, smartly dressed in a suit and silver tie, with a short biography next to his image. Laporte read that Strange was the lead sales representative at Desert Palms Golf & Country Club, a luxury villa resort in Dubai that catered to expats.

"Oh shit."

Laporte quickly picked up his desk phone, referring to a sticky note he'd placed on the bottom of his computer monitor for the number he wanted to call.

After a couple rings, a voice answered. "Purcel."

"Special Agent Purcel. This is Bruce Laporte, FBI up in Albany."

"Agent Laporte, yes. How can I help you?"

"Listen. I think your person of interest is getting ready to skip the country."

44

January 7, 2026. 23:19 hours local time.
Chaoyang District, Beijing, China.

The elevator dinged, signaling arrival at the fourteenth floor. As the doors opened and he made to step out, Li Yong checked his watch. Already, it was after 11:00 p.m. Tonight, for a change, telling his wife that he was working late had actually been the truth.

He was still having to deal with the fallout from the disastrous turn of events with the Ocelot drones. Just a couple of hours after Zhang had left his office following their stormy meeting, the remaining two drone feeds also showed nothing but static noise. They waited two full days, and there was no change. All seven feeds still displayed the same thing. The Taiwanese had done something to block their Trojan leak. Deng looked like a man heading for the gallows when he informed Li there was nothing they could do, that plans for an invasion should be postponed.

Unsurprisingly, his superiors at the MSS, along with various decision-makers in the Navy, Army, and the Politburo, had been apoplectic. One of the most important undertakings in the modern history of the People's Republic had suddenly been halted by...what? Deng nor any of the other technical experts at the ministry had an explanation. It hardly mattered.

Without the intel being leaked from the Ocelots and the inability to spoof the feeds, the naval landings had to be shelved—indefinitely, he was told—until another plan was formulated. Someone was going to have to answer for such a catastrophe.

In the intervening days, Li had used all his lawyerly skills to ensure it wouldn't be him facing the reckoning. He knew he could rely on his uncle and the influence the old man still held in the Politburo to keep him out of real trouble, but he had a fight on his hands to maintain his status in the ministry. He had designs on moving up the ladder, and this mess put those plans in jeopardy. Not even his puppet-master uncle could stop a demotion or a halt to promotion, not if the situation merited it.

Li was doing everything in his power to make it known that this was Zhang Hudao's doing. Was Zhang Li's subordinate? Sure, but Zhang had great autonomy in the Ocelot mission and had abused it. He may have reported to Li—and even that he failed to do properly—but the mission was his and his alone. And look how everything had turned out. Zhang was reckless, a self-professed lone wolf who believed too much in his own mystique. That, Li recognized, was part of his problem. Zhang was highly regarded among the rank and file. Li might have had the high-level connections, but Zhang commanded respect, and those above Li likely recognized that as well. That was the hurdle he needed to get over if he was to shift the blame onto Zhang.

Ironically, Zhang was helping Li's cause. Ever since their meeting that day when the drone feeds began to drop, no one had seen or heard from Zhang. If someone had, they weren't saying. That, Li pointed out during more than one of the ongoing inquiries, was evidence enough that Zhang acknowledged his own culpability in the whole affair.

As Li approached the door to his penthouse apartment, he let out a sigh. Part of what had kept him in the office so late wasn't even directly related to the Ocelot fiasco. On top of everything, Li was now having to field questions from counterparts in North Korea. Apparently, it had been some time since one of their agents who operated in the border region had checked in. Li knew that had to be the one called Chu. He had sent Zhang to Dandong to meet the Bowibu agent, and now the man's bosses were complaining he'd gone missing. Just another instance of Zhang wiping his dirty shoes on the carpet. Even as a ghost, Zhang was causing Li headaches.

He came to his door. After unlocking it and entering the apartment, the very first thing he noticed was just how cold the entire unit was.

"What the fuck? Why the fuck is it freezing in here?" he said aloud.

He flicked on the light to the living room that lay out before him. On the far side, he saw that one of the large sliding glass doors that led out to his balcony was wide open.

"What the fuck?"

He walked over and stepped out onto the balcony and looked to both sides. There was no one and nothing out there. He looked across towards the neighboring buildings, all mostly dark. He shook his head, dismayed at how the slider could be gaping open. Perhaps the cleaning lady had forgotten to close it. He would fire her first thing in the morning.

Li did not hear any movement come from behind him. Just before he turned around to head back inside, he felt a powerful shove into the middle of his back, sending his abdomen hard against the balcony railing. The force of the shove made him bend slightly over the railing, and then an arm that felt like a steel bar came across the back of his neck and pushed downwards. At the same time, Li felt his legs lift into the air as someone grabbed the back of his belt and pulled upwards.

He screamed just as his body was sent over the railing. So many floors up, and with the thickness of the windows that was standard in the city's newer buildings, no one would hear it. Li Yong plummeted into the cold Beijing night.

Zhang Hudao stood looking over the railing as Li fell to his death, and he watched as the body made a grotesque impact with the floodlit street below.

He stepped back into the apartment, leaving the slider open. He walked over to Li's large dining table and pulled a folded piece of paper from his jacket pocket with his gloved hands. He unfolded it and placed it on top of the table. Li's suicide note blamed shame over his role in the now-postponed invasion of Taiwan, mentioning that he had not lived up to the family name that had been so elevated by his father and uncle. The note was handwritten, in something very close to Li's actual handwriting. One of the very first things Zhang had learned all those years ago in spy craft was forgery. Next to the note, he tossed Li's key to the apartment. Zhang's skills as a pickpocket had not dulled over the years, either.

He looked around the apartment for a moment. There were certain elements of Li's death he would have preferred to be different. Li still wearing his winter clothes for his suicide might raise some questions. Zhang also would have liked to have waited for Li to sit down and have a drink, as he knew Li was likely to do. Not only did alcohol always help with the suicide narrative, but putting a glass with Li's prints next to the note also would have been a welcome touch. A folded letter wasn't ideal, either, but it was plausible Li had written it elsewhere and carried it back to where he decided to do the deed.

Zhang also wondered if the concierge downstairs would remember that it wasn't Li's voice that called down from the room just moments before Li had entered the apartment, saying that the expected guest, Li's call girl, was no longer necessary.

He wasn't too worried about these details, however. There was the note with the key next to it, and Li was under immense pressure lately. It fit. This was China, as well. Zhang knew how the police behaved. Li's aging uncle might make some noises, but no one working in Beijing Homicide was going to overanalyze this one.

Zhang went over to the apartment door, opening it a crack to peek out to make sure no one was in the hallway. He stepped out, quietly closing the door. Standing there, he produced from his jacket a copy of the apartment key and locked the door's top bolt. Zhang had known of Li's apartment and the purpose for which he kept it for some time now. At one point, he lifted the key from Li's office and made a copy for himself. One night, when Li had gone home to his wife, Zhang had snuck in and hidden a camera in the bedroom. He figured evidence of Li's extracurriculars would make for a nice insurance policy someday.

It wouldn't be necessary now.

45

January 8, 2026. 11:11 hours local time.
Air Force Office of Special Investigations Headquarters, Quantico, Virginia.

Henry Purcel flexed his right hand open and closed, trying to work out the discomfort in his arm. The injury he had sustained in Jordan still crept up on him occasionally, but this time, the blast of pain had been self-induced. He had just slammed his fist down on his desktop, an uncharacteristic burst of fury elicited by the call he'd finished a moment before on his office phone.

I'm sorry, Henry. We just don't have enough. Sometimes, the bad guys get away.

The weak words of comfort from Lieutenant Colonel Al Reed ran back through his mind. As Purcel leaned back in his swivel chair and tried to let the anger subside, he recognized that the lieutenant colonel was right. Not everything had a happy ending.

Despite evidence from the FBI Office in Albany that John Woods was now a flight risk, and despite all efforts and exhortations, neither AFOSI nor anyone at the bureau could get a judge to issue even a search warrant of Woods's home and office, let alone an arrest warrant. There simply was not enough solid evidence tying Woods to espionage at the time. Selling your home and moving abroad was no crime, particularly when your current residence had six months of winter and the destination had year-round warm weather. Furthermore, who could blame Woods for retiring and backing away from his company? The fallout from the Eddie Voss matter was sure to reverberate around BTP for years to come. As far as the judge was concerned, there was nothing suspicious about Woods's recent actions.

It was not lost on Purcel that the United Arab Emirates was yet another country that did not have an extradition treaty with the United States. Why there? Why are you selling your house in the dead of the Upstate New York winter? Why the sudden retirement from BTP? Even more saliently, who was it that gave you Eddie Voss's resume and asked that he be considered? Purcel wanted to ask all of these things and had pushed for the FBI to bring in Woods for questioning, but at this point, Woods would have to appear voluntarily. Even if he did so, Purcel could already foresee Woods providing only benign answers to the questions, and the age old *I don't recall* to the crucial last one.

Purcel was sure of Woods's guilt. As far as he was concerned, all signs pointed to it. What he couldn't understand was what had taken Woods over to the other side. What happened all those years ago in Vietnam? He sighed and ran a hand over his face, realizing that it was very likely he would never know the answer to that.

His desk phone rang, startling him out of his thoughts. He saw on the display it was Lieutenant Colonel Reed's number. He felt his pulse quicken. Was Reed calling back so soon after their conversation because he had an update? Something had come up, maybe a judge had a change of heart? They were arresting Woods after all?

He picked up the receiver. "Lieutenant Colonel?" He failed to hide the anticipation in his voice.

"Purcel, no I'm not calling with an about-face. Forget about Woods. Move on. Listen, I just got a call from Langley. Someone wants to speak to you in the SPAF."

———————

Five minutes later, Henry Purcel picked up the receiver on the phone in his building's secure conference room.

He spoke to the secretary who manned the SPAF's front desk, "Darla, you can put the call through."

After a moment of silence, a voice came from the other end. "Henry?"

"Yes, speaking."

"Hi, Henry, this is Chris at the agency. You remember, I help run our China desk."

"Yes, yes, of course. How can I help you, Chris?"

"Well, I'm actually just calling out of courtesy. I'm breaking protocol a little, but I thought you might be interested and deserved to know some recent updates we've had here."

"Um, sure, yes. What do you have?"

"Well, for one, I'm not sure if you recall the last conversation we had back here at Langley. I made reference to a training facility the Chinese have in the far north, a region called Inner Mongolia?"

"Hmmm, I vaguely remember something about that."

"Well, they have a facility there that is modeled on the Taiwanese Presidential Palace and the surrounding streets."

"Ah."

"Right. Anyway, I thought you might like to know that over the last couple of weeks, our satellite imagery has shown a marked decrease in activity at the facility. A number of personnel appeared to have pulled away, based on vehicle traffic."

"I see."

"In early December, we had also seen an uptick in naval exercises around some of the small islands between China and Taiwan. Those also died off suddenly. There has been no activity recently."

"Interesting. I—"

"There's one other thing. This just came in early this morning. I'm sure it will be on some news services later, but sources on the ground report that the head of foreign intelligence at the Ministry of State Security, which I can tell you would be the body behind your whole investigation, appears to have committed suicide."

Purcel raised his eyebrows in surprise and shifted his stance. He didn't say anything for a few seconds, until finally, "Really?"

"Yep. Jumped from a high-rise balcony. Quite a way to go out if you ask me, but I guess us spooks have a flair for the dramatic."

"Jumped to his death? Correct me if I'm wrong, but that sounds like a Putin tactic for people he'd rather not hear from again."

"Russia, China. You got to be careful near open windows and balconies in these places."

"I guess so."

"Anyway, I thought you should know. You did good work on that case, Special Agent."

"I...I appreciate it."

"Take care of yourself." Chris hung up.

Henry Purcel stood there for a moment, receiver still in hand. He thought about what the CIA man had just told him. For a moment, it called to his memory something he'd heard once, an actor on a podcast talking about tragedy in film or theater. The actor had said something about all tragedy being rooted in the lack of information, how no one really wins if nobody has the full story.

He knew the truth was that no one who'd been attached to the case, himself, Giresi, Chris, Chris's colleague Mike, Major Decker, none of them could say for sure what the Chinese really had in mind with Eddie Voss's handiwork. Even that itself was a bit murky, with Voss having done so much to cover his tracks. All that Chris had told him certainly pointed to Jason Lizac's RECORD, and by association, Purcel, having had a significant impact on things on a global scale, but it wasn't definitive. Could it all be just the normal machinations of a huge, complicated country like China? That, too, was possible. He would have liked to say for sure that all of Chris's information pertained to his investigation and the introduction of Jason's technology to the situation, but he would just have to settle for the notion that it seemed very likely.

He let out a sigh and then smiled to himself, his signature nearly imperceptible grin. Finally, he put the receiver back on its dock and turned to leave the SPAF, ready to get back to work.

EPILOGUE

March 17, 2026. 00:21 hours local time.
John F Kennedy International Airport, Queens, New York.

The line for passport control moved apace. Luckily for the passengers of Air China Flight 981, no other flights were arriving in New York City at a such a dark hour, and the flight was barely half full. Luckier still for Gao Heping, most of the passengers were either US passport or Green Card holders, and the line ahead of him for foreign passports was only a few bodies deep. Minutes after deplaning, he was next in line to face the Customs and Border Patrol agent.

Gao moved his head around side to side, up and down, trying to work out the kinks of the painfully long direct flight from Beijing to JFK. He dreaded the trip every time. Fifteen hours in those Air China seats—no way would a Chinese-state-owned company design anything even approaching comfortable—stuck in a metal tube with coughing people and/or crying babies. To him, stepping out of the stale air of the plane each time felt like being a prisoner finally released from an underground dungeon. No, it was not easy, but it was unavoidable. Now, it was time to get back to work.

He had been left somewhat in the dark about his last mission, the Voss mission. So much time, years, dedicated to it, and from what he surmised, all for naught. Gao's level of need-to-know regarding that particular piece of work did not go high enough, but even spies aren't immune to gossip and rumor. Colleagues of his in the intelligence community whispered that Bao Jiaotong, the other NOC he collaborated with closely on Voss, was in the wind. Gone. Gao had also learned, not long after it happened, that Eddie Voss had been killed in a shootout with an American federal agent. Those two things happening so near each other did not portend good news. At the end of December, when Li Yong contacted him to let him know it was time to go back into the field, Gao sensed all was not well.

The Customs and Border Protection agent, a portly, bald man with bags around his eyes, waved Gao forward. Gao smiled when he faced the agent and handed over his passport, a smile that was not returned. The agent first flipped through the passport to find Gao's visa, then went to swipe the passport, asking what the purpose of Gao's visit was as he did so.

"I'll be working at Purdue University under a research grant," Gao said in his near-impeccable English.

The agent nodded and looked at his screen. A few seconds passed. Gao tried staring ahead at nothing in particular but, in his periphery, noticed the agent shift in his seat, his face now showing concern.

After another moment, the agent picked up his desk phone, hitting one number. "It's Dawson. Someone meet me in the box." He then stood up, saying to Gao, "Sir, I need you to come with me."

———————

The *box* the agent had referenced was the CBP interrogation room tucked away in the back part of the airport customs office. Over an hour later, Heping Gao found himself sitting at the sole table in the tiny, stuffy room, his right leg bouncing up and down in a combination of impatience and anxiety. When he followed the bald CBP agent to the office, he'd asked if everything was OK and was told there was an issue and that someone would be in to talk to him. Another officer had let him into the room, providing a room-temperature bottle of water while saying that they'd be with him shortly.

What is going on? He wondered. All the times he'd come through US customs, many through this same airport, there had never been any issues. His mind had first gone to wondering if this had to do with the Voss situation. He was sure he was clean from all of that. After doing his part to get the Yang girl involved with Voss, Bao had taken over. They'd been sure to eliminate any evidence of communication between Voss and himself, and he knew Bao had a very strict system of communicating with Voss. Had the Americans somehow gotten to the girl? Gao couldn't see how. This was all years ago.

He rubbed his eyes, the exhaustion from the flight now starting to creep in, the adrenaline of being taken from the passport line and led here now wearing off. He was ashamed to admit that, if this waiting game was an American tactic just to wear him down and deaden his senses and awareness, it might be having the desired effect.

Suddenly, the door opened. Two men, both appearing to be in their upper forties or early fifties, entered the room. One wore a navy blue FBI windbreaker, the other a long black overcoat. Both carried file folders. The one in the overcoat took the seat across from Gao, while the FBI agent folded his arms and leaned against the wall to their left.

Special Agent Mark Bizon placed his folder on the table and folded his hands in front of him, offering Gao a congenial smile. It hadn't taken him long to get to the airport from his hotel; there was hardly any traffic at this hour. He had been ready to go, too, waiting for the call to come from the CBP agents. Both he and Agent Shea Winger from the Manhattan FBI office had arrived around the same time, about twenty-five minutes after being alerted, but kept Gao waiting. Bizon wanted Gao to stew a bit, to become uncomfortable and tired on top of the nerves he was inevitably feeling.

Despite what appeared to be a dead end back in November, Bizon hadn't wanted to give up on Gao entirely. He had no hope of tracking down Gao's alleged accomplice, the man from the travel agency, but he'd had a hunch that Gao's days of traveling to the states to work his craft weren't over just yet. It had taken some doing, including leaning on a friend who still had some connections at the State Department, but eventually, he'd been able to get word to the American embassy in Beijing to monitor for any visa application from Gao. He'd provided them with all the background on Gao he had obtained from the University at Buffalo. Don't deny the application, he'd directed, let Gao come, but Bizon wanted to know when and where. A month ago, he'd gotten the call. Gao's application showed a booked ticket for JFK arriving in the wee hours of March 17.

Bizon looked across the table at Gao. He hadn't changed much in the years he'd been away. Gao still looked like an engineering academic: slightly boyish, thick-rimmed glasses, bangs sweeping over his forehead. Not, Bizon thought, how one would envision a highly trained intelligence agent.

"Mr. Gao, I am Special Agent Mark Bizon with the United States Air Force Office of Special Investigations. This is Agent Shea Winger of the FBI. I apologize for keeping you waiting."

Gao didn't say anything. Just stared back at him.

Bizon opened the folder in front of him and cleared his throat. "Oh, before I forget." Here, he paused for dramatic effect. He couldn't help himself. He smiled again, this time wider, with satisfaction. "Sonya sends her regards."

———————

April 7, 2026. 05:55 hours local time.
Thong Nhat, Vietnam.

It was his cat, or rather its absence, that alerted him something was wrong.

Every morning, when Bao Jiaotong stepped into the kitchen of his tiny one-bedroom home in this rural hamlet outside of Lào Cai, his elderly orange cat would greet him by coming and rubbing against his legs. But not this morning. After standing for a moment in the door frame that opened from a short hallway into the main part of the home, the cat had still not appeared. Something must have spooked him.

Complacency had caused Bao to leave his pistol on his bedstand. He had a spare, a small Makarov in a kitchen cupboard next to where he kept his coffee. He reflexively looked to his left into the kitchen, gauging how quickly he could close the space between where he was standing and where the gun was.

As he did so, a voice came from his right, "It's not there," he heard in Mandarin.

Bao knew right away who his visitor was. The deep, gravelly voice was unmistakable.

He turned to see Zhang Hudao sitting at his small dining table in the corner of the room, his hands out of view underneath the table. The house was only now beginning to lighten with the early dawn, but Bao could still see Zhang was wearing his preferred leather jacket. In the early spring, mornings in the Vietnamese mountains could be chilly.

Despite having put on warm clothes after rising, Bao suddenly shivered in the morning cold.

Zhang motioned with his head for Bao to join him at the table in the other chair. Bao hesitated for a moment, considering turning and bolting for his bedroom and the firearm by his bed. But based on what he'd seen years ago in Africa, Bao knew that Zhang was a quick, agile man, despite his size. Bao wouldn't make it.

This is it. This is how it ends.

He walked over and sat down across from his boss.

Zhang considered him for a moment before saying, "Your father was stationed here. He was the king of intelligence in the China-Vietnam border region."

Bao nodded.

"You still have connections here. People you can turn to if you are on the run."

Another nod.

"Did you really think I wouldn't recall any of that?"

Bao didn't say anything. He had, of course, known that Vietnam would be one of the first places Zhang would consider, but he didn't really see what other choices were available. He spoke the language, blended in more easily, and as Zhang had said, he had resources on the ground, people who remembered his father and his influence. Unfortunately for him, Zhang's reach, particularly in this part of the world, was always going to be longer.

Zhang broke the silence. "You disobeyed an order. I know you went to see your asset and told him about what happened in Somalia."

Bao finally said something in response, "I don't know why I did that."

Zhang considered for a moment telling Bao how that small decision possibly—probably—contributed to the failure of their mission, indefinitely setting back the People's Republic's plans for landing an invasion force on Taiwan, which would have set history right and finally brought the island back into the fold. But he thought better of it. A dead man doesn't need so much information.

He brought his right hand, the one gripping his silenced CF98 pistol, up from underneath the table and fired one shot directly into Bao Jiaotong's forehead. Bao's facial expression immediately turned to one Zhang had now seen countless times, a death mask showing surprise at what fate had wrought. Bao's upper body seemed to suspend in the air for a split second before slumping forward onto the table with a loud *thump.*

Zhang stood up, unscrewing the silencer from the pistol then putting the pistol back in his shoulder holster and the silencer into a jacket pocket. He took an envelope made fat with a stack of Vietnamese currency from the other jacket pocket and tossed it on the table next to Bao's lifeless body, avoiding the pool of blood now forming on the tabletop. He then removed his cell phone and made a call. After a couple of rings, the Chief of Police for Lao Cai province answered.

Zhang said to him in stilted Vietnamese, "It's done. Come now. Remember, natural causes for the records. Cremate the body."

He hung up, pocketed his phone, and made for the front door. As he opened the door, he felt motion beneath him and looked down to see a cat dart outside. Zhang stepped out and slowly closed the door behind him, watching as the cat slowed to a walk where the grass of Bao's small yard met the dirt road.

The cat turned and looked back at Zhang, its eyes filled with a predatory malice. The two stared one another down for a moment before the cat turned and made its way into the morning mist.

AFTERWORD

This is a work of fiction. However, the *RECORD* technology portrayed within these chapters is very real, having been developed under the auspices of the Air Force Research Laboratory (AFRL) and licensed by Indiana Integrated Circuits (IIC), a real company.

The Ocelot drones are fictionalized. If any capability allowing for sensing of rare-earth minerals from the air exists, I am unaware of it. The facial recognition software used by the CIA referenced in the latter chapters is also of my making.

Several of the locations portrayed here, I have been to. These include: the Upstate New York locations (the building used for BTP's offices exists, but BTP is not a real company),

New York City's Chinatown, the *hutongs* of Beijing, the Bangkok locations, and the Buffalo, New York locations. I describe them as I remember. For other places featured, I had to use a mixture of my imagination (especially for government buildings) and assistance from Google Earth.

ACKNOWLEDGMENTS

Thank you to Dr. Paul Hrycaj and Steven Farr for being alpha readers and for catching my errors.

Dr. Paul Nielsen was kind enough to also be an initial reader, and his positive words on the work are very much appreciated.

Thank you also to Emily at Ten Hut Media.

A special thanks to my father, Dr. Kevin Kwiat, for the idea of casting a nascent Air Force technology into a narrative. The same for Jason Kulick. Their work on RECORD is what made this happen.

A thank you as well to Dr. Paul Ratazzi for his backing.

Thank you to my mother, Patrice Kwiat, for her continuous encouragement.

And, of course, to my wife, Gabi. Some things are just written.

ABOUT ADAM KWIAT

Adam Kwiat has a background in military intelligence, having worked as both a civilian employee and a contractor for the Department of Defense. Before graduating from the University at Buffalo, he spent his last semester living in Beijing, China, and is conversationally fluent in both Mandarin and Spanish. He currently resides in Sarasota, Florida, where he is working on a second novel.

To learn more about Adam and his books,
please visit: www.amazon.com/stores/Adam-Kwiat/author/B0G36C3RJZ

www.ingramcontent.com/pod-product-compliance
Lightning Source LLC
Chambersburg PA
CBHW031052020726
47495CB00007B/1844